MARY

C000129727

CATCHING UP

MARY LAY

First published in Great Britain in 2022
Mary Lay Stories

A CIP Catalogue of this book is available
from the British Library

ISBN 978-1-7396653-1-9 (Paperback)

First e-book edition May 2022
ISBN 978-1-7396653-0-2 (ebook)

Cover and layout design by Chandler Book Design
www.chandlerbookdesign.com

Self-published by Mary Lay Stories
www.marylaystories.com

Printed in Great Britain by
TJ Books, Padstow, Cornwall

1

FREDDIE

Caroline tore open the thin cream-coloured envelope and unfolded the single sheet of note paper it contained. There was a smear of mud where the paper had been folded.

7 October 1918
Chigny, France
Dear C,

Finally got a moment to myself to write you a few lines. These boys simply will not be quiet, however much I'd like them to be. I was glad to hear that your needlework project was a success. Will Mother wear the blouse do you think? Or perhaps she will keep it for special occasions. I shan't pretend to know what drawn thread work is, but it sounds a wonderful birthday present for her and I look forward to seeing it when I come home. Will you make Father a shirt next, perhaps for Christmas?

I won't bore you with the goings on here. Everything is mud for as far as the eye can see with just the odd blasted tree stump or litter of abandoned buildings. But spirits are as high as ever. I have a new company and we are to be moved to a small town shortly – I shan't say where, as the censor will only scrub it out! – for what they are calling one last push. Something about a canal and taking a strategic position. You may read about it in the newspaper before we even know for sure where we are, no doubt.

Thank Annie and Mrs Monger for the Dundee cake and the socks. Rations have been somewhat hit and miss lately and Perkins and Thorne appreciated the extra morsels I shared with them. I hope we shall keep in touch after all this has ended, they have been first rate pals over the past six months. Perkins has invited me to visit his family in Sittingbourne. Perhaps I shall take you with me. Would you like that? An adventure just for ourselves to deepest Kent? Now that you have finished with your classes, we should start thinking of how you will fill your days until we can marry you off to a suitable young man (neither Perkins nor Thorne fit that description I'm afraid. I would have no sister of mine marry any of these fellows, despite them being first rate soldiers!).

Do you hear anything of Alice Franklin? I was thinking of her the other day as I watched some local women laughing over a joke they shared in the street. I remember her laugh was like a babbling brook. Some news of her, and of course her family, would be welcome in your next letter, if you can find out anything.

Well, the rain has started again, so I should get back to my duties. Give my love to Mother and Father and tell them I shall write again very soon. And make sure Florence pays her share when you go to the picture house, there is such a thing as being too generous!

Yours affectionately
Freddie

girl of dubious age and parentage to her attic room. He was a soldier like hundreds of thousands of others. Like them, he was now dead but with no grave as his body lay at the bottom of the Sambre Canal where it had fallen as he had attempted to scale the northern bank under German fire.

He had lived with enthusiasm, convinced the war would be won by the British and French. His letters home, though infrequent, were full of positive encouragement and tales of good-humoured events between Company members. He had relished his occupation. He had drowned in a muddy, bloody canal and would not be coming home victorious.

Elizabeth Munhead had taken the news of her son's disappearance hard. Her beautiful son, her only surviving son from three pregnancies, on whom she had felt sure the world would shower goodness and fortune. But there was still the hope that Freddie would be found wandering, disoriented and confused in some little French village. She knew it could be so, she had read enough accounts of such things in the newspapers.

George read the telegram alone in his study before dinner. He took a moment to process the information, never a man to act in haste, and then walked through to the parlour where Elizabeth was seated, reading by the fireside.

"My dear."

She looked up. She read his face and saw the telegram still in his hand. The book fell from her lap as she stood and took the two steps into George's arms, and she sobbed. For Freddie to be cut down so cruelly, just days before peace had been declared, was a knife to Elizabeth's heart.

Some minutes later, with Elizabeth returned to her chair by the fire with the book closed on the table beside her, George emerged from the parlour and informed Mrs Monger that his wife would not be taking dinner that evening.

"I'm very sorry, sir."

"You knew?"

"We had assumed, sir. I'll make up a tray for the mistress, she might want something light later on. Will you be dining, sir?"

"Yes, with Caroline."

"Of course, sir."

"Would you ask Annie to call on Dr Riley and request he attend my wife this evening. I feel she may need a sleeping draught."

The sleeping draughts became Elizabeth's salvation. While they did not fill the void she felt every waking moment since that evening, they did at least enable her to slip away from it. She did not leave her room for a week after the telegram arrived. Doctor Riley visited daily, spoke calmly, and topped up her cache of little envelopes with the magic powder inside. In the late afternoon of Monday 18 November, George Munhead returned from work a little earlier than usual in order to speak with the Doctor. George sat in his study listening to the mantle clock tick away the minutes. Eventually a creek the stairs betrayed the approach of the Doctor. He knocked and pushed his head round the open door in one fluid movement. He looked somewhat dishevelled having spent most of the day at the station hospital with the influenza patients.

"George, you wanted to see me?"

"How is Elizabeth today?"

"No real change I'm afraid, although I convinced her to spend a few moments in the schoolroom with Caroline. She is still mute, but I believe that will pass with time as she adjusts to the reality of the situation. For now, a little mental stimulation daily will help. I'm sure Caroline will be invaluable with that. A little reading for example, for no more than ten minutes at first."

"The muteness is not a concern to you?"

Caroline read the letter at the kitchen table while the family's cook Mrs Monger beat eggs into sugar and butter for a Victoria sponge. Their maid of all work Annie was on her knees at the bottom of the stairs, sweeping the carpet with a dustpan and brush. Caroline's mother, Elizabeth Munhead, was at a meeting of the parish Mother's Union (she disliked the name but felt it her duty to attend and assist the poorer members of the congregation). Caroline's father George was at his employment as Manager of the Cheltenham branch of the Cheltenham and Gloucester Benefits Building Society in the town.

"Freddie says thank you for the cake."

"Aww bless his heart. I expect they don't see cake from one month to the next, save what gets sent to them from the families. How is he?"

"He sounds well. He says it is very muddy. Do you think they will be home by this Christmas?"

"We can only hope so. It's about time someone knocked heads together and ended all this fighting, I'm sure of that!"

"I'm going to make Freddie a birthday card. I'm going to paint some birds on it and the apple tree in the garden."

"That's nice, dear. Now, did you want to help me measure out the flour for this?"

It was almost a month later when the letter from Freddie's Captain arrived. Annie had heard the contents read out as she cleared the dinner plates from the dining room.

" ... I regret very much to inform you that your son Pte. F. G. Munhead, No. 455763 of this Company has been listed as missing in action as of the night of the 4th instance.

The Company was taking part in an attack and your son's gun team was one of those which advanced against the enemy. The attack was successful, and all guns reached and established new positions. However, a number of men were unaccounted

for after the crossing of the canal. While all endeavours will be
made to establish the whereabouts of your son, I feel it is my
duty to inform you of the current situation.
    Your son is an exceptional soldier....".

And with those words, a quiet had enveloped the house
unlike any Annie had experience before at 20 Glencairn Road,
or anywhere else. It was not a peaceful quiet. It was a quiet
that had jagged edges, sharp corners to catch oneself upon if
one's guard were dropped for a moment of amusement. She
had known instinctively that her normal duties must now be
done as silently as possible. Always the maid of all work should
be invisible, but now she must also be inaudible. It was not easy.

Thankfully Annie had only to endure the immediate quiet
until Saturday evening when she returned to her parents' house
and the noise of her sisters. She soaked it up, provoked their
giggles and chatter, and fell exhausted into bed beside them
that night. The following morning at the church of St Mark she
sang as loudly and lustily as she could, knowing she would soon
be back in the house that no longer seemed tense and sharp.

When the official telegram arrived the following week,
Annie recognised it immediately. Though she had never seen
one delivered to the home she shared with her family, she had
seen them in the homes of friends and relations. The black
edge standing starkly against the off-white paper. She was
unsurprised, yet still caught her breath as the postman handed
the paper to her with a mumbled apology before turning and
retreating down the garden path.

Annie stood in the hall with the telegram in her hand. Mr
Munhead was at work of course; his wife was taking breakfast
in her bedroom and fourteen-year-old Caroline was in the
schoolroom with her watercolour paints. Should she disturb
her mistress, or wait until the master returned a little after

five o'clock? The telegram was addressed to Mr Munhead. Annie walked through to the kitchen seeking counsel from Mrs Monger. This was too big a decision for a sixteen-year-old girl to make by herself.

"What you got there?" Mrs Monger, sleeves rolled to her elbows and hands deep in floured dough, looked up from her kneading.

"Telegram." Annie said simply.

Resuming the pummelling of the dough, Mrs Monger shook her head sadly, "I knew it. Didn't I tell you last week? Missing in action means dead but we can't find 'em. The Mrs is going to take it hard, bless her."

"It's addressed to the Master. Should I take it up to her anyway?"

"Lord no! That'd be tampering with the King's mail, you can't give a telegram to someone it's not written to. No, it'll have to sit in the study 'til he gets home later. Just you remember not to open the curtains in the morning, and I'll bring you a black pinny tomorrow as I suppose you don't have one of your own."

"Do I need a black cap too?"

Mrs Monger squinted at Annie across the scrubbed table. "That one will do, nice bit of black velvet ribbon threaded through the band would be respectful. Got any?" Annie shook her head. "I'll bring a length tomorrow as well then. Such a shame all this with the Armistice announced yesterday too."

Caroline, now the only surviving child of George and Elizabeth Munhead, stared hard at the sparrow perched on a branch a few feet from the schoolroom window. The schoolroom was really no longer required by Caroline or the family. Her schooling had been a mix of a shared governess with the twins next door, and later weekly attendance at Mrs Pendersen's school on the edge of Pittville Lawns on the opposite side of Cheltenham. There had been talk of turning the school-

room into a larger study for her father and his current study becoming a music room. She wondered when there would be music again in the house.

Freddie loved music. Freddie loved all of the arts and should have been studying at Oxford or Cambridge now. Caroline didn't understand how a person could simply go missing. Certainly not a person as tall and strong as Freddie. But her father had said that soldiers did often go missing and were as often found again, just not in the place they were expected to be, so she wasn't to worry. He had said it to her as the dinner things were cleared away on Friday. His eyes were looking into Caroline's, but his voice was rolling over her head and across to her mother on the other side of the table.

The sparrow flew away. Caroline looked down at her painting. It was an acceptable rendition of a dull brown and grey bird, not quite as good as the one she had painted on Freddie's birthday card. Had he received it? It occurred to her that as a silent occupation she could be spending a lot more time painting in the future.

The day after the end of the Great War, 20 Glencairn Road embraced full mourning for the loss of their son and brother, Frederick George Munhead, who had turned twenty-one just days before. But for a brief few days during the previous May when he had surprised the family with a week's leave, Freddie had been in training and then in France since early 1915. His only other short period of leave had been spent in Maidstone as after three days he was expected to re-join his Company in France. He had celebrated the evening of his twenty-first birthday with his Company playing an old harmonium in a bar in the centre of Saint Quentin, singing bawdy songs his mother would have been appalled to hear. He had drunk cognac and smoked continuously the whole evening before following a

girl of dubious age and parentage to her attic room. He was a soldier like hundreds of thousands of others. Like them, he was now dead but with no grave as his body lay at the bottom of the Sambre Canal where it had fallen as he had attempted to scale the northern bank under German fire.

He had lived with enthusiasm, convinced the war would be won by the British and French. His letters home, though infrequent, were full of positive encouragement and tales of good-humoured events between Company members. He had relished his occupation. He had drowned in a muddy, bloody canal and would not be coming home victorious.

Elizabeth Munhead had taken the news of her son's disappearance hard. Her beautiful son, her only surviving son from three pregnancies, on whom she had felt sure the world would shower goodness and fortune. But there was still the hope that Freddie would be found wandering, disoriented and confused in some little French village. She knew it could be so, she had read enough accounts of such things in the newspapers.

George read the telegram alone in his study before dinner. He took a moment to process the information, never a man to act in haste, and then walked through to the parlour where Elizabeth was seated, reading by the fireside.

"My dear."

She looked up. She read his face and saw the telegram still in his hand. The book fell from her lap as she stood and took the two steps into George's arms, and she sobbed. For Freddie to be cut down so cruelly, just days before peace had been declared, was a knife to Elizabeth's heart.

Some minutes later, with Elizabeth returned to her chair by the fire with the book closed on the table beside her, George emerged from the parlour and informed Mrs Monger that his wife would not be taking dinner that evening.

"I'm very sorry, sir."

"You knew?"

"We had assumed, sir. I'll make up a tray for the mistress, she might want something light later on. Will you be dining, sir?"

"Yes, with Caroline."

"Of course, sir."

"Would you ask Annie to call on Dr Riley and request he attend my wife this evening. I feel she may need a sleeping draught."

The sleeping draughts became Elizabeth's salvation. While they did not fill the void she felt every waking moment since that evening, they did at least enable her to slip away from it. She did not leave her room for a week after the telegram arrived. Doctor Riley visited daily, spoke calmly, and topped up her cache of little envelopes with the magic powder inside. In the late afternoon of Monday 18 November, George Munhead returned from work a little earlier than usual in order to speak with the Doctor. George sat in his study listening to the mantle clock tick away the minutes. Eventually a creek the stairs betrayed the approach of the Doctor. He knocked and pushed his head round the open door in one fluid movement. He looked somewhat dishevelled having spent most of the day at the station hospital with the influenza patients.

"George, you wanted to see me?"

"How is Elizabeth today?"

"No real change I'm afraid, although I convinced her to spend a few moments in the schoolroom with Caroline. She is still mute, but I believe that will pass with time as she adjusts to the reality of the situation. For now, a little mental stimulation daily will help. I'm sure Caroline will be invaluable with that. A little reading for example, for no more than ten minutes at first."

"The muteness is not a concern to you?"

Three weeks after Christmas Elizabeth woke on a Tuesday morning in a sweat and called out for Caroline. It was the first sound she had made since the previous November, but her voice was loud and strong. She had dreamed that Caroline had died and was laid out in a white coffin in the parlour. On waking she was gripped with a terror that the dream had been true, so much reality had been distorted by her laudanum powders that she could not be sure of anything. Caroline burst through the door, with Annie close behind.

"Mother?"

Elizabeth stared at her daughter. "You live?"

Caroline went forward, took her mother's hand, and perched on the edge of the bed. "Yes mother, yes, I'm here. You have found your voice again!"

Elizabeth withdrew her hand. She frowned. She swallowed, noticing her throat felt dry, "I shall take breakfast in the dining room."

There was no more laudanum. Doctor Riley had been surreptitiously reducing the amount of opium in each sachet of powders since Christmas, concerned that Elizabeth would develop too much reliance on them. Even so, Elizabeth suffered the withdrawal. Her nose and eyes ran the following day after a poor night's sleep. She felt nauseous, she paced, she picked at the skin around her nails. But she was vocal. She insisted on having Caroline in the room with her at all times she was awake at first, and only after some weeks relented when George intervened to explain it was unreasonable.

She began accepting social visits from her friends. At first, she would dictate letters for Caroline to write and Annie to deliver, but she grew to suspect that Caroline was not writing everything exactly as she had said it (in truth, Elizabeth often began to ramble, and Caroline could only keep up by paraphrasing) and took over the writing herself. Once her friends began to receive these communications, naturally they were keen to take tea and observe their friend's condition. As the year anniversary of the Armistice approached, Elizabeth declared she was sufficiently recovered to attend Christ Church for the service of remembrance.

Caroline adjusted. During her fifteenth year she had become nursemaid, companion, and secretary to her mother. She had had no plans for her own future; she absorbed what was required of her without protest. Only occasionally, when discussing some topic with her father over dinner, did Caroline catch a fleeting glimpse of a world outside of her existence. A world where trains carried passengers to distant towns and cities. Where women were taking seats in Parliament. Where men returning from the Great War were finding it difficult to obtain employment, despite the ravages of the Spanish influenza. Thankfully 20 Glencairn Road had escaped as influenza had stalked the country, mainly due to their focus on Elizabeth and the ceasing of social engagement during their period of mourning. George was careful to avoid anyone showing signs of illness on his daily train journeys, and instructed Annie and Mrs Monger to ensure they washed their hands in the scullery every time they entered the house. He did not instruct the same of Mrs Curtis the laundrywoman who came each Monday and Wednesday morning, as she did not venture further into the house than the kitchen.

Caroline's days revolved around attending on her mother, but after her father's intervention she was able to spend some time alone or with Annie or Mrs Monger in the kitchen. As the weather improved, Caroline would sit in the shade of the apple tree in the garden and if the twins who lived next door noticed she was there they would come out and talk to her. Florence and Timothy were the same age as Caroline; their parents were teachers, and the family rented the house with the benevolence of an elderly aunt who lived in Lansdown. Florence was destined for finishing school in Austria, and Timothy was expected to become apprenticed to an importer/exporter in Gloucester when he turned sixteen. Florence would frequently ask Caroline to go with her to the Daffodil cinema, but Caroline reluctantly declined.

Caroline's relationship with Annie was closer than would normally be approved of in a family of the Munhead's social standing. Servants were not peers or friends. Had Frederick returned from the war, and the family continued with their social activities, Caroline would undoubtedly have found herself courted by a number of clerks and legal assistants, perhaps friends her brother would have brought home on occasion. As it was, that avenue of social interaction had been cut off for Caroline and so she relied on Annie's stories of her little sisters and their family life to sustain her vicariously. Annie being two years older than Caroline and infinitely more worldly aware, naturally assumed the role of confidant and elder sibling, though she always addressed Caroline as "Miss".

Caroline's other outside contact was with two girls who she had been friends with during her time at Mrs Pendersen's school. They now wrote, intermittently, and their lives were so very different from each other's that they inspired questions and curiosity that maintained the friendships.

17 September 1920
Cheltenham
Dearest Midge,

It was so good to hear from you again. Your letters always make me smile; the antics of your brothers are so interesting to me! How on earth did they manage to crash the tractor? Are they all unhurt? I am glad to hear you were only spectating that time. I cannot imagine what Mother and Father would say if I arrived home on a tractor one day! Well, perhaps I could imagine it.

All of my news is domestic as usual. Mother has a routine now of receiving friends on Thursday afternoons while Annie is out of the house. I think Mother feels Annie would hear too much gossip if she were here to serve the tea and cake, because in truth that is all Mother's friends talk about. It has become my role to serve tea and cake instead, supervised by Mrs Monger of course, else I would surely forget the milk or slice the cake incorrectly. I do not care for Mother's friends, or the young ladies they bring with them. The young ladies do not talk, and I am rarely spoken to, so their contribution is rather unclear to me.

How exciting that you will be going to the theatre! Is Reading a very large town? As you know, I have only ever been as far as Gloucester, and I was very young then so I hardly remember it. Timmy talks of the docks to me over our garden wall, and of the ships and canal boats that come and go. He is so desperate to start his apprenticeship. The Palace Theatre sounds so very grand. But what will you wear? What is the fashion in Berkshire today? Annie went to see a production of 'General Post' a few weeks ago at our New Theatre for her birthday treat with the young man she is courting. He is the Coalman's son Jacob. Annie said it was a very funny play but that I might not understand it. I'm not sure why she thinks that.

Do tell me more about the tractor escapade! Also, I would love to hear how your baking fares at the Women's Institute Show.

Yours ever,

Caroline

Margaret 'Midge' Frampton, daughter of Reverend Thomas and Mrs Georgina Frampton of Pangbourne, Berkshire was an

"Not an immediate one, no. I have seen it before after a sudden shock of one kind or another. I am confident it will pass. In my opinion it is a psychological response to the trauma, not a physical one. Elizabeth can speak, she is simply experiencing a temporary amnesia of speech caused by the shock."

"There is no further immediate treatment you suggest?"

"None. I am very sorry for your loss, George. Frederick was a fine young man."

"Thank you. You will send details of the final account at the end of this month?"

Doctor Riley nodded, accepting that the interview was at an end. He offered his hand.

"Send for me if Elizabeth regresses, but I do not believe she will. And look after yourself, George." He closed the study door as he left.

Elizabeth heard the Doctor leave through a laudanum haze. She was vaguely aware a little later of George taking her hand in his; she knew it was him but could not follow what he was saying. She wanted to be alone.

A routine developed at 20 Glencairn Road. George would rise, dress, breakfast and leave to catch the train two short stops to the High Street Halt six days a week. He would take the return train ride each evening, and after handing Annie his coat and hat, he would climb the stairs to spend an hour with Elizabeth in her dark, stuffy room. Elizabeth gradually received him with more lucidity and progressed from lying prostrate to sitting up in bed, to sitting in a chair by her fire. After their interview, George would work in his study until dinner, where he and Caroline would talk quietly about anything other than Frederick.

Elizabeth's routine progressed as Doctor Riley had predicted. She would be increasingly aware of George's exit from the house each morning. She gradually accepted breakfast in her room on a tray, gradually washed and dressed at first with Caroline's and Annie's help. Sometimes she could be coaxed into the schoolroom, and sometimes Caroline attended her in Elizabeth's bedroom.

Christmas 1918 happened around Elizabeth. George and Caroline attended Christ Church together as they had each Sunday since they had moved into Glencairn Road. Caroline received a keepsake box from her parents, though she knew it was her father who had chosen it. She thanked him with a kiss, placed it under her bed that evening, and wondered what on earth she would find to put inside it.

The Munhead's house was not grand. It had been built at the start of the century for the then growing class of respectable professionals. Convenient for the railway and easily within walking distance of the town centre, George had secured the mortgage on their home through his job at the Building Society when Caroline was two years old and had moved his family from a smaller rented house just off the Bath Road. He had not over-stretched his finances. George had been impressed with the construction of the houses in Glencairn Road, the proximity to Christ Church and the open farmland of Arle to the north. He had felt justified in the expenditure, and naturally Elizabeth had been overjoyed to have room for a live-in maid. Their first maid had not been satisfactory, and neither had the following two, none of them lasting more than a few weeks and one being a positive threat to the family's dinner service. Then came Ruth, who had stayed with the Munheads until Caroline was eleven. Ruth had left their employment when she married a young man who worked at the Queens Hotel between Montpellier and Imperial Gardens. She had arranged for Annie, her niece then aged thirteen, to take on her role.

eminently practical girl having grown up with four brothers. Matthew and Mark were older than her. Luke was a year younger, and John followed three years later. Collectively the boys were known locally as the 'Gospels'. Midge had been sent to board at Mrs Pendersen's School for Young Ladies just before her eighth birthday, in an attempt to quell her boisterous and completely un-ladylike behaviour. Six years there succeeded in giving Midge all of the accoutrements expected of a young lady in polite society but did very little to smooth off her rough edges. She still spoke a little too loudly, was a little less concerned with her appearance than other girls and knew a lot more about the world through her brothers than was considered necessary. Her parents, while wanting to do the right and appropriate thing by their daughter, were also socialist in their outlook. Once Midge returned home, as long as she was engaged in some constructive or benevolent activity, they were content to allow her tomboy proclivities to remain.

In later years Midge would come to understand how unusual and yet beneficial her upbringing had been. Her father's parish encompassed the villages of Pangbourne and Upper Basildon, with poverty, industry and wealth distributed across the largely rural landscape. Industry was centred along the river Thames and the railway station at Pangbourne, with grain and other produce from the surrounding farms transported to Reading and on to London. A couple of miles from Pangbourne, the Basildon Park estate had been offered by the Morrison family as a convalescent home during the Great War. The servicemen were encouraged to create and help repair tools used on the estate and local farms, and to contribute to the local community. As Midge's parents spent a good deal of their time assisting with the administration of these activities, Midge and her brothers had the run of the estate. Matthew had served his country with the 8th Battalion of the Berkshire Regiment but had been wounded in the shoulder at Ypres and lost some of the use of his left arm. Mark had been given a medical exemption due to epilepsy, which thankfully gave him infrequent seizures. There was always an engine to dismantle and rebuild, an animal to be fed or treated for an ailment, food to prepare and share, stories to be told or listened to.

Caroline's other school friend could not have been more different to Midge, or to Caroline herself. Helen Postgate, middle child and third daughter of Colonel William Postgate and his wife Lady Rosalind of Plymouth in Devon. She had had all the advantages of a young woman whose parentage was at the outer edges of the aristocracy. Yet being the middle child with two older sisters and two younger brothers also had its disadvantages. She was aware of how her sex had been a disappointment to her parents. It had given her a sense of invisibility at times amongst her siblings, as she was in robust health (unlike Sophia the second eldest who was in the final throws of tuberculosis) and not in constant trouble like her wayward brother William or endowed with a brilliant mind like her youngest brother Jolyon.

Helen became a magpie, collecting interesting and amusing experiences through her siblings and their friends and associates, and never lacking for a topic of conversation at dinner. She regularly spent weekends at the houses and estates of her cousins or their friends, spoke fluent French and passable Italian, and had absolutely no intention of finding a husband. She had spent three years at Mrs Pendersen's while her mother had been travelling across Europe with Sophia in search of a cure. Helen's sister Roberta, twelve years Helen's senior, had been placed in charge of the two younger boys – a decision their father continually blamed for William's later indiscretions.

21 October 1921
Derbyshire
Dearest Caro,

How wonderful to hear from you, your letter finally found me at Morley House where I have been practically in an enclosed order for the past 3 weeks, attending to Sophia. I fear she is not long for this earth; it is so terribly sad for Arthur to be home only 2 months from their honeymoon to have his wife deteriorate so quickly. I do not make a particularly good nursemaid. Of course, the doctor is here often, and the servants take on much of the practicalities, but I do my best to be a companionable sister and read to her or mop her brow as is required.

Arthur's Mother is an absolute terror! Her word is law and even Arthur visibly shrinks in her presence. I fell foul of her on my first evening here, for daring to smoke after dinner in the drawing room. I was sent out on to the terrace like a naughty schoolgirl, without thinking to take a wrap or jacket out with me. Thank goodness for the darling old butler Rogers who snuck a rug out for me after a few minutes, along with an ashtray. We have become partners in crime since then, he brings me coffee or a glass of whiskey every evening onto the terrace and if the weather is too dreadful, I settle myself in his boot room with the Labradors and smoke for as long as I please without censure!

You reminded me, I must write to Midge. My cousin Gordon has invited me to weekend with him at Upton Park and we must have Midge to visit while we're there, along with the Gospels of course. Do you think she has grown any taller? Have you, dear Caro? Surely we all have in the four years since we were last together. Are you sure you won't join us at Upton? You know you are always welcome to join whatever party I find myself in.

Heavens, I must end here and take my bath before dinner.

You have no idea how dusty these big old houses are with their hundreds of dogs and staff roaming the halls!

Adieu ma cheri
Helen

Years passed. Christmases and birthdays, Easters and long, dusty summers filled with the scent of flowers from Curzon's Exotic Plant Nurseries which occupied almost five acres between Glencairn Road and Christ Church. Annie's entanglement with Jacob found its own routine between her duties at number 20 and his for his father's coal delivery business. Thursday afternoons they would walk into Cheltenham and take tea at the Cosy Corner Café before walking back again. Sunday mornings they would meet at the gates of St Mark's church and sing together in their Sunday best clothes. Jacob would spend a few minutes after the service talking with Annie's father and sisters before walking Annie back to Glencairn Road.

It was one Sunday afternoon in the early summer of 1924 when Annie told Caroline that Jacob had hinted at marriage on their walk from the church. The girls were in the kitchen, Caroline perched on a stool at the scrubbed table and Annie shelling peas into an enamel colander for the evening meal. Mrs Monger no longer cooked on Sundays for the family, and Annie had expanded her culinary repertoire to compensate.

"Not yet of course. It will take a while yet before we can afford our own home, but Jacob has been saving a little each week and he thinks in maybe a couple of years we might be able to settle down. His father says he's heard the town might be building some new houses on the old Arle Farm, and not just for servicemen either."

"Oh Annie, how exciting! But what does one need to be married, besides a dress of course and some flowers?"

Annie smiled, "A groom." Sometimes Caroline was just too easy to tease.

"Yes, no, I meant how does one do it? What happens?"

"Have you never been to a wedding?"

Caroline shook her head. She was aware of how little social experience she had had directly for a girl of her age. Indeed, by the age of twenty which she now was, many girls would have been a bridesmaid once or twice. Caroline had not. The closest she had come to weddings was to help with the floral decorations at Christ Church in advance of the ceremonies.

Annie popped a peapod and inspected the contents for worms before using her thumb to remove the row of peas into the waiting colander.

"Jacob will need to ask Father's permission to marry me. That's the first thing. Even though I'll be over twenty-one, I'd expect him to do that. Then we'd need to decide on a date and book the church. I'd like a spring wedding, all the flowers just starting to bloom. They have to read the banns, that takes three weeks unless the bishop allows you to have a special licence. That usually only happens when the man is leaving for war though. We won't need a special licence."

"What are the banns?"

"It's like telling everyone that you're going to get married, just in case there's a reason why you shouldn't. The vicar puts a notice on the church notice board for it and talks about it at the end of his sermon. Don't they do that at Christ Church?"

"No, the Reverend Canon doesn't do that, but I've seen the banns in the porch, I just hadn't realised what they were." She took a raw pea from the bowl and slipped it into her mouth.

"I suppose they would do it differently in the big churches. You're right, I'll need a frock, and Jacob will need a clean suit. And a ring. That's all really, anything else is nice to have but to be married you just say your vows in church and that's it. Jacob says he doesn't want us to live with his family, he still shares a bedroom with his brothers like I do at home with the girls. But people will always need coal, its steady employment, so Jacob says we'll be able to afford somewhere that's more than a couple of rooms in a basement."

Cheltenham was indeed a town for rent. Many of the larger town houses around the Suffolk and Lansdown areas stood empty, and the population was shrinking. The town council was trying to improve the facilities for visitors to take the Spa waters, and several private and public baths catered to those who perhaps could not afford European retreats. There were of course also areas of extreme poverty and deprivation in the town. The monthly council meetings of the Housing sub-committee were appraised of numerous properties inspected and found unfit for human habitation or in violation of the requirement for adequate ash and other waste disposal.

Insulated from all of this, Caroline's life now existed along the wide Queens Road and Christ Church and little further. She rarely left the house without the company of either her mother or father. She was not unhappy, that would have been unfair to her parents and especially her father who had done his best to encourage Caroline's interest in the outside world in so far as his reading of the newspapers would allow. He was well aware that she would otherwise have been enjoying a colourful social circle of friends, and privately he felt he should have been firmer with his wife's insistence that Caroline be protected from external dangers. He had been delighted with Caroline's curiosity about the excavations in Egypt of Carnarvon and Carter over the past two years. They had spent several very pleasant Saturday afternoons in his study poring over maps and through histories of antiquity to satisfy some, though not all, of her questions.

No, she was not unhappy, but Caroline was beginning to feel an unnamed and unrecognised restlessness. Her awareness of the world outside her own was gnawing at the tethers that kept her securely orbiting her mother.

"What does St Mark's look like? On the inside I mean." Caroline took a handful of peas this time.

Annie tutted. "It's not as big as Christ Church, not as gold. Wooden pews, two rows of big, plastered columns down the sides of the pews, arched windows. I don't know, it looks like a church I suppose! Come and see it next week if you like."

Caroline paused mid chew. Could she? How could she explain it to her mother? Elizabeth would not approve of her attending church with those of the lower classes. St Mark's was a rural church compared to Christ Church and was literally on the other side of the railway tracks. Caroline knew she would have to speak to her father first.

"What time is the service on Sunday morning?"

"It starts at nine, Miss, I can come here first and walk with you."

"I'll ask my father."

Annie understood.

"Of course not!" Elizabeth had been about to put a fork laden with green beans into her mouth. She held it as she spoke, one bean falling back on to her dinner plate.

"Elizabeth, there is no harm in Caroline visiting another church."

"She has no need to. Christ Church is our parish church and is the church we attend as a family."

"St Mark's is a perfectly respectable church, my dear. The Vicar is known for his work with the poor of his parish."

"And it's not as if it's a Methodist chapel, or a Catholic church," the words were out of Caroline's mouth before she could stop them. George put down his knife and fork and dabbed his mouth with his napkin, looking at Caroline as if to say, let me handle this. He took a sip of water.

"Caroline is not leaving the Christ Church congregation. She is simply viewing another form of service for one day. Is that not correct Caroline?"

"Yes, Father."

"And Annie will accompany you?"

"That's hardly a satisfactory situation!" Elizabeth protested.

"Yes, Father, she says she will come here first and walk with me, and we will return here after the service."

"Elizabeth, if Annie is acceptable to serve our food and polish our silverware, then I feel she is acceptable to accompany Caroline away from our sight for a few hours of daylight."

Caroline smiled to herself and continued with her roast mutton.

The sun shone brightly the following Sunday as Annie and Caroline approached the wooden gate of St Mark's. Annie's sisters broke away from the small knot of people in the street and ran up to them. Louisa was now sixteen, Julia fourteen and had just left school, and Sara a petite twelve in her best white pinafore. Caroline having never met them before was fascinated to see how much they resembled Annie, though she tried hard not to stare. Each had the same liberal allocation of freckles across the nose and forehead, and light brown hair that shone with golden highlights in the sun. They walked on together to the gate, where Annie introduced her father, whose freckles were present but with much less hair than his daughters. Jacob arrived taking off his cap and wiping his hand on his trousers before offering it for Caroline to shake. They moved through the gate, Annie making introductions all the way up the path and into the church, until their party were seated on the left of the centre aisle in a pew three from the front.

Caroline glanced around the other pews as the church quickly filled. She became aware that her clothes, though plain, were of better quality and repair than those of the congregation. She had worn a light coat and was thankful for it as the interior of the little church was cool after the heat outside. She took off her gloves as she noticed few of the other women were wearing any. Annie passed her a hymn sheet; again, Caroline noticed that few of the congregation were holding them, but she was interested in the hymns as they were unfamiliar to her with the exception of *Holy, Holy, Holy, Lord God Almighty*. She was a little surprised to see it listed for the service as she was more used to singing it at Pentecost. As the Vicar entered from the vestry, the congregation stood as one and the service began.

The experience was uplifting for Caroline. She had not imagined that the word of God could be spoken with such lightness and compassion. She had only ever heard long dull sermons proclaiming restraint and modesty, with the threat of damnation held over anyone who might take enjoyment from simply living. But this Vicar, though of a similar age to the Reverend Canon Lloyd, was a kindly soul. His love for his parishioners was clear. The sermon he preached that morning was based around Psalm 140:12 "I know that the Lord secures justice for the poor and upholds the cause of the needy". It was less a sermon about being thankful for what one has, which Caroline would have expected from the Reverend Canon, but more about how God loved the very least of mankind equally and that all would serve Him by serving others less fortunate than themselves.

Even the congregations' singing was different. Caroline quickly picked up the melody of each hymn, and found them a faster tempo to the plodding, deliberate hymns sung in Christ Church. She smiled as she sang and glancing at Annie found her to be smiling too. She could not remember enjoying singing as much as she was in that moment. At the end of the service, Caroline asked Annie if she could keep the hymn sheet.

The walk home with Annie and Jacob was equally uplifting. Caroline was full of questions about the members of the congregation, the hymns, and the Vicar, and the couple tried their best to answer them. Caroline left them to say their goodbye at the garden gate and trotted inside to get a drink of water. It would be another hour before her parents returned from church and Annie would need to start preparing luncheon. Caroline ran up the stairs and flopped down on her bed, hands behind her head, to digest all that she had seen and heard that morning. A few minutes later she got up and retrieved the hymn sheet from her dressing table. The typewritten text, with its smudged letters o and e was worth keeping as a reminder of the morning she decided.

She looked around her room for somewhere safe to put the hymn sheet. It could go flat inside a book, but what if she lent the book to someone and it was lost? As she sat on her bed, she moved her foot and her heel bumped against the wooden box she had been given years before by her parents. The Christmas present she had received the year that Freddie had died. She had pushed it under her bed, sure that she would never have anything special to keep in it, and there it had stayed. Caroline reached down and pulled the box out. It was covered in dust which did not all blow away when she tried. Using the corner of a blanket, Caroline wiped the lid and sides of the wooden box clean.

It was a decoupage box, approximately twelve inches by ten inches and four inches deep. The lid had two small brass hinges. The box had been painted black, then paper flowers cut out and pasted onto the surface, before the whole thing had been varnished in the Victorian style. Caroline had gone as far as to lay a piece of red crepe paper in the bottom but had not placed anything inside it. She tried the hymn sheet and found that it fitted over the crepe paper with an inch or so to spare around the edges.

On very hot days, the scent of roses and other flowers wound its way from Curzon's Exotic Plant Nurseries into the nearby houses on the breeze. Annie cursed the soot from the railway engines that speckled the sheets on the washing line. Thursday afternoons continued to be when Elizabeth received her visitors. The most frequent attendees were Mrs Salmond and her daughter Josephine, and Mrs Tomlins and her daughter Eliza. Both women were married to employees of banks in the town, and felt their social standing was equal to Elizabeth's. One afternoon in early September, they were assembled in the parlour. Mrs Tomlins had been describing her recent visit to the Pump Rooms to the party.

"Of course, one can never be completely sure of the restorative qualities, but Doctor Vaughan recommends it."

Mrs Salmond saw an opening to impart a piece of news she had been sitting on since she arrived.

"I hear, on very good authority, that the Vicar of St Mark's intends to take a young curate to relieve him of some of his duties."

Caroline's curiosity was piqued, but she did not speak.

Elizabeth sipped her tea and said, "He is an older gentleman, is he not?"

"The Vicar? I believe so. The new curate is not. He is to come up from Bristol, some arrangement between the Bishop and our Bishop of Gloucester as I understand it. And his wife is," she paused for dramatic effect, "coloured."

Elizabeth carefully placed her teacup on its saucer.

"Caroline, would you fetch some more hot water." It was not a request, Caroline knew. She rose and took the jug out of the room, straining her ears unsuccessfully to catch any of the rest of the conversation.

Later that evening Caroline found Annie in the kitchen by the range mending some linen.

"Mrs Salmond told Mother today that the new curate at St Mark's has a coloured wife, is that true?"

"I haven't met her, Miss, but I believe so, yes."

"Have you ever seen a coloured person before?"

"No. Have you?"

"No. Well, there was a girl from Ceylon at school, but her father was British. She had a photograph of him. I remember she had incredibly long black hair. Timmy says there are coloured men who work on the ships that come into Gloucester. Annie, when do you have your harvest festival service at St Mark's? I should like to attend."

"It's next weekend Miss. As I understand it the new curate takes up his position at Michaelmas, but he might be attending the harvest festival. It's a good way to get to know us all, everyone will be there for the harvest supper on the Saturday. You could come along to that maybe?"

"No, I don't think that would be appropriate. Mother would be horrified. But I think Father will allow me to attend the service on the Sunday."

The weather had not been kind to the farm labourers that week. In the fields around Cheltenham heavy rain created new streams, bogged down carts and tractors, and stranded a small flock of sheep on an island at Uckington as the river Chelt overflowed nearby. The majority of farms in the area produced fruit from vast orchards, and the itinerant labourers swelled the numbers of farm workers in the town considerably during August and September.

The harvest festival service at St Mark's was one of the best attended of the year, as usual. The congregation being mostly labouring classes, naturally wanted to give thanks for another bountiful harvest. They were also keen to receive any provisions donated but unused from the harvest supper the evening before. Trooping into the cool of the church from the torrential downpour and howling unseasonal wind outside, the congregation were a dripping and sniffing collection of souls. Caroline again sat with Annie and her family, having stowed her umbrella in the corner of the entrance porch.

Annie's assumption had proved correct. After welcoming everyone, and the singing of the first hymn to warm them all up, the Vicar asked his new curate to step forward and be introduced. Philip Rose was a bespectacled young man with neatly oiled dark hair. Even from three pews away, Caroline noticed his particularly long and slender fingers.

"Would you like to say a few words, Philip?" the Vicar asked.

"Indeed, Vicar, thank you. Everyone, I am honoured to be nominated for the position of curate here, and I cannot think of a better man to take instruction from. I do hope that I, along with my wife, can serve you all as we serve God and continue with the Vicar's work here in the parish of Saint Mark. Mary, join me..." He held out his hand towards the front pew. Caroline had noticed a neat hat in front of her but had not seen the individual wearing it. "...I am sure we will both be very happy here."

There was an audible intake of breath from somewhere behind Caroline as Mary turned to face the congregation. She wore a simple navy-blue coat, belt tied at the waist, trimmed with white piping along the wide collar, white gloves and a navy cloche hat. She looked out at the faces looking back at her and lifted her chin a little, relaxing her shoulders. Philip was beaming next to her and seemed oblivious to any tension. Feet shuffled. A baby grizzled. Annie's father cleared his throat, then began to clap his hands. Annie nudged Jacob and they joined her father, and in a wave the welcome applause was picked up around the pews. Caroline enthusiastically joined in with a grin and caught Mary's eye. Mary smiled and Philip laughed, and the Vicar looking around in surprise clapped for a moment also before raising his hands to quiet the congregation again.

"Thank you, my friends, thank you. Now, hymn number 47 if you please Mr Peters."

Lunch that Sunday was tense at 20 Glencairn Road. Caroline had asked her father's permission to attend St Mark's but had not mentioned it to her mother and had left the house without seeing her that morning. Caroline was sure her parents had disagreed about it, but they would not do so in front of Annie. Elizabeth made a point of eating very little and placed her cutlery onto her plate with more volume than usual. She declined dessert, and excused herself as quickly as she could, retiring to her room.

"Father, I should like to attend St Mark's occasionally but next weekend I will go with you and Mother to Christ Church. I don't want to cause any upset."

George leaned back in his chair and dabbed his mouth with his napkin.

"Your Mother wants the best for you Caroline, as I do. However, we do not always agree on what that might be. I think it would be a welcome gesture if you would attend with us next Sunday." He looked at Caroline, and she noticed the first grey hairs at his temple and some new tiny purple thread veins on his left cheek.

Throughout the rest of September and October the Mun-head family attended services together at Christ Church. Caroline decided that it would be simpler to acquiesce to her mother's wishes than to fight to attend St Mark's. The anniversary of Frederick's death was looming. November would never again be a month of anticipation for Christmas at number 20; Freddie's absence, and the absence of a graveside to properly mourn at, lay in heavy folds on beds and chairs throughout the house. It swept around the rooms with the pulling of thick brocade curtains and chilled the food so that it caught in the throat unexpectedly. As the daylight hours decreased and darkness stretched the evenings into lamplit sombre tableaux, the occupants felt themselves both shrinking and swelling at the same time. If we can just get through November, was silently muttered a hundred times every day.

Sunday November 2nd dawned with a frost and a cold fog enveloped the town. Caroline woke as Annie brought a jug of hot water into her bedroom.

"Sorry for waking you Miss, but breakfast is waiting."

The small wooden mantle clock said eight-fifteen. Caroline waited while Annie poked the embers in the small fireplace and brought them back to life, adding a few nuggets of coke from the scuttle. When Annie had gone, Caroline quickly washed her face and dressed in woollen stockings and woollen vest underneath her black woollen dress. Always black in November. She sat at her dressing table and brushed her long hair. She tried to remember Freddie as he had been before he enlisted. Tried to imagine him now, a man of twenty-six, perhaps married, perhaps with children of his own. It was no use; the image would not come. She put down the brush.

How old am I? Will I repeat this performance every November for the rest of my life? Will I stay here in this room, here in this house, slowly aging as Father and Mother are?

Her stomach growled. She went down to breakfast.

Christ Church was, despite the recently installed heating system, freezing cold. The gentlemen removed their hats on entry, but the women kept theirs firmly on their heads. Coats remained on their owners, fur and wool pulled closer to the skin, toes wriggled inside boots and shoes. The choirboys had been permitted to wear sweaters beneath their surplice. The Reverend Canon took his place at the pulpit to the left of the great arch where the altar stood. A serious man, authoritative in speech and deed, he surveyed his shivering flock.

"Hebrews, Chapter eleven. A study in faith. Verse 32, 'And what shall I more say? For the time would…'"

At midday the ladies and gentlemen and their children of the parish of Christ Church made their way from the cold of the church to the cold of the foggy street outside. Caroline followed her parents, her head slightly bowed, her attention not drawn by the small groups forming near the wide double doors as it usually was. She was thinking about the words of the sermon. Words that had echoed around the gallery and wove around the muffled bodies assembled; words proclaiming that with faith, anything was possible. With faith, the mouths of lions could be stopped. With faith, women received their dead raised again.

She continued to walk a few paces behind her parents all the way home, an idea growing in her mind. It resonated with her thoughts in front of the mirror that morning, what would Freddie be doing now? Why should she be constrained in the shroud of his mourning? At lunch, the family were naturally quiet, each thinking their own thoughts. Caroline declined to accompany her parents to the evening service. She needed more time to think.

It was Monday after dinner, when Elizabeth had retired, that Caroline felt ready to articulate her request as she sat in the parlour with George.

"Father, I shall be twenty-one next year."

"Indeed, you shall."

"I do not feel that I have seen as much of the world as any other twenty-one-year-old woman."

George put down the evening newspaper. He had wondered when this conversation might happen. He wanted to give Caroline his full attention; he could see she was carefully selecting her words.

"Perhaps not."

"I have declined invitations that I should have liked to accept. I fear that if I continue, those invitations will cease to arrive. I have been thinking of Freddie, of how joyful he always was, how he got stuck into things. Father, I do not feel that I am doing justice to Freddie's memory by becoming an old maid." She looked up at her father, frown lines creasing her brow.

"Freddie was fearless. Had the war not taken him from us, it is possible that some other escapade or adventure would have. Boys are made for such things, Caroline."

"And what of girls? Freddie was a bright light, and I do not honour him by living in shadow."

"What do you propose?"

Caroline took a deep breath. "I should like to say yes to things, Father. I have no real plans, but I do have faith that opportunities will present themselves to me, and I should like to be able to grasp them as they emerge. I want to talk of more than parish news and new shoes. I want to experience whatever God has in store for me. I may already be too late, but women are forging new occupations and movements and I want to be part of it all."

George held his daughter's gaze. How much she looked like Freddie. How he had frowned in the same way when announcing his desire to enlist. George could never have stopped Freddie, and he was sure he could not stop Caroline now. But he would need to handle the request with more diplomacy and forethought than ever, and especially with Elizabeth. He would need to consider all arguments and have answers at the ready.

"Your mother will not be enthusiastic."

"I am not asking to emigrate. I am not asking to become a policewoman or fly an aeroplane. At least, not yet. But I cannot be my mother's lap dog!" she said with exasperation.

"There are things to consider, Caroline. Let me consider them and speak with your mother. You were not intending to embark on this adventure immediately?"

"No… Yes, should an opportunity arise!"

"But one has not yet presented itself?"

"No."

"Then I will consider how we might facilitate you. Have faith in me also."

Caroline excused herself the following evening after dinner, and lay on her bed, fully clothed, straining her ears to pick up any morsel of conversation between her parents in the rooms below. She knew she had to break out of the cocoon of mourning, she was too young to spend the rest of her days gossiping over tea and cake. Her gossip was limited in any case as she rarely saw anyone outside of her mother's circle. Her mother's friends would not be interested in the people Caroline had met at St Mark's, with the exception of Philip and Mary of course.

Caroline had felt a kinship with Philip and Mary that had surprised her. Philip's beaming smile, and Mary's quiet self-assuredness, spoke to Caroline of the world beyond Cheltenham. Mary was exotic, intriguing. Even if her father did not manage to convince her mother to agree to Caroline's request, Caroline resolved to spend more time at St Mark's and try to make a friend of Mary – heaven knows Mary might need one given the initial reaction of the congregation.

George had been considering Caroline's request all day and had spent some time before dinner in his study, checking through some documents. He had also decided on the way to broach the subject with his wife. They retired to the parlour after dinner. George picked up the evening newspaper and Elizabeth her current novel, sitting either side of the fire that burned brightly.

After a few minutes, George rested his hands on the arms of the chair and looked at Elizabeth. "My dear, I have been thinking about Caroline's future."

Elizabeth placed her bookmark into the novel and closed it, holding the book in her lap. She was on guard but looked across at her husband. "Indeed." She said, cautiously.

"I believe it is time that she made her way in society. She will not find a husband if she spends all of her time here in the house."

"There is little society in Cheltenham, George. It is her duty to remain with us. She is still so young."

"She is almost twenty-one. I would very much like her to remain with us, but I do not think young women today are satisfied with the occupations that our generation have been sustained by."

"Nonsense! Young women want nothing more than a home to manage, and Caroline will have that here with us."

George folded his newspaper. "Caroline, I think, will want more. She may stay with us while she finds it, but she has a curiosity Elizabeth, and that will not be satisfied within our limited acquaintances. I have decided to make her an allowance, to enable her to make her own way," his voice was quiet but clear, "should she want to."

"An allowance? Her needs are already met through our accounts. I really do not see the need for this, George."

"An allowance, of £50 for the next year. The money we had put aside for Frederick's university expenses will be adequate to cover it, and I will of course make some conditions." This was, he knew, a risk. To mention Freddie, and in this context, could provoke Elizabeth.

Her hands gripped the book in her lap. The reminder that Freddie would not need a university education was a cold, stark reality that she did not want to face. Her voice trembled, "I need her here George. I need to keep her safe. We will need her as we grow old. She is the only one left."

"My dear, we did not have children so that they might nurse us in later years. We had children because it was God's will. It was His will that Freddie was taken from us. I feel it is His will that we provide a sound basis for Caroline's foray into the world. Believe me," he leaned forward, "I feel she will spread her wings whether we assist her or not, and I would be failing as a father if I did not provide for her as best I can."

"Has she said as much? I knew that church would be a lowering influence. Consorting with the servants, unthinkable when I was a girl. We have been too generous already George, we must put a stop to it now!"

"We must not, Elizabeth. I have decided. The allowance will be Caroline's from January the first. I do not think she will become extravagant overnight, but I shall make it clear that there will be no further amount available. And of course, if she were to travel, I will insist that she corresponds with us on a regular basis."

"Daily, I should think."

"That may not be practical, my dear. I think it reasonable to require a weekly letter."

"And what if something terrible happens to her? How would we know? Oh George, the risk is too great!" Elizabeth could hear the note of panic in her own voice.

"I propose to inform Doctor Riley and ensure that Caroline has his telephone number for emergencies. But really Elizabeth, I am sure that nothing serious will occur."

Elizabeth knew she was overruled. She dropped her gaze and opened her book. "Yes, George."

"Fifty pounds! Father, that is too much!"

They were standing at the window of George's study the following Saturday after lunch. A cold rain fell steadily outside, and the lamps were lit in the house opposite.

"I do not think so. It is not so great an amount more than Annie earns in a year. However, there will be conditions. The money will be available to you from January 1st, for you to spend however you choose and I have opened an account for you at Lloyds Bank in town. But this should be an exercise in learning for you, not just one of extravagance, therefore if you wish to receive the same allowance the following year, I will require you to have retained at least the fifty pounds in full by the final day of December 1925. And you must refrain from immoral or illegal means of recovery, naturally."

Caroline's mind fizzed with excitement, but she wanted to be sure she understood her father's terms.

"So, I am to earn money as well as having the allowance? And if I end the year with fifty pounds in my account, then I can have another fifty pounds for the following year?"

"No, my dear. If you end the year with fifty pounds in your account, you will be able to keep it for another year. I am making you a donation that need not be repaid but would also not necessarily be repeated. Should you not recover the fifty pounds by the end of next December, then our... experiment will come to an end. Is that acceptable?"

"Oh yes, Father!" Caroline threw her arms around her father and kissed his cheek. He placed his hands on her shoulders and gently moved her backwards, smiling.

"If you are to be a lady of the world, you would do well to remember the deportment Mrs Pendersen must have taught you."

27 November 1924
Pangbourne, Berkshire
Dear Caroline,

What a turn up for the books! You, a lady of leisure for a year, well I never! Goodness but I am thrilled for you of course. I have often wondered how long you would remain your mother's companion, it seemed so at odds with how you were at school.

Now, let me start you off on your adventure, and invite you once again to spend a few days with us here before Christmas. Do say you'll come this year! The weekend before Christmas would be suitable for us, and one of my brothers will meet you at the railway station in Pangbourne on the Friday if you let us know by which train you will be arriving. We can make up a spare bed in my room, well away from the boys! It will be just like the old days at school, at least for me.

Bring some old clothes with you, as well as a smart outfit. No doubt we'll end up in a muddy field or knee deep in the river while you're here. Oh, it will be such fun to have you here!

Write as soon as you can, dear

Midge

MIDGE

Caroline stood on the station platform, her small suitcase at her feet, staring hard at the station name painted on the wall opposite just to be absolutely certain she was in the right place. It had been an exciting journey, though of course one made by travellers across the country daily. She had only rarely travelled in a train carriage before. Though her father preferred the train to go to work, if Caroline had ever needed to go into Cheltenham for shopping, she and her mother had taken the tram or had walked. That morning Annie had accompanied her to the station, carrying Caroline's case, and made sure that she purchased the correct ticket. Her agreement with her father was not due to begin for another three weeks, but Caroline had a few pounds in her account from previous birthdays and could cover the expenses herself.

Making the change at Oxford had been bewildering. The conductor made sure she got off the first train at the correct stop, and then the station porter had kindly carried her case and deposited her in exactly the right spot on the platform so that she could board the next train due to Pangbourne station.

And here she was. The steam drifted across the platform as the train pulled away with a toot of its whistle. It had been frosty that morning and the frost remained in corners untouched by the weak sun that was now attempting to break through the clouds. Caroline checked her watch by the station clock, picked up her case, and began to walk in the direction the other travellers had taken towards the exit.

Midge had said she would be there to meet Caroline. How much would she have changed since their school days? Caroline needn't have worried. As she rounded the corner of the ticket office and passed through the picket gate and into the street, someone shouted her name. She turned to see Midge, it had to be her, waving frantically from a trailer attached to a bright blue tractor. In the tractor driver's seat, a young man with a strong resemblance to Midge was concentrating on directing the activity of two other young men who had the side flap of the tractor's engine open and were bent over it together. Midge jumped down from the trailer and trotted across the yard.

Standing five feet and two inches tall, Midge Frampton wore trousers tucked into her wellington boots, an old woollen jumper over a collarless shirt and a tweed jacket with patches on one arm and a missing pocket. On her head, apart from her spectacles, she wore a knitted woollen pompom hat pulled down over her dark shoulder-length hair. Underneath the hat, a tortoiseshell clip ensured that no hair fell over Midge's spectacles.

The girls hugged a little awkwardly and then both giggled.

"It's so good to see you again! Let me take your case…"

"No, really, I can manage. Everyone else has been carrying it for me all day."

"Mother is so thrilled that you are staying, she has been baking in a frenzy for days! Now, if you wait a moment, we've got a box for you to step up on. The cart is perfectly clean to sit in, I made sure of that myself – I wasn't going to leave it to them."

Midge slid Caroline's case onto the floor of the trailer, and pulled out a crate, placing it on the ground. Then she held Caroline's hand as she stepped up from crate to footboard and onto the trailer bed. There was no time to be hesitant, Midge retrieved the crate as soon as Caroline's foot had left it and stowed it again next to her case. The girls sat on the wooden bench seat just behind the tractor.

"Matty, say hello to Caroline."

Matthew turned in his seat and smiled Midge's smile at Caroline. "Pleased to meet you, Caroline. I won't shake hands just now, a bit oily I'm afraid. The old girl was running perfectly yesterday but we're just making sure now that we can get you home." He turned again to face the tractor and instructed the others to close the flap as it was time to move out.

Two heads appeared, one with the same dark hair as Midge and Matthew, the other with a sandy, wayward mop. They quickly scrambled into the trailer and as Matthew coaxed the tractor out of the yard, they introduced themselves as Mark and Luke. John, they reported, was at work on the river and would meet Caroline that evening at dinner. Mark, Caroline learned, was the real mechanic of the family. He had asked for the afternoon off from his job at Emery's Garage in the village so that he could drive the tractor to collect Caroline, thinking that Matthew would be working on the Basildon Park estate. Matthew had had the same idea, and Luke was home from the University College in Reading where he was studying medicine, so all three brothers had braved the cold to help their sister.

The Vicarage was a Victorian gothic jumble of gables, wings, projections and embellishments. It stood in almost an acre of garden just outside the centre of Pangbourne and faced the river Thames with a sweep of farmland behind. It had two staircases, one at either end of the ground floor, and five floors including the cellar and the attic rooms. The Reverend and Mrs Frampton kept no live-in servants but had a cook, a maid and a gardener who came and went at various times of the day, mostly organising themselves. As long as meals were prepared, fires lit and fed, and the laundry undertaken, the Framptons were very much loath to ask too much of their staff; it went against the grain.

The girls alighted the trailer in the street outside the Vicarage at the garden gate and walked up the brick path to the house while the Gospels took the tractor on to the farm sheds where it was kept. Midge explained that they would probably not appear again until dinner time, as they were generally governed by their stomachs.

"Mother and Father are at the church hall. The Christmas bazaar is tomorrow, and they are organising. We can go along once you've unpacked."

Midge led the way around the side of the Vicarage to the kitchen door, explaining that they rarely used the front door. Caroline was struggling to keep up with the commentary of her friend, the new sights, sounds and smells, and as they passed through the large kitchen, she was suddenly aware that she was hungry, having only had a sandwich on the train that Annie had wrapped in waxed paper for her that morning.

"I say Midge, could I have a glass of water please?"

"Goodness, mother would shoot me for not offering you something to eat and drink! I'm so sorry Caroline, what can I get you? Here, there is some soup still warm on the range, would that be alright with some bread and cheese? It's leek and potato, we had it earlier."

Not waiting for a response, Midge quickly ladled soup into a bowl and cut a thick slice of bread from a loaf covered with a cloth on the kitchen table. Caroline took off her coat, hat and gloves and sat down, grateful that Midge had been so perceptive of her needs. Two glasses with thick bottoms were filled with water from a jug on the dresser, and Midge sat opposite her friend and handed her a napkin.

"Did you enjoy the train ride?"

Caroline swallowed and dabbed her mouth, "Oh yes, it was exciting. I've never been on one this far before."

"We take the train to Reading quite a bit, especially when Luke has a free afternoon. He has rooms in Wantage Hall just next to the hospital, which is quite a walk from the train station, so we usually meet him at Lyons and then take a walk around the Forbury. A band plays there in the summer. I do like a good brass band, though Father prefers piano pieces and Mother loves to sing." She took a sip of water.

"We've got the weekend all planned out for you, Mother says it might be a bit much, so do say if you feel tired or don't want to join in with anything, we shan't be offended. I forget sometimes that other people don't live like we do! We'll get you unpacked, and I'll show you the house first, then we can walk down to the church hall and meet Mother and Father and see if there is anything left to do for the bazaar. The boys will be back for dinner, and then we read or play cards in the library. Father might have the wireless or gramophone on."

Caroline's heart skipped, music!

"Tomorrow morning we'll walk up to the Park. You can borrow John's wellingtons. We'll call in at the hospital so that you can meet Kate. She's Matthew's girlfriend, she's a nurse, they met when he was recovering." Midge paused, aware that Matthew had survived the war and Freddie had not.

"I should like to meet her," Caroline said, finishing her bread.

"Super! Then we'll go to the bazaar in the afternoon, and we'll probably be roped in to help clear up afterwards too. Sunday will be church of course, then lunch, and then in the afternoon John says he can take us out on the river if you'd

like, or Mark could borrow a car and take us for a drive. My
brothers refuse to let me drive anything and I have no idea why.
Anyway, you see, there is lots to do." She beamed at Caroline
across the table, almost bouncing in her chair with the joy of
having her friend there to entertain.

The tour of the Vicarage began on the ground floor, with
Caroline's belongings left on the bottom stair of one of the
staircases. It had a familiar smell of polish and coal dust. Midge
kept up a commentary of humorous family incidents that had
happened in each room as they passed through them. The hall
was large; wood panelled and with a black and white tiled
floor on which the green glass in the front door cast patterns.
The library was twice the size of Caroline's father's study and
contained an assortment of chairs and low tables as well as a
writing desk in the window bay where Midge's mother would
compose her correspondence. The front parlour held settees and
worn upholstered fireside chairs, occasional tables and a small
piano. The dining room and the Reverend's study completed
the ground floor family rooms.

On the first floor was a large nursery room that the children
had now outgrown. It held sporting equipment of all kinds
including a set of skis and a toboggan. Midge's mother had a
bedroom and a dressing room on this floor; her father also had
his bedroom and dressing room, there was a bathroom and a
separate toilet, and John's bedroom. Caroline was very interested
in the bathroom; Glencairn Road had an indoor toilet, but the
family bathed in their own bedrooms with Annie bringing up
jugs of hot water for the large tin bath.

The second floor held the remaining bedrooms for Matthew,
Mark, Midge and Luke, plus another bathroom. Midge's room
looked out over the river at the front of the house. Having
walked from one side of the house to the other on this floor,
the girls took the opposite staircase to the attic rooms. There

were two, previously used by former staff of the Vicars before Midge's father arrived. The second staircase meant the staff could access the kitchen without bumping into the residents or guests. Now they just provided extra surfaces for the maid to clean.

Midge explained that while there was electricity on the ground floor, the rest of the house remained unwired. The bedrooms had fireplaces and gas lights, which was just as well because the draughts would often blow out unprotected candles. Back in Midge's room, Caroline was left to unpack by herself while Midge went to answer a caller at the front door. A bed had been made up as promised for Caroline, and space cleared in a drawer in the large chest by the door.

Opening her case, Caroline was unsure if her wardrobe would be suitable for the activities Midge had outlined. As instructed, she had packed an old sweater and had on Mrs Monger's suggestion, found a pair of Freddie's trousers that fitted reasonably well with the aid of a belt. She had not told her mother about taking them. She had two day dresses plus the one she was currently wearing, but only stockings and no socks. She felt that this was a vital omission and when Midge returned, she explained her situation.

"Not to worry, I have tons you can borrow! I spent all last winter knitting pair after pair just to learn how. Here, take these." She produced three dark blue socks from the top drawer of the chest, and then rummaged for a fourth to make two pairs. "You can keep them."

"Oh, I couldn't possibly…" Caroline began.

"Yes, you could, silly thing, see how many I have!" Midge scooped up the rest of the socks from the draw which filled her arms and her beaming smile returned.

The church of St James the Less stood to one side of Pangbourne's main street, near to the George and Dragon Hotel which was the central focus of night life in the village.

The church hall had been built three years before on the edge of the field next to the church yard. Its wooden exterior was painted cream with bright green trim around the windows and green double entrance doors. Inside it was well provisioned with a small kitchen, a toilet, a storeroom, a large hall with a raised stage at the end opposite the entrance door, and behind that, an area that could be called a dressing room or 'backstage'. The hall had electricity, and its own committee as a sub-committee to the Parish Council. It was the pride of the village.

As Midge and Caroline arrived, the double doors were open despite the cold wind. Two men in work clothes were carrying crates of milk bottles from a small truck parked outside into the hall. Inside, tables were arranged in a row along the two longer sides of the hall with a few feet of space allowed between them and the wall for each stall holder to stand. This being a Christmas bazaar, several of the stalls were covered with red or green cloths and had a variety of home-made gifts displayed. On a long table near the stage, a group of women were sorting through a pile of clothes.

"Mrs Frampton, here's your Midge with her young friend."

Georgina Frampton turned to face the girls, a child's yellow dress in her hands. She was neither short nor tall but had an elegance of movement that was exaggerated by the flowing, brightly coloured coats and dresses that she favoured. Her hair was worn in the Edwardian style, rolled with whisps escaping and softening her face. Her spectacles hung around her neck on a thin chain. Caroline had met her just once before when Midge's parents had visited Mrs Pendersen's school at the end of term to collect their daughter.

"Caroline, dear, how lovely to see you again! Has Midge fed you? Yes? Good, well perhaps we could adjourn here for a moment and take a cup of tea in the kitchen. Ladies would that suit you all?"

Grateful nods all round from the other women who were glad of a chance to sit for a few minutes. Georgina kissed Caroline on the cheek and shepherded the girls back to the kitchen where a large water urn was grumbling to itself. Cups and saucers were piled on to a tray, the teapot filled along with a spare jug of hot water, and Caroline carried a bottle of milk back into the hall behind Midge and her mother. This was no tea ceremony as Caroline was used to on Thursday afternoons at home. She was asked direct questions by the ladies as to where she was from, what Cheltenham was like (one lady had an aunt who lived in Gloucester, did Caroline know her?), and what her father did for work. The chink of Staffordshire china and the general chatter of the ladies echoed around the hall for twenty minutes or so before Georgina announced that there were two crates of hyacinths in pots to be unpacked and set out on a table if the girls wouldn't mind. They did not.

Caroline had not considered before the effort that was required for a successful bazaar. She listened carefully to how the other ladies discussed the presentation on each table, interlaced with comments about other villagers who might like something or other 'put by' for them, or indeed might chance taking an item without paying the full price for it. She did not notice it had grown dark outside as the hall lights were already turned on when they arrived. The Reverend Frampton appeared just as the last boxes were being stowed underneath tables, and after welcoming Caroline, announced his admiration for all the work done that afternoon. The cakes and pies to be sold would be brought to the hall in the morning, and so the ladies filed out of the hall and the Vicar turned off the urn and the lights and locked the double doors.

Dinner that Friday evening was Caroline's first experience of a large family meal with the Framptons. Having been told not to dress for dinner, and being somewhat relieved at that,

Caroline followed Midge into the Library where opening a cupboard set into the outer wall but away from the fireplace Midge revealed several shelves of beer bottles as well as some wine bottles on their sides and some other tall bottles standing upright.

"We keep them in here so that we don't have to get in cook's way getting to the scullery. Would you like a beer?"

"I've never tried beer, usually we just have water with our meals. But yes, please, I would like to."

Midge opened two bottles and poured the contents into the heavy bottomed glasses that seemed to be distributed throughout the house.

"The froth will take a while to settle, but cheers!"

"Cheers!"

"Ho, Midge, pass me one old girl" Matthew called as he came into the library followed by a large black Labrador. Caroline had not expected to see the dog and took a step back, nudging a side table and rattling a rack of pipes that stood on it.

"Don't mind Meg here, she won't hurt."

The dog wagged its tail and sniffed around Caroline's legs before sitting at her feet and licking its front paws. Caroline let out a breath of relief. She was not used to dogs although she wasn't especially worried by them.

After passing a bottle to her brother, Midge suggested she and Caroline go into the dining room with their drinks and left Matthew and Meg to entertain Mark and Luke who could be heard approaching down the stairs. Georgina and the Vicar were already seated at the dining table, both with spectacles perched on their noses and reading newspapers. Caroline was directed to sit next to Georgina, with Midge on her other side. The room was warm with a fire burning in the grate, and Caroline cautiously sipped her beer remembering the warning Mrs Monger had given her about drinking too much without eating first. Mrs Monger had not explicitly mentioned beer, but Caroline liked the rich malty taste and hoped there might be more to come after the meal.

As they talked, the maid brought in the first of the dishes and informed the party that John had arrived home and would be joining them shortly. The three older brothers entered the room together, still discussing the tractor. Their father inquired how the machine was running and was given a full appraisal with each son adding information in turn. Finally, John arrived having washed and changed from his work clothes, and after a short prayer of thanks, the meal began.

As the girls lay in their beds later that evening, Caroline felt as if she were glowing inside and out. She had thoroughly enjoyed the relaxed atmosphere over dinner and afterwards learning to play bridge with Midge and her brothers in the library. All of these new experiences made her feel more alive than she had been for years. She had even found herself petting Meg and giggling at the dog's warm tongue on her hand.

"You must be tired," Midge said across the room for the tenth time that evening.

"Yes, now I am. I have had such a wonderful evening though Midge, truly I have."

"I'm pleased. We don't always have all of my brothers at dinner together, this evening has been lovely for me too."

"Your family is very kind. I feel as if I have always been here." She paused as a thought came to her, "I wonder what Freddie would have made of your brothers. I think he would have liked them all as I do. I wonder if we would have had evenings such as this at home if Freddie had survived."

Midge considered her response. "I think Freddie would have been very welcome here too."

Saturday dawned cold but dry. Caroline woke but kept her eyes closed, listening to the sounds of the Vicarage. She thought about the evening before, particularly how the Framptons seemed to completely fill the spaces they inhabited.

Caroline had joined in with their conversations, chiefly encouraged by Midge, though she found herself saying she didn't know rather more than she would have liked. She had also had time to observe the ground floor rooms in more detail. Caroline was curious that although on a basic level they were no different to the rooms she was so familiar with at Glencairn Road, there were differences. She began to understand that here, items were left, dropped, rested and discarded until needed again. Mementos and personal trinkets shared space with spiky horse chestnut cases, shoes, and a magnifying glass. Every table was littered with a miniature collection, a study of Frampton-ness. At home in Cheltenham, everything had a place and was expected to be returned to it, she assumed so that one would know where to find it the next time it was needed. Not so in the Vicarage. Here, the hunt for an object appeared to form part of the general entertainment for the family.

Another thing Caroline had noticed was that nothing was still in the Vicarage. Even as she lay there with her eyes closed, snug under several blankets, she could hear voices and creaking floorboards, the sound of a pan being dropped from the kitchen. So used to quiet, almost silent evenings at home with her parents, each of them reading to themselves near the fireplace in the parlour, the turmoil of the card games and chatter last night had been almost overwhelming at times. And yet the Framptons seemed to sense that too; they had an uncanny way of knowing what she needed or was thinking.

The most surprising thing she had discovered was that Meg the Labrador did not belong to Matthew. In fact, Meg didn't seem to belong to anyone at all. She regularly followed Matthew home from Basildon Park, but just as often could be

found in the George and Dragon saloon bar in front of the fire
or wandering around the village and in and out of the gardens
and kitchens eating whatever anyone offered to her. No one
knew how old she was, but everyone called her Black Meg.

Caroline opened her eyes and realised Midge's bed was
empty, the covers thrown back and crumpled. There was no
clock in the room, but Caroline's watch said almost a quarter
to nine. Just as she was wondering if she should wash her face
in the bathroom or if someone would bring some hot water
to the bedroom for her, Midge gently nudged the door open
and put her head round it.

"You're awake! Jolly good. Would you like a bath or breakfast
first? The boys have all gone out, so you don't have to worry
about bumping into them in your night clothes."

"Could I have a bath? That would be lovely."

"Right-ho. There should be enough hot water left in the
tank. Come down to the kitchen when you're ready." Midge
disappeared.

Caroline was puzzled by hot water being in a tank but
reassured that she could get from the bedroom to the bathroom
without seeing anyone (it was only across the landing after all),
she left the warmth of the bed and wrapping a blanket around
her shoulders, went to investigate the bathroom. It took a few
moments for her to understand how the bath would fill with
cold water from one tap and hot water from another, and that
the hot was really just warm so that she wouldn't need to add
any cold. There were towels laid out on shelves, and smaller
cloths neatly folded next to small packets of soap cakes.

Caroline looked at herself in the large mirror while the bath
filled. Her long hair was dishevelled; she had plaited it before
going to sleep but strands always escaped during the night. She
pinned up her braid on top of her head and bathed as quickly
as she could as she was beginning to feel hungry again.

As Caroline entered the kitchen, Meg was laying by the range and thumped her tail on the floor to signal her approval. Midge looked over her shoulder from the bacon she was frying.

"Was it hot enough?"

"The water? Yes, thank you. Is there anything I can do here?"

"Cut some bread if you would, this is almost ready."

Caroline looked for the bread and a knife and continued to marvel as she had done descending the stairs at how easy it was to move around when not wearing a long skirt. She had never worn trousers before, though she was aware that some women did including Midge. Now she understood why, so much more practical. She cut two slices of bread as thinly as she could as Midge arranged the bacon on a plate. There were boiled eggs, butter in a lidded dish, a pot of jam with a spoon resting in it, and a large tea pot covered in a cosy stood on one side of the range to keep warm. Midge produced knives, forks and spoons and two large teacups without saucers, placing them directly onto the kitchen table.

"Tuck in old girl!" she instructed Caroline as she helped herself to an egg and began hammering it on the table to break the shell.

After breakfast, and after washing the dishes together in the scullery, a short hunt produced a pair of wellingtons that were just a little too large for Caroline's feet. A further hunt provided an old tweed jacket, similar to Midge's, along with a woollen hat, scarf and gloves. Meg accompanied the girls out of the Vicarage and along the lane towards Basildon Park, but eventually disappeared on a quest of her own. Midge explained as they walked that the Morrison family who owned the Park were rarely at home but had a few staff to keep the place ticking over. Since the war the recovering servicemen had slowly left the village and the house had reverted to a country home, but the Frampton offspring could come and go as they always had, as did many other children from the village. The woodlands were the preferred recreational area, as the vast lawns at the front of the house had little for entertainment, and the fountains had not been turned back on.

Matthew worked on the estate as a general gardener and handyman, though his injury meant he was unable to do any heavy lifting work. He had been offered a cottage but decided to stay at the Vicarage for now. Midge thought he should ask Kate to marry him and then they could both take the cottage. She explained that they would probably see Kate at the bazaar later so there was no need for them to call in to the cottage hospital. Instead, the girls walked around the lake to the folly, a white stone construction set on a raised mound with a domed roof supported at the front by Doric columns and at the back by a solid wall with a ledge projecting at a comfortable height for sitting on. It was too cold to sit for more than a moment, despite the view of the house being prefect from that aspect.

As they headed back towards the Vicarage, Midge with her usual directness asked, "How do you intend to make fifty pounds to repay your father?"

In any other situation, Midge's question would have been considered incredibly rude, particularly for a girl. Caroline had been giving it some private thought and found Midge's straight forward question put everything into sharp focus.

"I honestly have no idea, Midge," she sighed. "I don't even know what fifty pounds looks like, and I'm sure it will be impossible for me to earn that much in just a year. I'm not allowed to rob a bank for it, and I haven't the imagination to write a novel. I shall have to find a job of some kind, but then how can one have adventures if one is working?"

"That would depend on where you work, surely? I think Kate must have adventures all the time, with all the sick people she nurses."

"But I am not a nurse, and I don't think I can be one in just a few months. Oh, I know they did in the war, but that was different."

"True. But I still think an exotic job might be the answer. You could join a circus!"

"I don't think that would pay fifty pounds, do you?"

"Perhaps not. You could invest it, but then you wouldn't have it to spend this year.... Oh, I know, you could become a reporter for a newspaper."

"I wouldn't know where to start!"

"So, what have you to lose?"

"I think I shall just have to keep meeting interesting people and keep my ears open for interesting positions. If nothing turns up, at least I shall have had one year of experiences. What are you going to do with yourself next year?"

"Mother mentioned teacher training college a while ago. In fact, she mentioned several, and I'm sure at least one was in Cheltenham. And of course, there's Girton, where Mother studied. I rather like the idea of Cambridge, now that I've seen Luke's digs and read some of his notes."

"You were always the best of us at school."

"Better than Helen at any rate! But you were always the better artist. Hey, perhaps you could sell some paintings?"

"It's been a while since I painted anything that was any good. What would you study?"

"At Girton? I'm not sure. Politics perhaps, or economics. Though I wouldn't be awarded a degree certificate."

"Why not?"

"Because Cambridge doesn't allow women to matriculate. Thinking about it now, perhaps it would be better to try Oxford and get a degree at the same time. I don't know.

I could always do something with the church, go to Africa or South America."

"Now that would be exciting! And terrifying too, to go by oneself."

"One wouldn't be completely alone though; they place you in a community. There would be other English people there too. Perhaps I should study English at Girton and then go out to do some good in the world!"

The Christmas bazaar that afternoon began at two-thirty and Midge and Caroline had been asked to arrive at two o'clock. Caroline had decided to change into a day dress, though she kept her borrowed socks over her stockings inside the wellingtons for warmth. She thoroughly enjoyed the afternoon, having been placed on a table where books were for sale. It was explained by her tablemate, Mrs Anderson, that there would be two waves of customers; those who came as the doors opened and wanted the best items, and then those who would come at the end of the day and want the best bargains from whatever had not yet been sold, at a knock-down price. Mrs Anderson appeared to be correct, and in a lull after the first hour, Caroline was given a few minutes to take a look at the other tables and make a few small purchases for herself.

At four o'clock the Reverend Frampton began drawing the tombola tickets, and by 5pm it was agreed that no more customers would arrive. The doors were closed and the clearing up began. Caroline had never worked so hard physically since leaving school. The morning walk, coupled with being on her feet for most of the afternoon in ill-fitting boots, and the melee of people to talk to was exhausting. The hall had to be cleared completely, ready for Sunday school the following morning, and it wasn't until just after seven that Caroline sank into a chair in the Vicarage library, hungry, worn out, and thoroughly happy.

After church and lunch on Sunday, Caroline and Midge had declined John's offer of a boat trip to Mapledurham Mill as he could only borrow an open barge and it would have been very cold to sit in. Instead, Mark's suggestion of a drive over to Silchester to look at the Roman town site was accepted. He had the use of a four-seater Albert motorcar for the day, and Luke made up the party, carrying rugs and blankets from the Vicarage to keep the chill from the girls in the back of the vehicle. It was another new experience for Caroline, to be riding in a motorcar. She had been thankful for the comforting familiarity of the inside of St James the Less that morning, the hymns and the prayers. One needed some continuity if one was to also embrace change, she decided.

Luke took charge of the tour once they arrived in Silchester as he had been to the site several times. While his main interest was medicine, he had also excelled at history at school. He strode about the site in his green suit and flat cap, pointing out where objects had been found and the suspected location of several buildings. Caroline was fascinated and asked many questions, which encouraged Luke further. It was some time before Caroline realised that Midge and Mark had returned to the car, and reluctantly she admitted that she was starting to feel the cold and perhaps they should join Luke's siblings as it would be dark soon. As they turned towards the car, Caroline bent down and picked up a pebble.

"Did you drop something?" asked Luke.

"Oh no, I just thought I would take a pebble to remember the day by."

If Caroline had expected Sunday evening to be a more restrained affair at the Vicarage, she was wrong. After dinner, instead of retiring to the library, the family filled the parlour, and each took a turn in singing and playing the piano or violin. It was not a sedate recital. The songs were from popular music hall acts, none of which Caroline was familiar with. Some of the words were also a little embarrassing to her, but she laughed along with the others and tapped her fingers to the tunes. John provided a very convincing portrayal of Charlie Chaplain, miming a comical episode with a cricket bat. And then it was Caroline's turn.

The family were good natured in their encouragement, and Caroline took the piano seat reluctantly after protesting that she had not played for some time. A booklet of sheet music was placed on the music stand for Caroline to sight read, and with a few stumbles at the beginning she played her way through two numbers from the comedy musical *A Night Out* with the family providing the lyrical accompaniment. As the second number ended, Caroline looked around the room at the laughing, smiling faces of her hosts and felt that her smile would be joined by tears of joy if she didn't extract herself and give up the piano to someone else.

"Excuse me miss, you were wanting the Cheltenham High Street or Malvern Road stop?"

Caroline had been just resting her eyelids as the carriage rocked its way through Gloucestershire, the end of the daylight fading ahead of her. "Malvern Road please."

"Two stops then Miss. I'll be back for your case."

"Really, there's no need, it's not heavy." But the guard was gone. These small things, Caroline mused, were more tiresome than not being able to matriculate at Cambridge as Midge had described. One wouldn't assume that would be possible, but to carry one's own case should at least be permitted. She opened her bag and made sure she still had her ticket. She wanted to keep it safe so that she could add it, with the pebble from Silchester, to the box under her bed.

She had had a very enlightening weekend in Pangbourne. It had felt familiar and comfortable yet at the same time new and fascinating. If this was what she had been missing out on all of the years she had spent comforting her mother, then she certainly wanted to make up for lost time. But the nagging question of how to sustain her income would not go away. There was a newspaper on the seat opposite, left by a previous traveller. Caroline picked it up and saw that it was from Oxford. The train was pulling into the High Street stop so Caroline decided not to start reading then and there, but to take it home with her and see what situations were vacant after she had unpacked and had a good night's sleep in her own bed once more.

3

MARY

It was the first Tuesday in February and Caroline had gone to St Mark's to help arrange some flowers for Epiphany. It had become her habit since the first time she had visited with Annie, to attend one service each week though not the Sunday services which she returned to Christ Church for. She had also offered to collect the flowers from Curzon's Exotic Nursery, using a large trug-shaped wicker basket. The act of carrying the basket herself and walking the just over a mile to the church by herself, became a tiny act of independence in defiance of her mother that she wanted to protect.

Today she had carried a collection of dogwood, viburnum, and daphne stems, some late hellebore and early daffodils. Mr Curzon had picked them all out for her to collect, as several of his employees attended St Mark's though he himself was a Methodist. Caroline enjoyed being inside the glasshouses and breathed in deeply while she waited for the new stems to be brought for her basket. Most of the flowers and plants that Mr Curzon and his staff grew were destined for London, as well as the grand houses along the route between Cheltenham and the big city who dedicated their glasshouses to exotic fruits rather than inedible flowers. Caroline had wondered if there might be a way she could work in the glasshouses, not so much for the money but to simply spend as much time amongst the flowers as possible. However, the heavy lifting and long hours did not fit into Caroline's concept of enjoyable employment.

Saint Mark's church door was open, and inside it was very cold. Caroline walked up the central aisle and placed the basket on the floor by the first pew, her breath visible in the air. Mary was already at work with a large pair of scissors, trimming the ends of some daffodils she had brought from her own small garden. She wore a thick woollen coat, with a knitted scarf wrapped several times around her neck so that it covered her chin and mouth.

"Good morning," Caroline said with a smile, knowing that would elicit one from Mary in return. Caroline was entranced by Mary's smile, the way it lit up her whole face, but also the whiteness and straightness of her teeth against her dark lips.

"Good morning to you Miss Caroline," Mary replied.

Her soft Caribbean accent had been tamed by years of living in Bristol with her mother as her father fought with the West India Regiment of the British Army in Africa. Unmarried women of her own age and younger she addressed as Miss, and after some confusion at first when Caroline thought she was adopting Annie's habit, it had become a natural welcome.

They had talked as they worked on the flower arrangements over the weeks, slowly and cautiously asking questions of each other. Caroline did not have Midge's directness, and Mary was aware that her presence was one of curiosity in the town. She had been reluctant to leave Bristol when Philip had first suggested it. She had her mother there and a number of Caribbean and African friends and relations close by. Of course, there was hostility sometimes, she had grown up with it, accepted it, but to be the only black person, the only black woman in a new town was frightening and she had not wanted to go. It had been her mother who had finally convinced her. She had explained how arriving in Bristol with Mary as a small child and her husband overseas, Celestine had known no one. She had only the address of a boarding house near the docks, her small suitcase and five pounds in her purse. But she had found the boarding house and been accommodated by the older black woman who ran it; given a room and use of a bathroom with just one other black couple, and fed two meals a day in the large kitchen where Mary eventually learned to read and write.

There were good people in the world, Celestine had told Mary, and they would always be found if you looked for them. But it was not God's will for a husband and wife to be parted, of that Celestine was convinced having spent so long apart from Mary's father. Mary must go with Philip wherever God sent him. And so, she had arrived in Cheltenham.

That February morning Mary seemed preoccupied. Caroline noticed a couple of times that Mary had stopped what she was doing as was staring up at the stained-glass window depicting Saint John with a lamb in his arms.

"Mary, are you quite all right?" Caroline asked.

Mary turned from the window to face Caroline, "Why yes, but… I need to go home to see my mother. And I don't want Philip to come with me, not this time."

"Whyever not?"

"Because he would be too kind about it all and I need to see Mother first," was Mary's cryptic answer. Caroline didn't understand.

"Does your mother live near the docks still?"

"No, she has a small house near to the eye hospital. I was thinking of going next week or the week after."

"Is Bristol terribly big?"

Mary chuckled, "It is many times bigger than Cheltenham, Miss Caroline. Cheltenham would fit into the docks with plenty of room to spare. There are so many more people, and shops and theatres and museums. It is always so very busy."

"I should like to see it one day."

Mary tilted her head and looked at Caroline. "Why not come with me then? That may help Philip feel more comfortable with me going without him, that I would not be travelling alone."

"Do you mean it? Gosh, that would be exciting!"

"We would stay the night with my mother, would that be acceptable to you?"

"Of course, if it would be no trouble to her."

"Nothing is trouble for mother," Mary smiled again, with a look of relief in her eyes this time that Caroline did not notice. "We could visit the cinema, and I may need to do some shopping."

Elizabeth had been very much against Caroline's trip with Mary. Not only because it was to Bristol and that they would be staying overnight. George had had to raise his voice, a most unusual thing at 20 Glencairn Road, to stop his wife's tirade of imagined perils and clear hostility towards Mary and her kind. Caroline had heard the argument from the garden and had almost changed her mind about the trip.

It was two weeks later when Caroline and Mary stepped off the train at Temple Meads station and made their way through the tunnel under the tracks and out into the street. A light misty rain was falling, though not enough for an umbrella, and the trams were crowded with travellers and workers making their way into the city centre. Caroline immediately noticed that Bristol smelled different. Not the slightly musty damp smell of steam and rivers that had been Pangbourne's aroma. Bristol smelled of industry, oil and coal, horses, malt, and tar. Everything was in constant motion, and the noise level was something she had not considered before arriving. If this was Bristol, she thought, what on earth must London be like!

She next noticed the softness of the accent, as she tuned in to the conversations in progress around her. Caroline didn't consider herself to have an accent, but she had understood that people from other places as well as other classes often did. Annie for instance sounded very similar in her speech to Caroline's fellow tram passengers, although as far as Caroline knew Annie had never been to Bristol. Mary's accent was softer still and rolled like the hills with a lyrical melody. Her Bristol upbringing was evident, but also her Trinidadian parentage.

The conductor on the tram was a stout man with a moustache and spectacles; he barked "Where to?" at Mary and she handed him the pennies for the fare. Caroline had expected to need some cash for her trip having used almost all of the change in her purse in Pangbourne before Christmas, and George had brought home two pounds changed into various coins for her the day before. As she reached for her purse, Mary pressed a ticket into her hand.

"Oh, but I have change!" Caroline said, rather disappointed.

"You can give it to me later," Mary replied quietly.

"But why didn't he ask me for my fare too?"

"Because he thinks I'm your maid," Mary's eyes were downcast as she spoke.

Caroline blushed helplessly. "But that's ridiculous! Of course you're not, we're friends, why on earth.." and then she understood. "Mary, I'm sorry."

"You have nothing to be sorry for. We can settle everything later at my mother's house." Caroline could tell by Mary's tone that there was to be no further discussion.

The walk from the city centre with its busy tram lines criss-crossing in the streets and people scurrying here and there was not a long one but was uphill. The women left the major activity of the Horsefair and walked through St James before starting the climb along Dighton Street and finally into Dove Street. The houses had become smaller in size and with less rendering on the brick facades as they moved away from the city centre, and here they were elevated above the main roadway by some ten feet. Caroline was glad she had only brought a carpet bag with her overnight things and not her suitcase; she hadn't expected quite such a walk. There were small children playing in the street, and a few women gathered around one open doorway chatting. These houses were made of a honey-coloured brick and stood in a terrace of twelve, two stories above street level, but narrow with only a door and a small window showing the ground floor accommodation.

Mary stopped at dark green door, the paint starting to crack and showing the undercoat of grey. She unlocked the door and walked in, with Caroline behind her.

"Mother!" Mary called, though she knew her mother would be at home, sitting in the small kitchen with a black range and table pushed against a side wall. The hallway was very narrow, and stairs had been built in between the kitchen and the front parlour with no window. Caroline followed Mary through the house after closing the front door behind her. It smelled even more strange than the outside of Bristol and the inside of its trams. Here was a smell of fried food, fruity, mixed with tobacco and something else Caroline could not name.

Celestine Vincent hauled her considerable frame to her feet to welcome her daughter effusively with a hug and a kiss. Then Mary introduced Caroline and Celestine smiled and tilted her head to one side as she appraised the young woman stood before her.

"Welcome, welcome," she murmured, then smiled showing several missing teeth, "we will feed you up, have no fear!" and advanced on Caroline, wrapping her in a big hug which literally took Caroline's breath away.

When she was released and could speak, she said, "thank you, Mrs Vincent."

"Celestine! Everyone call me Celestine. Now, you will have the front bedroom, Mary you will come in with me. I put clean sheets out this morning, I knew you'd be wanting them. Now tell me, are you girls hungry for some chicken?"

It wasn't really a question, as Celestine turned as she spoke and took the lid off a pot that was sat on top of the range. A more pungent fruity smell filled the little kitchen and Caroline couldn't help but feel hungry. Mary led her up the dark stairs to the front bedroom to leave her bag, hat and coat while Celestine dished up the meal.

"Your mother, Celestine, is very... friendly," Caroline remarked as they quickly made up her bed.

"She is everyone's friend. The house is usually full of people, I think she must have asked them to stay away as she knew we were coming. Now, our food may not be what you are used to Miss Caroline, and we only have an outside water closet so there is a china pot under the bed here in case you need it in the night. I know, now that I am used to the amenities at home, I do not like to go outside in the dark."

Caroline considered the chamber pot, and the darkness of the stairs, and resolved to not be silly about such things. She had braved the outside water closets at school, which were little more than benches over an open trench inside a long low shed, and she could retain her dignity by using the pot if necessary.

Celestine called up the stairs, "Your food is on the table now, come and eat while it's hot!"

Caroline soon discovered what Celestine meant by 'hot'. It was not so much unpleasant, as unexpected. The sensation on her lips and in her mouth after taking two or three small bites reminded her of nettle rashes she had suffered as a child. But the food tasted good, and she was hungry, so she ate with as much good grace as she could muster. Celestine had a habit of asking Caroline questions just as she had a mouthful of food, and Mary filled in much of the information that Celestine required.

"I thought we might go to the picture house this evening. Would you come with us?" Mary asked her mother as they cleared the plates away.

"I shall! I have a new hat! Them see me walking round town looking mighty fine." Celestine beamed, "You girls sit in the parlour and Celestine be with you in no time. No time at all."

"You don't mind, do you Miss Caroline, about mother coming along with us I mean?"

"Of course not. She's a dear thing."

"Only she doesn't go out very much, as I said everyone comes here. And it will be better for us when we are walking after dark."

Caroline didn't understand that last remark but was happy to let Mary navigate her through Bristol by whatever means. "It has been a long time since I last visited a picture house. Florence and I used to go often, but then… I imagine the ones here are much larger than the Daffodil?"

"It is magical Miss Caroline, magical. There will be lots of people, it is always full in the evenings. There's a band, they play music, and sometimes there is writing in between the pictures if it is a news report."

"It sounds very exciting! What time do we need to get there?"

"The show will start at six, so we have plenty of time. Would you mind if I go and help mother, there is something I need to ask her?"

"Not at all, I shall be perfectly comfortable here."

Later that evening as some five hundred Bristolians emerged into the crisp night air outside the Metropole picture palace, Caroline's smile was as wide as the river Avon. She had been dazzled by the opulence of the building, the size of the interior, and the ornate carvings along the walls. She would have liked to have kept the ticket for her keepsake box, but the doorman had torn it in two and kept one half as they entered the main auditorium. The main feature had been Douglas Fairbanks in *The Thief of Bagdad*, with the star himself climbing and leaping across the screen with cat-like athleticism, accompanied not only by the small orchestra in the pit by the stage, but by the "Oh!"s and "Ahh!"s of the audience.

Caroline had found herself sitting next to another lady of ample stature not unlike Celestine who sat to the right of Mary. The lady to Caroline's left had crocheted all through the performance, without taking her eyes from the screen. Caroline was very impressed, if a little distracted on occasion by the movement of the lady's elbow against Caroline's arm. Celestine had enjoyed herself immensely, eating bonbons from a small paper bag and whooping with joy at the antics on screen. Her hat was indeed a triumph of millinery couture, with a long feather which curled around from front to back obscuring the view for anyone a good three rows behind her.

When a young man asked her, "Madam would you mind removing your hat?" Celestine turned a gave him a hard stare.

"This hat? This fine hat cost me six shillings young man! I ain't taking it off for nobody, nobody! D'you hear?"

The young man, suitably chastened, moved to a vacant seat with a better view of the screen.

It was a relief to be out in the fresh air and away from the smoky inside of the cinema. Caroline had tucked the remaining half of her cinema ticket into her purse, so that it would not get lost before she had a chance to put it into the box under her bed at home. She could not understand why she had stopped going to the cinema in Cheltenham. She supposed that with Florence leaving for finishing school, there had been no one for her to go with. It was not an occupation that her mother ever indulged in.

As the ladies walked along towards Dove Street, a cry went up from across the road.

"Celestine! Celestine Vincent! Would you come and have a rum with your old friend?"

A black man in a bowler hat and a dark suit stood tall against the doorway of another of Bristol's narrow buildings. There was a bright light inside, and the sound of several voices.

"Tawny you old rascal. I'm out in me new hat, d'you see? And with Mary and her friend." Celestine crossed the road, oblivious to a man on a bicycle who swerved and narrowly missed her. Mary and Caroline followed at a distance.

Tawny grinned and nodded. "And a fine hat it is Celestine Vincent. Come in now and have a glass of rum with your old pal Tawny."

Celestine was obviously considering the offer seriously. Caroline could now see through the open door a smoky room with several middle-aged men, some black and some white, sitting around a table playing cards. There was a large bottle on the table and smaller glasses for each player. Other men were leaning on the mantle above the fire, which was low in the grate, or sitting on stools in a second circle around the card players at the table. There were no women present.

Mary said gently, "Mother, we should get Miss Caroline home. And I's tired too, Mother."

Celestine shook her head dramatically at Tawny and wagged her finger at him. "You leading me nowhere Tawny Antoine, no-where! I go home now with my girls to look after, you bad man."

Tawny let out a loud laugh, "Bad! Woman you have no idea! You take those lovely ladies home and then come back. Tawny will keep your drink warm."

"I shall not! If my Samuel was here now, he would strike you down!"

With that Celestine grabbed Tawny's glass and before he could say any more, she had drained the contents and placed the empty glass on the windowsill beside him, turned on her unsteady heel and was shepherding the girls back across the street and towards home.

"Come now, we go. We don't stay with Tawny Antoine and his wickedness."

As Caroline sat on the edge of her bed that night, brushing her long hair, Mary tapped on the door and came in carrying a clay bottle with a cork stopper.

"I thought you might want to warm your bed," she said offering the bottle to Caroline who took it with thanks and tucked it under the covers. Mary sat on the bed next to Caroline. "I'm sorry that we met Tawny."

"Is he a family friend?"

"I have known him all my life yes, though he comes from Tobago, not Trinidad. He and my father did not get along though they are distant cousins. I think he comes here more now I am not here with Mother." She yawned.

Caroline didn't know what to say. The lives of these people seemed far removed from her own. She was soaking up the experiences like a sponge, but she still had no idea how to behave around them. All she knew was that her parent's ways were not shared by many of the people she was starting to meet, and she felt a deep sense of what she would only describe if asked as fear. Fear of the new. It was terrifying, but also so exhilarating.

"Miss Caroline, would you like to go shopping tomorrow before we catch the train back to Cheltenham? There are a few items I would like to purchase while I'm here. I think you would like the shops near to the University. And we can take the tram from there to Temple for the train."

Caroline was happy to change the subject. "Yes, let's do that. And you must let me pay for the tram this time Mary."

Mary smiled her warm smile again, stifling another yawn. "Yes, you can give me the fare before we get on."

It was the following week when Caroline arrived at St Mark's with her usual basket of flowers from Curzon's Exotic Plant Nurseries that she learned the reason for their trip to Bristol.

"A baby?! Oh, how wonderful Mary! You must be so very delighted!"

"I am. We are. But Lord knows I am so tired with it all!"

"Goodness do sit down. Do you feel faint? Shall I call for Philip?"

"No, no Miss Caroline, I am well." Mary chuckled, "And Philip would have me confined to bed for the next 5 months if he could! No, I just need a little broth in the mornings and a nap after lunch."

"Well, look here, you can sit on the pew and pass me the stems from the basket and tell me how my arrangement is coming along. A baby. How exciting!"

1 March 1925
Derbyshire
Dearest Caro,

What adventures you are having indeed. We have coloured people here in Plymouth of course, mainly around the docks, but I have yet to mingle with any locally. Their hair fascinates me. And their skin, the way their hands are paler on the palms.

I have sad news. Despite living for so much longer than anyone could have imagined, Sophia passed away last week, and Arthur is distraught. He refused to leave her bedside for two whole days, and we had to ask the Game Keeper to manhandle him out in the end. The funeral is to be on Thursday, and I cannot wait to leave this mausoleum and return to the giddy heights of Lipson once again.

Papa is thinking of buying a new house out on the moor. He says it will be for us all to use, and it is on the edge of the golf course in Tavistock. Such a parochial little town with its Bedford granite stamp on every corner and sheep in every lane, but William says the golf course is exemplary and the fees are very reasonable. And cousin Gerald is taking a house on the other side of Tavistock for Easter, Endsleigh Cottage I believe he said. Do say you'll join us for a few days? I find it so tedious when Gerald insists on tennis every afternoon. And I have someone I would very much like you to meet, so let me know as soon as you can dear.

I won't draw this out, Rogers will be waiting for me on the terrace with my ashtray and rug.

Much love

Helen

P.S. Midge tells me you were a hit with brother Luke!

4

ELSA

"Annie, I really must find some employment. I do not see how I will have time enough to repay Father if I leave it much longer."

The two young women were in the kitchen of 20 Glencairn Road, in their usual positions of Caroline perched on a chair with her elbows on the table and Annie busy preparing food. This time, potatoes were being peeled into a large pan, with the peelings dropping into a galvanised bucket on the red tiled floor.

Annie wiped a hair from her eyes with the back of one hand. "I don't know, Miss. Is there nothing in the Chronicle this week at all?"

"Nothing suitable. I think half of it is that I truly don't know what I would like to do."

Annie decided not to comment on Caroline's luxury of having a choice. "Don't you have a dream job? If I could do anything in the world, I should like to be a Governess. Except I don't read or write anywhere near good enough."

"A dream job? I do but promise you won't laugh."

"Never, Miss."

"Since I saw Douglas Fairbanks at the picture palace in Bristol, I would give anything to become an actress."

Annie raised an eyebrow. "An actress? But Miss, you know what people says about them. Most are no better than they should be and that's a fact!"

"No, surely not! And even if some are," Caroline pondered, half to herself, "that's not to say one would have to be the same."

"No, Miss. With all these strikes, I'm not sure there will be employment for anyone soon."

Caroline got up and returned after a moment with the newspaper from the previous evening. She spread it out on the kitchen table and began to inspect the pages of fine printed columns. When she reached the situations vacant column she read aloud.

"Educated gentleman or lady required in Cheltenham to act as sole agent for a strictly scientific apparatus for electro-galvanic treatment at home. Small private means necessary." She looked at Annie, "What do you suppose that means, electro-galvanic treatment at home?"

"I'm sure I don't know, Miss."

"Sole agent. I think that means a salesperson. I shall ask Father." She continued down the column. "Wanted. Cooks and cook-generals, thirty to eighty pounds, good service town and country. Apply to the Agency. But I'm not a cook, am I?"

"No, Miss, although maybe it's time we taught you some basics?" it was Annie's turn to ponder. "Perhaps you could speak to the agency and see if they have any other situations?"

"Would you happen to know where the agency is?"

"I believe it is along the Prom, Miss."

After confirming with her father later that evening that 'sole agent' did indeed mean a salesperson, Caroline resolved over breakfast the next morning to take the tram into the town and enquire at the Agency. She didn't know exactly where on the

Promenade the Agency was situated, but it was a bright and dry morning, and she felt some fresh air would do her good.

Cheltenham in late February, in years when there had been some warmth from the sun, was coloured with cherry blossom and daffodils. Caroline had dressed with care, though her wardrobe could not be thought of as extensive. She wanted to make a good first impression and chose a sage green woollen skirt that was rather longer than the current fashion, and a cream crepe blouse. Her black shoes were a little worn at the heel but would have to do. As she pulled on her hat and gloves in the hallway, her mother had asked where she was going.

"I am going out to purchase a gift for Mary's baby," she had never uttered an outright lie to her mother before, and she hid her eyes by looking down and smoothing her coat.

"I wish you would refrain from mixing with the people of Saint Mark's, they are not appropriate for a girl of your status to spend so much time with." Elizabeth had expressed similar statements over the past few months. Caroline had come to understand that by "people of Saint Mark's", her mother explicitly meant Mary. It had been a revelation when she had realised it was the colour of Mary's skin that her mother objected to, and Caroline was irritated by her mother's continued comments.

"I'm sure Philip would be upset to know you thought he was unsuitable company for me, mother, but I really must be permitted to choose my own friends." Caroline moved to the front door.

"Philip would indeed have been good company for you." Elizabeth stated pointedly. Caroline did not reply.

As she walked along Queens Road towards the tram lines, Caroline found she was shaking. She loved her mother, but she could be intolerable. Conversations had taken a strange turn recently between Caroline and Elizabeth, with unsubtle hints that Caroline should now be considering her future with a 'suitable gentleman'. It was not an immediate future that Caroline intended for herself; she had far too much of the world to explore and understand, and so much catching up to do with her peers, to even think of romance. Caroline reached the line of waiting passengers for the next tram and composed herself, taking some deep breaths. The sun shone through the large Horse Chestnut trees that lined both sides of Gloucester Road; they had bare branches but with more sun they would unfurl their buds and soon provide much needed shade. Caroline turned her face up to the sun and closed her eyes for a moment. How different Cheltenham was to Bristol. How quiet, despite the railway station and tradespeople occupying the nearby shops.

Fifteen minutes later Caroline stepped off the tram in Winchcombe Street and walked back towards the centre of the town. She had considered her 'lie' and had resolved to purchase something for Mary's baby after all. The lie would then not exist, and she would not feel such a weight of guilt for speaking it. Though she was familiar with the shops in the town, she had never needed to look at baby items before. She stopped at a window display of paper spring flowers decorating a range of wooden toys, dolls and teddy bears. Not much use to a new-born baby, even Caroline was aware of that. She moved on and headed towards the large department store in Cavendish House where she felt sure she would find some baby items. The store had an entrance on the Promenade so she would be able to exit and be in the right place to find the Agency.

Caroline walked down Regent Street with the Theatre in her line of sight. She was daydreaming about performing on the stage when a young man came out of a shop directly in front of her and they collided. He caught Caroline's arm and saved her from an embarrassing fall into the street, losing his hat in the process.

"I am so sorry! That was completely my fault, I should have been looking where I was going."

"I beg your pardon madam, forgive my clumsiness! Are you hurt?"

"No, really, I am quite alright, thank you. I really should have been paying attention. Oh, your hat!" The young man bent down to retrieve his hat and brushed off the street dirt.

"No harm done there. Can I assist you to your destination? I feel I should make amends."

The young man was a little taller than Caroline, with sandy hair under his cap, pale blue eyes and a pale complexion. His suit was a little short for his arms so that his shirt cuffs showed, though his trousers seemed a little long for his legs. He wore no overcoat.

"Well really I am on my way to Cavendish House, so there truly isn't..."

"Then I shall escort you the hundred yards to its very door!" he said with a broad smile and swept his arm towards the store.

Caroline giggled, "If you insist, Mr?"

"Shaw. Arthur Shaw, at your service madam. Artie to my friends, of which I would hope to include you?"

"And where were you going in such a hurry, Mr Arthur Shaw?" Caroline felt Arthur's smile was an invitation to ask as they walked although it seemed that his voice and eyes did not share the smile's warmth.

"I have some business to attend to in the Lower High Street. But perhaps you would agree to join me for lunch today, when we have both completed our appointments for this morning?"

Caroline thought quickly. She wanted to say yes, and this young man appeared respectable, but he was also very forward. She decided to decline.

"I'm afraid I won't be able to join you for lunch Mr Shaw. But thank you for your invitation. And here we are." They had arrived at the entrance to Cavendish House. "Goodbye Mr Shaw."

"I'm sorry to hear that. But perhaps you would tell me your name? As we are now so well acquainted," again the warm open smile, again not reaching his eyes.

"Caroline Munhead. Thank you again Mr Shaw, please don't let me keep you." There was something about the young man that Caroline felt instinctively wary of.

She turned and pushed the door open and walked into the store. Arthur stood on the street for a moment as she left, removed his hat and scratched his head. How could he engineer another meeting with that lady? He would need to ask his associates if they knew her family though her name had rung a bell.

Caroline spent a while being attended to by the shop assistant in the children's department of the store. She sat on a hard chair while the assistant brought her tiny vests, bonnets and dresses. She was less interested than she might have been, something was itching her mind and that something was Mr Shaw. Where had she heard or seen his name recently? She couldn't place it, but she knew she had.

"I'll take the bonnet with the lemon ribbons. Please put it on our account, the name is Munhead."

"Certainly madam. Would madam care to take the item with her now, or have it delivered?"

Caroline had only brought a small handbag. "Please deliver it, thank you."

In the street on the Promenade side of Cavendish House, Caroline applied herself to the original reason for her excursion that morning; to find the Agency. She had an idea that it would be in some rooms above another shop, Annie had said it was a door with a name plate to one side. Caroline walked down the gently sloping street; it had been designed as a wide, open expanse for the town's people to see and be seen, with yet more horse chestnut trees in rows on either side. It was busy with many people riding bicycles and carrying shopping baskets. After passing a few shop fronts, Caroline saw one that had a notice fixed in the window. It read:

ASSISTANT REQUIRED
ADMINISTRATIVE DUTIES AND SOME STOCK
MANAGEMENT. ENQUIRE WITHIN.

Caroline stepped back to appraise the shop. Above the door read a sign 'E. A. House, Photographic Portraiture'. The window itself had photographs in ornate frames against a black fabric background. On the other side of the door, a second window had a camera on a tripod stand, again against a black fabric background. Caroline gathered herself; some greater hand had placed this in her path rather than the door to the Agency. It would be rude to ignore it. She pushed open the door and a bell rang somewhere deep inside the building.

With the shop windows covered with fabric, the only light that entered the shop came through the glass in the door. It was a dark welcome; there was a counter along one side of the room, a pair of comfortable upholstered chairs stood opposite with a low table between them, and a large palm tree in a pot completed the furniture. Four steps at the far end of the room led up to another partially-glazed door that was ajar and Caroline could hear footsteps approaching. She then heard something fall onto the floor, and some muttered profanity, before the door was pulled open and E. A. House stood in silhouette before her.

"Good morning, how may I be of assistance?"

"Good morning. You have an advertisement in the window. I am inquiring about it."

As the figure descended the steps, Caroline could see that E. A. House was a woman, though she was dressed as a man would, in a white shirt and black waistcoat and trousers, and her hair was short and slicked back from her forehead. Caroline was taken aback but swallowed and stood her ground.

"Please, take a seat, Miss…?"

"Caroline Munhead. Thank you. And you are?"

"I am E. A. House the second," she smiled, "my father was the first. Edward Andrew House. I am Elsa Amelia House. This is my business. Photography. Portraits mostly, as it pays the bills, but I am interested in capturing movement and experimenting with exposures and developing techniques."

"By movement, do you mean moving pictures?" Caroline was immediately very interested.

"Not as you would see in a picture house, no. Capturing movement using still photography. Obtaining the essence of movement, without the blur or distortion. Can I offer you a drink Miss Munhead?"

"Tea would be lovely, thank you."

Elsa went through to the back room and Caroline heard the sounds of china being placed on a tray. Caroline took off her gloves and folded them in her lap with her bag. She wondered how a woman came to dress as a man for more than a walk in the woods. She had enjoyed wearing trousers when she visited Midge but would not have considered doing so again now that she was back in Cheltenham.

Else returned and placed the tray on the low table. "There's no sugar I'm afraid. Help yourself. Have you any experience in administration?"

Caroline paused, "No, although I'm sure I can organise anything you might require me to." She was pleased with her answer, unrehearsed as she was.

"Any experience with photography?"

"No, I'm afraid not."

Elsa crossed her legs and looked at Caroline over the edge of her teacup. She studied Caroline's round face, her slightly crooked nose (the result of a fall down the stairs as a child), and her full lips. Her unfashionable long hair, curled and pinned into a bun at the back of her neck.

"Have you worked at all?"

Caroline held Elsa's gaze. "No."

"Why do you want a job now?"

"I... I intend to pay back an investment."

"Pay back? Someone invested... in you? Interesting," Elsa smiled, "I need someone perhaps three or four mornings each week, and on Saturdays. Clearly not enough for a man to undertake. Would that be suitable for you?"

"That would be eminently suitable, I could still help at St Mark's. Which mornings would you require me?"

"Shall we say Monday, Wednesday and Friday? And all day Saturday. I open the shop at nine-thirty and close for lunch at one. I spend the afternoons developing the images. On Saturdays I open in the afternoon at one until six. We have enquiries as other businesses are closing for the evening. I am willing to remunerate you with a guinea a week. Is that agreeable?"

"Yes! Err... yes, very agreeable. And when would you like me to begin?"

"Do you have any engagements this morning? You could begin by removing the advertisement in the window."

After a tour of the premises, which consisted of the kitchen-come-parlour through the glazed door with a staircase up to an open studio space on the first floor with a small, partitioned area full of shelves, and a bedroom and darkroom on the second floor, Caroline and Elsa spent the next hour going through the appointments book and the catalogue Elsa had started some time ago of her negative plates and developed images. She had not got very far, and that was one reason she gave for needed an assistant. There was a sitting in the appointments book for 11am, a Mr and Mrs Samuel Jones, and Elsa explained to Caroline how she usually welcomed her clients and arranged them in the studio.

"Do you think you can jump straight in?"

"Of course. Let me just go through it with you once more. When they arrive, I ask them to sit down in the shop and then come and tell you they are here. When you are ready you will come down and we will all go up to the studio together where I take their coats and help you with any props. Then I return here, and when you show them down, I make a second appointment for them to view their images."

"Excellent! A quick learner is just what I need. I think this is going to work admirably Caroline." Elsa smiled.

At one o'clock Caroline turned the sign on the front door to say 'Closed' and took a moment to sit down before gathering her coat and bag. She hadn't spent that long on her feet since helping at the bazaar in Pangbourne. Even when she was helping at St Mark's, she could sit on a pew every now and then. But she hadn't felt she should sit down in the shop, just in case a customer chose that exact moment to come in.

Caroline had been surprised at just how many people had come to the shop that morning. She understood quickly how Elsa could not manage everything by herself, yet the work was not physically difficult, and Caroline felt a surge of accomplishment in not only having obtained a position but to also completing her first shift, all in the same morning. She heard Elsa descend the stairs and quickly stood up and started to put on her coat.

Elsa had been impressed. More than that, she had been giving silent thanks to any God who happened to be listening all morning to have found such a capable, attractive and willing assistant. Even with unemployment rising across the country, Elsa had started to wonder if she would ever find someone suitable. She knew what many people in the town thought of her, which was mainly why she chose to socialise in Gloucester when the mood took her. Dressing as she did, with an occupation largely regarded as a male province – though she followed the progress of notable American photographers such as Fannie Benjamin Johnson avidly – she knew she fuelled the town gossip mills. In fact, she was surprised that Caroline seemed to have no idea about Elsa's sexuality or the occasional salacious details that were manufactured about her.

"Have you enjoyed this morning?"

"Oh yes, very much. I feel I shall want to come back again tomorrow instead of taking the flowers to St Mark's, but I know we agreed on Wednesday."

"Yes, Tuesdays I usually spend either out and about trying to capture movement somewhere, or pestering publishers to take my work. As the weather improves there are often requests for outdoor sittings, so I try and book those for Tuesdays and Thursdays – something to remember if anyone enquires."

"Of course. Well, it's been lovely to meet you Elsa and I will see you on Wednesday morning at nine thirty, sharp." Caroline held out her hand, which Elsa shook perhaps a little too gently and quickly.

When Caroline arrived home, she went straight through to the kitchen in search of Annie to tell her the good news.

"That's a miracle Miss, and no mistake!"

"Do you think so? It felt as if the advertisement had been placed there just for me to see, and Elsa is so in need of an assistant. We got along famously. And now I am ravenous! Goodness it's almost two o'clock!"

"I saved you some lunch, it's on the plate on the stove. You take your coat off Miss, and it'll be here when you come back down."

As Caroline passed the parlour again, her mother called from within. "Caroline, is that you?"

Caroline entered, "Of course, Mother."

"Did you find what you were looking for this morning?"

For a moment Caroline forgot about the bonnet for Mary's baby and wondered how her mother could possibly know about Elsa and she shop so quickly. Then she remembered. "Oh, yes, a little bonnet. Cavendish House will be delivering it this afternoon."

"You have been rather a long time."

"Yes, I ... I just walked around, lost track of time somewhat. Mother I must put my outdoor things away, Annie has some lunch saved for me and I am famished."

Without waiting for her mother to comment, she turned and almost ran up the stairs to her room. Why did she feel like a naughty schoolgirl? Why did she feel the need to lie to her mother? It was thoroughly uncomfortable, and she decided that at dinner that evening she would tell her parents together that she had taken the photographer's assistant position.

"Part-time you say?" George was deliberately keeping his eyes on his dinner as he spoke, not wanting to look up and see Elizabeth's reaction.

"Yes, Monday, Wednesday and Friday mornings and Saturday afternoons. And all for a guinea a week, isn't that wonderful?!"

"It certainly sounds most suitable." He had prepared the ground and now looked up at his wife, "don't you agree Elizabeth?"

"You did not mention this when you came home, Caroline. I see no reason why you should practice deceit if this is such an excellent position."

"I wanted to tell you both together. I had not completely decided to take the position when I came home; I have decided this afternoon." Another lie: this really must stop she thought to herself.

"But if you are employed, will you still be able to visit your friends as you had hoped this year?" George could feel the tension between his daughter and wife.

"I might not be able to stay with Helen for as long, but I shall cross that bridge when I come to it, Father."

Elizabeth put her knife and fork neatly onto her plate, despite having only eaten a small amount. "Tell me again the name of this photographer."

"House, Elsa House. On the Promenade."

"I know of it," said George, keeping exactly what he knew to himself for now.

"I believe I have a headache. I shall retire to my room." Elizabeth got up with exaggerated stiffness and left.

"Caroline, this Elsa, what kind of photographs does she take?"

"Portraits mostly, and some of movement she said. A couple came in for a sitting – that's what Elsa calls it – while I was there so I got to try out for the position straight away! It was so very interesting, to watch how Elsa placed the couple and the lights to create the scene. And there are so many plates and negatives and old photographs to put into some kind of order…"

"Older photographs?"

"Yes, some are from when Elsa's father ran the business. Elsa wants them catalogued by date and subject. Her father kept notes in his appointment books so that he could remember which prints went with which sitting."

"I see. Well, I am pleased that you have found something that you seem to enjoy."

Caroline and Elsa worked well together. Caroline had a knack of suggesting just the right prop or angle for light and shade, her artistic talent drawn out by having someone willing to listen and respond to her. She also suggested some small changes to the shop, including a portable screen that could be used to hide the kitchen as clients were shown upstairs to the studio. She was polite but did not fawn over customers. She made sense of Elsa's haphazard accounts and approached the cataloguing of the stock and library in a methodical way.

Caroline felt at home in the shop and studio and could not have been happier.

Elsa too could not have been happier. She knew she was becoming infatuated with Caroline, knew also that it was not reciprocated. It was not the first time this had happened, though Elsa had been uninvolved for several years since returning from a short spell in London. She appreciated Caroline's quiet efficiency as well as her obvious artistic understanding. However, she was also Caroline's employer, and her senior by six years, and it was her responsibility to maintain both their reputations.

They made plans to attend the Cheltenham Gold Cup horse racing meeting; Elsa wanted to capture the crowds rather than the horses and Caroline simply wanted to experience the event. It had been held for the first time the year before, and generally agreed that it would be a boost for the town as attendance at the various spa rooms and baths continued to wane. They talked of arranging sittings in Montpellier Gardens after Easter, and Caroline suggested several other opportunities for Elsa to expand her clientele, such as publicity photographs for the spas and graduation photographs for the students of St Paul's and St Mary's Colleges. Elsa said she would be happy to accommodate Caroline's trip to Devon, "take the whole week" she had said. Anything to see Caroline's smile.

It was the Friday of Caroline's second week at the shop, and Caroline arrived home at a quarter to two as had become usual. She took her coat and hat off in the hallway and went straight through to the kitchen to retrieve her lunch from the stove where Annie had left it covered with a plate. She heard her mother's bell ring from the parlour, and Annie's footsteps on the stairs. A moment later Annie entered the kitchen.

"Your Mother would like you to join her in the parlour when you've finished, Miss."

"Thank you, Annie. Where did the bowl of hyacinths in the hallway come from? They smell divine!"

"Your mother had a visitor this morning, Miss, he brought them."

Elizabeth had read the calling card, glanced at the bowl of bright pink hyacinths and had almost declined the request for an interview. But she was curious as to why this young man should want to speak to her. It really was time that Caroline should find a suitable husband now that she was twenty-one, and perhaps this would prove an opportunity to extend their circle somewhat. One might hope for nobility, but one was aware of the lack of such titles even in Cheltenham.

"Mr Shaw, Ma'am," Annie announced and then left them in the parlour to ready tea things should they be required.

Elizabeth appraised the young man as he removed his bowler hat. A little short, a little pale though clean at first sight, and a little nervous perhaps with the way his eyes darted this way and that. "Do sit down Mr Shaw. What can I do for you?"

"Thank you. Yes, I won't beat around the bush with you madam; I am acquainted with your daughter, Caroline, and I have come into some information that I believe you should be made aware of."

This was unexpected, and Elizabeth detected a harshness in the young man's tone. "Information of what kind?"

"That which I am sure your friends and neighbours would be most distressed to learn." Arthur looked directly at Elizabeth now, having appraised the room. He had done his research and knew Caroline's father was involved with the Building Society. He had briefly considered a traditional short courtship, she was pretty enough, but then another piece of information had come his way and suggested a faster and more lucrative means of funding his growing gambling habit. Seeing the quality of the furnishings, he increased the amount he had been considering.

Elizabeth felt cold. She had heard the rumours of course, and as soon as Caroline had announced the name of her employer Elizabeth had feared some kind of scandal. She had told George he must insist that Caroline resign immediately, and he had refused saying that Caroline would surely do so herself if she felt in any way compromised. He had faith in her, he said. Elizabeth did not. And now this young man sitting not six feet from her in her own parlour had come to expose some sordid detail that involved her daughter and could ruin the family's name! She would have to approach this carefully. She did not offer him refreshment as she might otherwise have done.

"I am most certain, Mr Shaw, that my friends take no notice of common gossip."

"I would hope not, Mrs Munhead. The same could not be said always for one's neighbours."

"Whatever you think you know, Mr Shaw, might I suggest you furnish me with the details so that I may reassure you of their lack of importance, and indeed certainly their falseness?"

"Your daughter Caroline is engaged as an," he paused for effect, "assistant at a local photography studio."

"Go on."

"You are aware of the nature of a number of the photographs that this studio has produced in the past? You are aware that a local dignitary was involved in a nasty little affair three years ago, where those photographs were of great importance?"

"Make your point, Mr Shaw."

"My point is this, Mrs Munhead. Your daughter, by association, is likely to have been corrupted by Elsa House and her disgusting habits. I am aware that they have plans to attend the Gold Cup race meeting next week. Naturally the newspaper I represent would under no circumstances purchase or use any photographic material produced by Miss House. But should one of our own photographers happen to capture Caroline and Miss House together, in a moment of exuberance perhaps, it would be difficult for me to give any assurance that no story would find its way into print. It is an unfortunate association, Mrs Munhead, I'm sure you will agree. One that any decent bachelor would shudder to contemplate and with Caroline being unmarried, such a shame for her to find no man willing to take her off your hands..." He left the sentence hanging between them.

Elizabeth weighed the situation. He was not suggesting he had any proof of any wrong-doing or anything that could be suggested as inappropriate, but he was willing to create a story out of nothing none the less.

"You have no proof." Elizabeth said flatly.

"They do say the camera never lies, Mrs Munhead. I have a duty to report in the public interest, and surely you agree that warning of corruption and deviancy is indeed in the public interest?"

"What is it exactly, Mr Shaw, that you want?" She knew instinctively, but she wanted him to say it.

"I am giving you this information for your own benefit Mrs Munhead. A public service, if you will. I am undoubtedly doing myself out of financial gain here, as I will need to invest considerable time and effort into filling those column inches with some other notable news event. I believe it would be morally appropriate on your part to agree to cover my expenses. Shall we say ten pounds?"

"This is blackmail, Mr Shaw!"

"My dear lady, such a sordid term. I am merely requesting payment for services rendered. What you choose to do with the information is absolutely up to you and your husband. If Caroline were to be forbidden to attend the races, then no photograph could be taken."

Artie left the second half of the sentence unspoken, but they both heard it in their minds "*Though the story could still be written*".

Elizabeth stood up. She crossed to the writing bureau under the window and unlocked a small draw. When she turned round, she had two five-pound notes in her hand.

"Mr Shaw. I was not born yesterday. Blackmail is indeed a sordid business, and I would appeal to your sense of shame, yet I see clearly you have none. Take five pounds. If no mention of my daughter, either by name or inference, appears in your newspaper for at least one month after the Gold Cup races, you will receive the other five pounds."

Artie began to speak, but Elizabeth hadn't finished and held up the hand containing the notes.

"You will not call at this house again, the money will be sent to your newspaper offices. And should my daughter's name *ever* appear in your newspaper for any reason other than her wedding or to celebrate her success in some field, I can assure you Mr Shaw, you will find it impossible to secure credit anywhere in this county. Something I assume a person of your social standing requires at all times."

Artie calculated the implications of her terms. Five pounds would cover some of his debts, and others could be put off a while longer. What did he care for the stupid girl anyway? Elsa House would slip up again eventually, her kind always did, and then he would get a real story. He rose deliberately to his feet, aware that he did not exactly tower over Mrs Munhead in stature or presence.

"I agree to your terms, madam. As I said, it would be in your family's interest that Caroline does not attend the races." He took the note offered to him and left.

Elizabeth had been alternating between rage and despair since Artie's visit. How dare that man? How could George have been so naïve? Why must Caroline be so wilful, and so like her father? First consorting with the lower classes and that woman Mary, and now this. How on earth would she secure a respectable marriage for her daughter if she insisted on courting scandal at every turn? She was still rolling these questions around in her mind like a bag of marbles knocking against each other when Caroline came into the parlour.

"Good afternoon mother, Annie said you wanted to see me, but would you mind if I ate my lunch first? I am rather hungry."

"Sit down." Elizabeth commanded. Caroline sat. "You have plans to attend the Gold Cup horse racing next week?"

"Yes, Elsa and I are going to take some photographs there and …"

"I have no interest in Miss House. A horse race is no place for a respectable woman. I do not want you to go. Indeed, I have come to the conclusion that Miss House does not offer you suitable employment, and as such you must hand in your resignation."

"Mother, what on earth are you talking about? Lots of women attend horse races, some even own racehorses! And as for resigning, I enjoy working with Elsa and I see no reason why I should." She felt her face flush and her pulse quicken, but she had to stand firm. She knew her mother had been against her working with Elsa from the start but had no idea why.

"That kind of environment, with crowds of men, bookmakers and gambling, encourages unattractive behaviour. I will not have you associated with it!" Elizabeth raised her voice slightly to make her point. She did not want to have to spell out what her concerns were, and she could see Caroline's stubborn face set with her lips pressed together thinly. "I do not want to discuss it further now. Your father will want to impress upon you the importance of maintaining standards, for us as a family, when he comes home later. Go and eat your lunch."

"I don't understand. Why are you so against Elsa?"

Elizabeth did not reply. After a moment Caroline got up and went back to the kitchen. Annie had found occupation in the garden; it was difficult not to overhear conversations in a house that size, and she did not want to be drawn in on one side or the other. She was aware her relationship with Caroline was closer than any servant would normally have, and she hoped that once she and Jacob were married and had a family that she and Caroline could remain friends without the barrier of class. The world was changing, the Great War had seen to that. Annie resolved as she pegged out napkins on the washing line that her daughters would never go into service. She would be the last of that line.

Caroline was upset. She pushed the food around on her plate and went over the brief conversation with her mother again. Something must have happened. Who was the visitor that morning? She felt sure the two were connected. And what had that to do with Elsa? Caroline understood that Elsa was what many people called eccentric. Her style of dress, her preference for coffee over tea, the slim cigars she liked to smoke, all the small things that made Elsa who she was. Yet she was intelligent, polite, certainly not coarse in her speech, and had taught Caroline so much just in the past two weeks about the techniques of photography, she was an excellent teacher. How could Caroline give that up? It was impossible. Ridiculous.

Caroline finished her lunch and left the plate and cutlery on the table. Putting her coat on as she left the house, she felt oppressed at home in a way she had never done before. How different things had felt at the Vicarage with Midge and her brothers. She needed air.

A milkman and his cart stood at the end of the street where it met Queen's Road. The horse switched its tail, the only sign of impatience as the milkman chatted to another man over a garden gate. Caroline crossed the road and walked towards Lansdown. The towering, curved terraces of houses and apartments drew long shadows on the streets, but Caroline walked briskly as she thought and did not notice the cool air. She found herself after a while in Montpelier. She crossed the street and entered the public gardens. The bandstand was empty; the lunchtime concert had ended, and the band decamped to the Queen's Hotel bar. The tennis courts were deserted, and the flower beds circles of green foliage waiting for the tulips to push up through and open. Caroline sat on a bench.

Being independent was a complicated maze for a woman. So many considerations that men simply did not have. How would she ever be able to earn fifty pounds in a year if she was prevented from taking a paid position? The guinea a week she was paid by Elsa was really an extraordinary sum given that she only worked part time, even Caroline with her small knowledge of finance understood that. As she sat on the bench, Caroline considered how little she knew and understood of the world. It was slowly becoming clear to her, and she often felt foolish for asking questions that Midge or Helen or even Annie clearly took for granted knowing the answers to.

But I am not stupid, she told herself. I simply do not know what I do not know. I will catch up; I am catching up. And I am bound to make some mistakes and get into scrapes along the way. I'm just doing that as a woman instead of a young girl. I wish Freddie was here, he would tell me what I should do. He always knew the right thing.

Caroline closed her eyes. She remembered a conversation she had with Freddie when he told her he was enlisting.

"Can't stay here for ever," he'd said with a smile.

No, she thought, we can't stay here for ever.

When George arrived home after work that evening, Elizabeth was waiting for him. She quickly recounted the events of the day while he sat in his study and listened intently.

"She simply must leave there." Elizabeth ended, almost pleading.

George looked down at his desk and the letters and newspaper unread and waiting for him. He was annoyed that Elizabeth had given in to blackmail so easily, yet he understood her fear and even commended her quick thinking to add conditions of her own to the transaction. He did indeed have the ear of many important and influential residents of the county through his employment, and although it was distasteful to think of using those connections to out-manoeuvre an enemy, he would do so if it became necessary. Perhaps it would not become necessary; perhaps Caroline could be persuaded, although it may become necessary to explain to her in greater detail the reasons why she would have to give up her position. That also, to George, was distasteful.

Elizabeth fidgeted with her shawl. She knew better than to interrupt her husband's train of thought. After a few moments more, George looked up from the desk.

"I shall speak to Caroline after dinner."

Not wanting to face the strained tension that would surely exist over their evening meal, Caroline had elected to eat in the kitchen and then retire to her bedroom. George found her there, with the door open slightly, sitting in her comfortable chair by the window, reading.

"May I come in?"

"Of course." She placed the bookmark between the pages.

"I would like to discuss today's events with you." George, ever the diplomat, knew he would only have one chance to get Caroline to agree before he would have to give instruction. He so wanted her to be a successful, confident, happy woman, it pained him physically to have to clip her wings just as she learned to fly.

He sat on her bed opposite her chair and noticed her keepsake box on her dressing table. "Have you found anything to place in your box?"

"Two or three things. I'm sure it will fill up this year."

George nodded, "Caroline, do you remember three years ago, there was a scandal here in Cheltenham involving a man named Jonathan Priestley? It caused a great stir at the time."

Caroline's brow furrowed as she thought backwards, but in the end, she shook her head, "No, I don't recall anyone of that name."

"Perhaps his name is unimportant. You might remember that some photographs came into the possession of the national newspapers. Photographs of young men. As Priestley had property in Cheltenham, our local newspaper ran amok with the story at the time."

"Ah, were those the photographs where the men were kissing? I do remember that, yes."

George shifted uncomfortably on the bed, "That was what was reported, yes. And do you remember who it was who is said to have taken those photographs?"

Caroline suddenly understood. "Not Elsa?! Surely not!"

"Yes, my dear."

"But that was years ago. Father, I have seen the archive Elsa has, it's part of my employment to catalogue the contents, I can assure you there are no photographs of that nature there at all!" Which might not be strictly true, she would concede, as she hadn't seen the entire catalogue yet.

George was relieved that he did not need to be any more explicit.

"Your mother is very concerned that you do not become involved in any other unfortunate scandal by associating with Miss House. I am sure she is a thoroughly decent young woman who simply misjudged the situation and found herself compromised, but it is all too easy for you to become painted with the same brush I'm afraid."

Caroline was dismayed. "But Father, I so enjoy working with Elsa." She found herself trying not to cry, this was too unfair.

"We must find a way to limit any damage before it occurs. Your Mother has your best interests at heart, and you must understand that one day you will want to get married and to have to constantly worry about who may say the wrong thing at the wrong time to potential parents in law…"

"I would rather not marry if the man thought of Elsa as a dirty secret!" Caroline snipped. Truly this constant talk of marriage was more likely to turn her against the idea completely.

George felt the conversation slipping away and tried to refocus his daughter.

"That may be so. Caroline, please consider all our reputations in this matter. Your Mother would want you to terminate your employment immediately. I am willing to concede that this would not provide you with a reference should you need one at a later date. It is a month until Easter and I know you intend to visit your friend Helen then. I propose that you tender your resignation to take effect on Good Friday, but on one condition."

"What is that?"

"That you do not attend the Gold Cup race meeting with Elsa."

Caroline's tears spilled onto her cheeks. She suddenly felt as if she were ten years old again and had cried when Freddie refused to take her into town to see the elephants at the circus.

"But I so wanted to go! Why can't I go with Elsa? We'll be in public Father, what could possibly be wrong with that?"

George offered his handkerchief. He felt like a cad, but she had to see for herself.

"There, dear, dry your eyes. I know you want to go. But to be together in public is exactly why you must not. Elsa will not be the only photographer there. And there will naturally be reporters too. And really the class of people who…"

"But you're wrong Father, and Mother was wrong about that too. Horse racing is not just for the lower classes to get drunk and gamble their money away! Lots of wealthy people attend the meetings, women as well as men. Helen has been to race meetings and she is of our class."

George had one card up his sleeve. He had not discussed it with Elizabeth, but the Building Society were considering sponsoring a race at the following year's Gold Cup meeting, and as such George had been asked to attend this year as a guest of the Jockey Club. He had no interest in horses and did not think it was necessary to sponsor as race, but the opportunity was there to find a compromise with Caroline.

"You may still go to the race meeting, my dear. But I will go with you."

The following Monday, Caroline told Elsa that she would be leaving, and that she would not be able to go to the races as an employee. The women were taking coffee in the back room of the shop. Elsa had asked if Caroline was feeling unwell as she had been particularly distant that morning. They had just finished with a client and Caroline had been polite but had not shown her usual enthusiasm for the composition. Elsa had her back to Caroline while she stood at the tiny stove, and Caroline blurted out the information. When Elsa turned around, tears were in Caroline's eyes again.

Elsa's stomach dropped. "You know. About Priestley."

"Yes. Oh Elsa I don't care about that, it was years ago, but Mother and Father are so insistent that my, our, reputation is at stake while I work here. I'm so very sorry, I don't want to go but it is impossible for me to stay, don't you see?"

"What if you moved out? Found your own digs here in town? Moved in here even?" She heard the panic in her own voice and was ashamed. How could she be thinking of herself, when this poor girl would never be anything more than a friend.

"Elsa, there is no room for me here, where would you sleep? No, I don't think I'm ready to find my own apartment just yet, and I couldn't afford it in any case. Please believe me, I do not want to stop working with you. I simply have no choice. If you want me to leave now, I will of course understand."

"No, no not at all, you goose! I want you to stay. But I do understand. I understand completely Caroline. You do have your reputation to consider and mine went to pot years ago so it is completely unfair of me to bring you or anyone else down as well. Here, let's drink our coffee and then get ready for Mrs Daley and her daughters. Let's just enjoy the time we have together before Easter."

Caroline and her father took the train to the Prestbury Park station and walked the short distance along with hundreds of other race goers to the course entrance. Caroline had her arm through her father's, and had agreed that should they bump into Elsa, she would simply smile and move on. Elsa had understood, and had even considered writing to Caroline's parents and apologising for the situation they all now found themselves in. At the last moment she decided to wait until Caroline was no longer her employee. There would be time later.

The day was cool with a mist shrouding the top of Cleeve Hill which loomed above the track and enclosures. The grass was dewy underfoot, and Caroline congratulated herself on wearing her old, buttoned boots rather than her slightly more fashionable shoes. She was becoming increasingly aware that she did not look like other girls of her age with their shorter skirts and dresses, their shimmering stockings and their even shorter hairstyles. She wondered how Helen looked now, and if she would recognise her at the station in Plymouth. Helen had always been the tallest of the three, a striking girl with black hair and almost oriental skin. An inheritance from her mother's side of the family.

The crowds had been gathering from ten o'clock in the morning although the Gold Cup race would not start before ten minutes to four. George had passes for the winners' enclosure and planned to spend most of the day there talking to various other sponsors and horse owners. The first race was at midday and Caroline and George watched the horses parade in the small circle roped off for this preview. The jockeys sat high on their mounts; the perspective disguising just how short in stature some of the young men were. The favourite gained a ripple of polite applause as it made its way into the parade ring and the jockey lifted his whip in recognition. His horse was spirited, excited by the occasion and ready to run. The stable lad had difficulty in controlling it as it pranced sideways and bumped into the ropes near to where Caroline and George were standing. The crown as one took a pace or two backwards, aware of the damage half a ton of horse could do to one's foot.

Another horse raised a small cheer from a group of soldiers on one side of the parade enclosure. This time it was the jockey that caused the interest. He was a local lad, the son of a well-known horse trainer in Cheltenham who had until recently owned a stable yard at the back of Lansdown Road. Albert French had since taken early retirement, but his son Cecil had spent time at a racing stable near Newbury and was now returning to his hometown to race.

As the horses were led out of the ring and down to the racetrack most of the crowd followed. Caroline noticed a range of accents as she walked with her father, some more exotic than others. A group of men stood together with small notebooks, and George explained that they would be taking bets on the horses.

"Will we be placing a bet?" Caroline asked.

"I do not think that would be appropriate for me as a representative of the Building Society, or for you as a woman. Indeed, gambling should not be encouraged, particularly with those men. If I were to place a bet, I would be sure to contract with the official bookmakers, the ones standing by their chalk boards." He added piously.

"Father, I don't understand how you can say that and yet at the same time want to associate the Building Society with horse racing, when you know it is a common place for gambling."

"Sponsorship is a form of advertising. As these races become more popular, more local people will attend and to have the name of a business in a prominent position will be good for that business. What people choose to do alongside the main activity is of no concern to the business. Do you see?"

"I see that it is a complicated relationship." As most relationships are, thought Caroline.

They had brought a small pair of binoculars so as not to have to get too close to the racetrack yet still be able to watch the races. Caroline had never used them before, and so practiced by surveying the crowds. She picked out Elsa who had set up her camera just beyond the finish line but facing the crowd in order to capture their movements. Caroline suddenly felt a wave of sadness that she could not be with her friend, helping with the plates and light meter. George sneezed beside her, and Caroline considered that it was also nice to spend some time with her father outside of their home for once. She continued to scan the crowd, and her eyes found another familiar face. It was Artie Shaw, and he was walking up the grassy slope towards them.

Caroline had discovered his involvement in her present situation when she noticed his calling card on the writing bureau in the parlour. She knew his name, and now she knew his profession, and could guess how he might have wanted to use her friendship with Elsa to his own advantage. She did not know about the blackmail. She lowered the binoculars as he approached and quietly alerted her father.

"Mr Munhead, I believe? I did not expect to see you here today sir, but I see you are accompanying your daughter just as any conscientious father would. How are you, Caroline?"

His informality annoyed her now more than before. "Very well, Mr Shaw."

George took Caroline's arm. "Yes, we were about to make our way to the track side. I think you will find the bookmakers gathered just up this hill. Good day to you." He steered Caroline down into the thicker crowd and out of earshot. "Odious little man!" he muttered.

After the first race, they took lunch in a large canvas tent erected for the purpose. Both Caroline and George were on high alert should Artie emerge through the crown in their direction again, but he did not. Caroline did manage to catch Elsa's eye as they were eating lunch and Elsa entered the tent in search of a drink. The women smiled at each other across the sea of heads, and then both resumed their occupation. The afternoon was rather more boring for Caroline as she accompanied her father to the winner's enclosure and smiled and nodded to the wealthy men he spoke to there. She noticed some appraising her as if she were a horse, their eyes travelling up and down, perusing her flanks and hocks.

The horses were led steaming around the enclosure before being held in position by the grooms. Only then did the jockeys dismount and shake hands with the owners and their entourage. The spectators here were exquisitely dressed, in sharply tailored suits and elegant dresses. Several military officers gathered around one of the winners, apparently all with a share in its ownership.

Caroline decided that being unfashionably dressed was indeed a good thing that day at least. One of the owners gave her a red ribbon with a pin; he had brought several to hand out if his young horse won its race, and it had. His jockey's colours were red with a white chevron. Caroline understood it was another form of advertising but took it all the same. It would make a nice memory for her box.

They decided not to stay for the main Gold Cup race. A train was due at twenty to four, and George explained that as soon as the race ended there would be a mass exodus of race goers clamouring for the next available train away from the site. He had spoken to enough men to know that sponsorship would be a good thing but that terms would naturally have to be agreed more favourably in the Building Society's favour.

Caroline was due to travel down to Plymouth on Maundy Thursday, and so agreed with Elsa that her last day at the shop would be the Wednesday of that week. There were no portraits booked, and both were thankful that they would not have to put on a show of bravery. Only one customer had called in to the shop that morning, and Caroline dealt with them swiftly as Elsa sat in the back room, elbows on her knees and head in her hands. The bell rang as the customer left and closed the door, and Caroline came through the glazed middle door and around the screen.

"Shall I make us some coffee, dear?"

"No. Sit down for a minute please, would you?"

Caroline sat on the chair next to Elsa, their knees almost touching.

"Elsa, you're crying! Here, take my handkerchief," Caroline produced the cotton square from the pocket of the overcoat she wore in the shop, but Elsa waved it away and ran her hand over her face.

"I simply don't want you to leave, Caroline. You have been a saviour to me these past few weeks. Not just here in the shop, though you've done an admirable job in sorting out the prints and frames, but I hadn't realised how lonely this work had become for me. It has been wonderful to work with another, to get your perspective, your insight. I don't know how I will go back to working by myself again."

"But you'll manage, just as you did before. And I'm sure someone will want the position. We should put the notice back in the window today, someone might see it straight away and inquire."

"They won't be you," Elsa's eyes threatened to overrun again, and she blinked and looked up to the damp and nicotine stained ceiling.

The wall clock in the shop ticked onwards to itself. Caroline did not understand the depths of Elsa's distress, but she knew she shared her sadness at how this episode had turned out for them both. It was almost one o'clock, almost time for it all to end. Caroline reached over and rested her hand on top of Elsa's.

"When we are older, we will still be friends. I don't think anyone will be able to stop us then. Everyone is so consumed with protecting my reputation at the moment. But when I am older and no one cares about such things, as I'm sure they will not, then we will still be friends."

Elsa nodded her head and turned to a pile of papers behind her on the windowsill. She thumbed through them quickly, pulled out a postcard and handed it to Caroline. It had a portrait of Elsa on the front, taken two years before as an advertisement. Elsa had had twenty printed and still had more than ten left. Caroline said nothing but took the card, suddenly feeling close to tears herself. Then she got up and went to place the advertisement in the shop window.

5

HELEN

Another railway platform, steam billowing in the breeze and shouts from the porters and passengers. Helen Postgate stood with her younger brother William, both smoking cigarettes.

"And the next one due will be Caroline's?"

"It should be. I do hope I recognise her it's been simply years since we saw each other last."

"All you gals look the same these days, I doubt I could pick you out in a crowd and I've known you all my life," William chuckled and flicked his cigarette end onto the track, "tell me the plan again, just so I get it straight in my head."

"William, honestly, how you manage to get through each day is beyond me! We'll stay with Mother and Papa, and then Saturday we take the train up to Bere Alston. Gordon will meet us at the station there and drive us over to Endsleigh Cottage which is in Milton Abbot. We'll stay a few days there with his party and then move on to the new house in Tavistock. And that's where you are meant to be joining us, so try not to forget darling."

"All right, no need to be Mother! I'll be there before you gals arrive anyway, I'm supposed to be engaging some staff. The Colonel wants some retainers though lord knows where from. Tavistock is full of farmers and little else by all accounts."

William and his brother Jolyon always referred to their father as the Colonel. William held the rank of Captain, quickly promoted at the end of the war as senior officers fell. Jolyon had joined the navy briefly, and held a desk job in the dockyard, resuming his legal studies as soon as he could. He now practiced as a solicitor with a large firm in the centre of Plymouth, with offices in Exeter, St Austell and Truro. William often made use of his legal advice for free, as the brother who most frequently found himself on the opposite side of the law.

Caroline's train arrived and she stepped on to the platform followed by a guard with her case and carpet bag. She peered through the steam, and then heard a shout. She turned to see Helen advancing towards her at a trot, and William swaggering behind.

"Darling Caro! You haven't changed one bit!" Helen hugged her friend, almost dislodging both their hats.

"How are you? Was the journey too awful? William will bring your case. It is so good to see you again! We will have such a fun time while you are down here in the wilds of the west country! And I have some people I am absolutely certain you should meet. Come along, we have the car outside, it's only a few minutes to Lipson and we'll get you settled in."

Caroline was swept away, Helen's arm through hers and William sauntering behind with her luggage.

While Caroline had met Midge's parents when the girls were at school together, she had not met Helen's. She was aware that Helen's mother Rosalind had been a distant part of a European titled family, possibly Romanian or Hungarian. Helen's father William senior had distinguished himself at the third Anglo-Burma war and the Sikkim Expedition rising to Colonel. He was some years older than Rosalind, and both were some years older than Caroline's own parents.

Helen explained that her father spent much of his time at his club which overlooked the Hoe, even sleeping there several nights each week if his bridge games went on long into the night, so Caroline would probably not meet him. Her mother however was at home and was delighted that Caroline would be staying at their villa before the girls moved on to Milton Abbot. They were introduced after Caroline had unpacked and changed in what she considered to be a rather extravagant bedroom with faded fabric on the walls instead of wallpaper on the first floor of the Postgate's substantial home.

Rosalind was a small woman with a sharp intelligence and a passion for women's emancipation, much to her husband's disgust. She had marched with the Suffragettes through Plymouth and Exeter and was active in the campaign to improve women's maternity care. On good terms with Lord and Lady Astor, Rosalind was respected in her own right in the county and beyond. She had travelled extensively and could rely on her maiden name to open stubborn doors across Europe. Her dark eyes glittered as she poured tea for Caroline into a delicate china cup.

"And your mother, what does she do?"

Caroline was struggling a little to keep up with Rosalind's accent and her questions with the twists and turns of the conversation. "Mother doesn't really do anything much I'm afraid. She was terribly affected by my brother's death in the war. She rather withdrew from society."

"Is she an invalid?"

"No, well, for a time I suppose she was, yes. What a lovely room this is Lady Rosalind." Caroline felt a little awkward using the woman's first name, but it was how Helen's mother had insisted she be addressed. It saved any embarrassment over a mispronounced surname.

"Thank you dear. We are very lucky to have this house, so fortunate to live away from the dockyard. Do have some cake. And William tells me you will both be staying at our new house in Tavistock next week. Helen, your father asked that you engage a cleaning woman while you are there if William forgets. Your father will be having some of his friends to stay for the golf after your visit."

"Yes, Mother. I don't think William should be engaging any young women." A look passed between mother and daughter.

"Perhaps if you could find an older, more experienced housekeeper?"

The Postgate's villa was constructed of locally available granite and stood in almost an acre of mature gardens on the gently sloping Lipson plane. It was far enough removed from the city centre to have a village feel, but close enough to be on the tram line and for easy access to the shops, entertainment and railway. The girls went into the garden after taking tea and sat in folding deck chairs on the lawn in the shade of a large copper beech tree with its new season's leaves on show.

Helen took out a cigarette and offered Caroline one. "I didn't ask before, so sorry old thing."

"That's quite alright, I don't smoke."

"I wouldn't be surprised if you do by the time you leave here! Everyone smokes."

The late afternoon sun was warm, and bees clambered over the tulips and anemones in the flower borders. A blackbird inspected a patch of lawn a few feet from the girls' chairs, cocking its head to the side before stabbing its beak into the grass. In the distance, Caroline could hear seagulls calling. It was the closest she had been to the sea since she was a little girl.

Helen sat back in her chair and blew smoke out of her nose. She was rather concerned at the lack of luggage that Caroline had brought with her, considering she was expecting to stay for ten days. One could only mix and match separates so far before the illusion of different outfits was discovered. Caroline's hair was also an object of curiosity. Helen wondered if a trip into the city on Saturday morning should be proposed, and a visit to her favourite salon included. As she considered this diversion, she smiled to herself. What fun it would be to take this caterpillar of her friend and transform her into a beautiful butterfly to show off to her cousin and his weekend set.

Caroline had been having very similar thoughts. This was a completely different family dynamic to that of the Vicarage in Pangbourne and their relaxed, informal ways. In some respects, it was more like her own home, but she felt she might not live up to Helen's expectations when they moved on to the cottage they would be staying at with Helen's cousin. Caroline wondered how they would all fit in to a cottage, as it sounded as though Gordon would have several friends to stay.

"This is a lovely garden, Helen. And your mother is lovely too, not at all how I had imagined her."

"Really? She's a dear old thing. Quite the force of nature when her nose catches the scent of an underdog mind you."

"I had thought she would be taller, as you are."

"Oh no, my height is from Papa's side of things. Although Mother did once tell me of a distant great aunt back in the old country who stood six feet tall in her stockings and terrorised the locals by riding around on a bull."

"Goodness, how exciting!" Caroline looked at Helen, not sure if she were being teased. Helen remained relaxed in her chair with her eyes closed, drawing occasionally on her cigarette.

"I say, how about we take the tram into Plymouth on Saturday and buy a new frock or two for the weekend? My treat," Helen added quickly.

"I'd love to, but Helen that's too generous of you, really."

"Nonsense. Papa opened an account for my birthday at Spooner's and it would be rude not to use it. We could have some lunch there and then go on to the station afterwards."

"I did wonder if I might need one or two more outfits."

"That's settled then. I will telephone Gordon this evening and let him know we'll be on a later train."

Spooner's Department Store filled an entire corner of St Andrew's Cross in Plymouth city centre and looked out over Plymouth Sound as a proud advertisement for commerce in the city. Principally a homewares store, in recent years it had opened a whole floor devoted to women's fashion and beauty with a small salon in one corner and regularly held catwalk fashion shows. Caroline had never seen anything like it. Everything was so bright, sleek and modern, the female assistants so polite and attentive. It made Cavendish House in Cheltenham seem positively Victorian.

Helen breezed about picking out outfit after outfit and dispatching the assistants to collect them from the storeroom, Caroline assumed for Helen to try on in the fitting rooms. She was amazed when Helen turned to her and announced they were all for Caroline to try on while Helen sat in the waiting area.

"But I thought you were shopping for yourself!"

"Yes, I rather like this scarf. Now run along, we have a hair appointment in an hour."

Caroline meekly did as she was told and paraded several times in front of Helen and the assistant in a variety of outfits for day and evening wear with matching shoes and other accessories. When Helen was satisfied, she led Caroline to the salon and instructed the hairstylist to give Caroline something more manageable. Helen then disappeared amongst the cosmetic displays as Caroline was shrouded in a thin gown and sat in front of a basin.

Caroline tried to take everything in, but in the end, she found it easier to clear her mind completely and try to relax. She was unused to someone else touching her hair and she wasn't sure she really enjoyed it to start with. However, once the cutting began and there was no going back, she became intrigued at how her hair started to frame her face and change her familiar features. Nothing would change her nose though, Caroline thought with resignation. The instruction had been 'not too short', and Caroline's hair naturally started to develop waves as the length was reduced.

Helen returned as the stylist was using a hand mirror to show Caroline the rear of her head, and proclaimed the transformation a success. Caroline had to admit, she liked her new style and found it difficult not to keep touching it. Her hair felt softer than she remembered, and so much lighter.

Over lunch on the top floor of Spooner's, Helen explained that she had bought a few other items of a more personal nature for Caroline, and everything was being delivered to the villa that afternoon. They were sat at a table by a window that looked out over Saint Andrew's Church, with a tablecloth and napkins of coral pink and a small green glass vase in the centre of the table holding a single white freesia stem. Once Caroline had repacked for their weekend away, they would be driven to the station in time for a later train. It would only take an hour to get to Bere Alston and they would arrive in time for dinner that evening.

"You are so good at planning, Helen," Caroline said a little louder than usual over the sound of the band that was playing in the restaurant.

Helen smiled. It was a skill she felt would be most useful to her throughout her life, and one she enjoyed practicing.

The boxes were piled on Caroline's bed when they returned to the villa. She thought there must be some mistake, there were so many. She went through to Helen's room.

"I think all the boxes have been put in my room, can you come and show me which ones you wanted me to have please?"

"All of them, darling."

"But... no, Helen, I couldn't possibly…"

"Caroline, I had such fun this morning, choosing the outfits for you and your new hair style is simply gorgeous. Please don't spoil it for me by being such a fuddy duddy," she patted the bed next to her, "come and sit down for a moment."

Caroline noticed three small boxes on the floor by the wardrobe and was a little relieved to think Helen had at least bought something for herself.

"Darling, there will be people at the cottage this weekend that could be extremely useful to me, and to you too. Gordon has some rather influential friends and acquaintances, and if a girl wants to get on in life, she needs as many of those as she can get her hands on. Figuratively, at least in the most part. We're not getting any younger, are we? Somewhere in the near future both of us will need to decide how the rest of our lives will be lived, and I don't know about you my dear, but I do not intend to spend mine with a brood of children and a husband who spends more time at his club than with me. In fact, I do not intend to have a husband at all, but one must have the means," she bit her lip, considering how to continue, "we must look the part. We must blend in."

"Helen, I'm not interested in finding a husband either. Not yet at least. Mother has been hinting for weeks now and it's simply out of the question when I have so much catching up to do!"

Helen smiled at her friend. "That's the spirit, dear heart! Now, you will find some small items for your personal grooming that I picked out for you, a lipstick and some rouge, some earrings, and you'll need one of these too," she leaned across to her bedside cabinet and took out a disposable razor. Caroline had never seen one before and Helen immediately realised this.

"For your under arms, darling, and your legs. And anywhere else you might want to remove hair from," she demurely lowered her eyes at this last piece of information.

The train from Plymouth rolled around the edge of Dartmoor as the sun glowed golden along the border with Cornwall. Gordon had sent one of the staff from Endsleigh Cottage to meet them in his brand-new maroon standard tourer motorcar. Milton Abbot was a few miles from the station at Bere Alston and Caroline peered out into the darkening countryside to get a glimpse of the cottage. As with many buildings of its name, it was no more a cottage than a stable. There was a small gatehouse, along with a Swiss style chalet, a couple of follies and a stable block, a walled kitchen garden, tennis courts, a croquet lawn, a lake stocked with fish and several acres of woodland. Endsleigh Cottage itself was a well-proportioned Georgian house extended and improved over the previous hundred and fifty years and now boasted twelve bedrooms, four with their own bathrooms, a large evening room with three sets of French windows that opened onto a long terrace, and ample staff quarters.

As they drew up to the front steps, Gordon bounded out to greet them followed by two other young men and a woman in an orange evening gown who leaned against the door frame, a cocktail in her hand. They were all dressed for dinner.

"Helen, darling, I was beginning to think you'd blown us off!" They kissed each other's cheeks, "And who is this fine filly?"

"Gordon, behave yourself. This is Caroline, I told you, my friend from our old school days. Be a darling and fix us martinis while we run up and change. You can introduce us properly when we come down."

"Right-ho. I've put you next to Vic, top of the stairs third door on the right, and Catherine, no, sorry, Caroline isn't it? Caroline is next to you so fourth on the right. Akers will bring up your things won't you old man."

They filed into the spacious hall with its tiled floor and chestnut panelling, Akers the butler balancing as many bags as he dared at once behind them. Caroline noticed the woman in the doorway greet Helen with a kiss on her cheek too and their eyes lingered on each other slightly longer than Caroline expected. Then the woman withdrew, and Helen led the way up the stairs.

Ten minutes later Helen knocked on Caroline's door and then entered at Caroline's acknowledgement. Helen took in the young woman before her with a critical though pleasantly surprised eye. Yes, the new hair cut really did suit Caroline's face. She wore a sleeveless beaded dress of royal blue, with peacock feathers embroidered on the band that sat just on her hips.

"Let me do your lipstick darling and then I simply must have a drink!"

"Must I?" Caroline heard herself sound like a petulant child.

"Yes indeed. It might not be quite the right shade for you, but it will do for this evening. Now, pretend to kiss but with your mouth open, like this," Helen drew the red lipstick expertly around Caroline's lips and then offered her a handkerchief to blot them on before applying a second coat.

"You won't leave me stranded with all these strangers, will you Helen? I don't know anyone and I'm sure I won't know what to say." Caroline frowned; she was really rather nervous of making her big entrance down the long staircase.

"I promise, tonight I will not be more than a few feet from you at all times. But really you have nothing to worry about. Gordon is an excellent host and people will want to talk to you. Just be yourself," she smiled, took Caroline's hand and they went out on to the landing.

With Mrs Monger's warnings about alcohol again ringing in her head, Caroline accepted her martini and sipped tiny amounts until she was able to eat something. She was a little embarrassed to see the lipstick transfer itself from her lips to the glass, but a furtive glance told her that the same was happening for the other ladies present too.

The party gathered in a drawing room just off the main entrance hall for their pre-dinner drinks. Caroline was guided around the group by Gordon and with Helen by her side, until she had been introduced to everyone though she could only remember two or three names by the end of it. There were to be fourteen people staying over the weekend, she learned, with some arriving the next day and not staying the night. There would be ten for dinner that evening; six men, and Caroline, Helen, the mysterious woman who knew Helen and had been introduced as Lady Victoria but whom everyone seemed to call Vic, and another young woman who seemed as nervous as Caroline and was called Emelina, or Lina for short.

Lina was a distant cousin of Tommy, a young man that Helen appeared to know very well. He had a mop of dark hair and wore a velvet suit in a deep plum colour. He was loud, his laugh was more of a giggle, but Caroline warmed to him and Lina instantly. She was relieved that Tommy was nominated to escort her to dinner, and that he was seated on her left while another man was to her right. Helen sat opposite but one seat removed, much to Caroline's relief as it meant she could watch Helen across the table and copy her manners. It became almost a game between them; when Helen drank, so did Caroline, when Helen put down her knife and held only her fork, so did Caroline. Tommy noticed as they came to the end of the main course, and began to copy Helen as well, which then alerted Gordon and uproar ensued as Helen's movements became ever more extrovert. Everyone was laughing, even Caroline after an initial horror of making a fool of herself could see the funny side of it all, and when Helen scooped up a handful of cream and early strawberries with her fingers and put them in her mouth, everyone at the table followed suit to squeals of laughter.

The ladies retired to clean off the remnants of their dessert before joining the men in the evening room, where the French doors were open, and lamps had been lit out on the terrace. Tommy played the piano for a while, singing a few humorous songs that most of the party seemed to know. Caroline sat on a sofa with Lina and chatted about film stars. Lina mentioned that there would be someone joining the party the next day who made moving pictures, and she was excited to be meeting him. Caroline said she was too and meant it. Then one of the young men asked the girls if they would make a four for bridge, and when Caroline explained she didn't really know how to play well, he insisted that he should teach her.

The bridge game broke up at almost eleven and Caroline looked around to see where Helen had got to. She was not in the evening room. Caroline got up and went to make one last drink at the tray of bottles on a small table by one of the French doors. She glanced out on to the terrace, and saw Helen with Vic. They were locked in an embrace, and Caroline stepped back from the door a little shaken. She composed herself; of course, she thought, that would explain the coolness Vic had shown towards her during the evening.

Caroline woke on Easter Sunday with a thumping headache. She carefully opened one eye to look at her watch and groaned as she saw it was almost eleven. She should be at church. Was there even a church nearby? Why hadn't anyone woken her? She sat up gingerly and saw to her horror red lipstick on the pillowcase. Now she remembered being so tired when she finally came to bed, she had dropped her clothes on the floor, yes there they were still, and collapsed into bed without washing her face. She needed to use the bathroom, so gathering her housecoat around her she slowly went to the door and peeped out into the landing. All quiet. She crossed the landing and quickly did what she had to in the bathroom, noticing that only a small smear of lipstick was on the side of her face and that her hair seemed to have been very well behaved overnight, before returning to her room.

She sat on the bed and wondered what to do next. The house seemed very quiet, but surely someone must be awake. She picked up her clothes from the night before and dressed in a simple pleated skirt and blouse. No lipstick, she decided, and no jewellery, just her watch.

Downstairs she found Lina in the drawing room where they had had cocktails the night before.

"Oh Caroline, I'm so glad you're here! I don't know where anyone else is, I've been sitting here for almost an hour, and I'm famished. Do you think there is any food to be had?"

"I do hope so. I would like some tea at least and maybe some toast. Shall we explore, see if we can find Akers?"

After trying three smaller rooms and walking through the evening room, they found a room at the corner of the ground floor with a long dining table and chairs similar to the dining room they had used the evening before. This one had a heated cabinet along one wall and under various metal domes the girls found bacon, eggs, kippers, mushrooms and to one side a rack of cold toast. Coffee and tea were on the table, and the girls helped themselves to breakfast. The sun streamed through the windows, and dust floated and swirled, illuminated like glitter.

"Are we really the only ones awake do you think?" Caroline asked as she buttered some toast.

"I think we must be. I went to bed at midnight, and I know there were still a few of the chaps drinking in the library. I don't know where Tommy got to, I don't remember seeing him after we'd played bridge. And Helen and Vic disappeared too. I'm glad you're here though. This is my first time at a house party like this and I really don't know the form."

"Neither do I. I was hoping Helen would be around to ask. You don't think they have all gone to church without us, do you?"

Lina giggled, "How Catholic! I very much doubt it. But listen, is that a bell for the front door?"

"Gordon did say some more people would be arriving today."

The girls continued their breakfast and presently the sound of voices could be heard approaching.

"You found the morning room then, bravo!" Gordon made straight for the coffee and poured himself a cup, dropping two sugar cubes into the cooling liquid. "So, what do you fancy today, ladies? We have tennis, croquet, a spot of fishing in the lake, perhaps? A ramble through the woods? Or are you the type to just sit and watch the rest of us exert ourselves for your entertainment?" Lina and Caroline exchanged smiles at Gordon's playful chatter.

"I rather think croquet might be fun," said Lina, "but won't your other guests be here soon?"

"Already here, dear girl. The last one just arrived and is making himself at home as we speak. Really, this coffee is cold!" He got up and pulled a handle on a chain. Moments later Akers appeared in the doorway.

"Some hot coffee if you please, Akers. And can you bring the tennis rackets and croquet mallets into the evening room for our guests?"

He turned back to the girls.

"Make yourself at home won't you, come and go as you please, do whatever you find most entertaining. We won't stand on ceremony here, except for cocktails and seven and dinner at eight. If you're hungry or thirsty at any other time, simply find one of those bell pulls and give it a tug. Akers will appear like a genie and be at your service." He looked up as a tall man entered the room. "Ho James, all settled? Good man, have some coffee, oh perhaps wait for the fresh pot, eh?"

"Thank you, Gordon, but I can wait, I had breakfast on the way."

Gordon remembered his manners, "James this is Tommy's cousin Lina and Helen's friend Catherine. No, dash it! Caroline. I do apologise, I am simply terrible with names. However, ladies, I am very proud to introduce the film-maker extraordinaire, Mr James Baker."

James shook hands with both girls, "I now have to live up to my introduction!" he smiled.

Before the girls could reply, Tommy and another of the young men from the night before burst into the morning room in search of food.

Caroline was watching Lina and a young man called Albert play croquet from the comfort of a cane chair on the terrace when Helen found her later that afternoon. Helen lit a cigarette and leaned her bottom against the low stone balustrade so that she faced Caroline.

"Are you enjoying yourself?"

"Yes, thank you. Everyone has been very friendly. Almost everyone anyway. Did you hear the commotion earlier when Tommy fell into the lake?"

"I should think the whole of Devon heard it! What an ass he is. How did he do it? All I saw was him dripping along the landing to his room."

"He found a rowing boat and took it out on the lake, and then he got an oar caught in some weeds and stood up to free it."

Helen drew on her cigarette, "you said almost everyone had been friendly?"

"Yes, well, I haven't really had a chance to speak to everyone."

"Anyone in particular?" The women looked at each other. Caroline waited. Helen dropped the end of her cigarette and pushed it into the gravel with the toe of her shoe. Then she sat on another of the cane chairs and looked out across the lawn.

"Victoria is a very close friend of mine. We have known each other almost three years, we met in London. She will

inherit a fortune when she is 25 next year. Until then, we can
only meet occasionally, as we are here."

"Is that what you meant when you said you had no intention
of finding a husband?"

"Yes. Caro, I simply have no interest in men that way. It's
not something I can explain, and here I don't feel I have to. Vic
means the absolute world to me. Once she has her inheritance
and is free from her guardianship, we will leave this mean, petty
little island and go somewhere where no one cares how we feel
about each other. Buenos Aires or Morocco perhaps. But until
then we have to be careful, and she is always guarded around
people she doesn't know."

Caroline thought of Elsa. The way Helen spoke of Vic was
how Elsa had spoken to her on her last day in the shop. She
was beginning to understand that the world as it appeared on
the outside was not how it worked on the inside. There were
different costumes to be worn, in much the same way Helen
had given her dresses for this occasion. Different parts to play
depending on the audience. A thought occurred to her.

"Is Tommy… is he like you too?"

Helen chuckled, "Darling, Tommy is absolutely like me as
you put it! Though of course, he has no interest in women.
Lina knows, I'm sure, but it's simply not a topic of conversation
amongst friends. We all know, and there is nothing to discuss.
Do you understand?"

"I think so. But not everyone here this weekend is… like
you, are they?"

"No, not at all. The couple that arrived this morning,
Gloria and Bill, happily married as far as I know. Neighbours
of Gordon's a few years ago when he lived in Kent, and
now they have a house somewhere near Okehampton. Lina
is definitely looking for a possible husband, and perhaps
Albert will fit the bill there, they do seem to be enjoying
each other's company. And then there is James of course.

Definitely as straight as an arrow, that one. So no, Caro, not everyone is like me."

Caroline turned in her seat and tucked her legs underneath her.

"Can I ask you about it?"

Helen smiled, "Of course, though I might not answer. Some things are private you know, even between old friends."

"Of course, oh goodness, tell me to mind my own business, but this is just so… I want to understand."

"Go on."

"How did you know? When did you know? How would I know?!"

"Darling Caro, I can tell you that you are as straight as Mr James Baker."

"But if I don't know, then how can you possibly?"

Helen was trying hard not to laugh out loud now. Caroline's earnest expression and her determination to understand human nature were so endearing Helen almost wished she were 'like her'.

"I knew when we were at school. There were other girls. Like me. And then at home young soldiers at house parties, friends of Papa, with their fumbling and their heavy breathing. I just knew. But I also knew that it wasn't to be spoken of openly. Eventually you meet other people, go to the right clubs, you find a way. It's rather easier in London than down here. That's why weekends away with friends are the very thing to do."

"I still don't understand why you never approached me," Caroline shook her head.

This time Helen did laugh, "Because you are not like me Caro. Not one bit."

Dinner that evening was a less raucous affair, and Caroline found herself seated next to James. She hadn't seen him at all that day since breakfast, and as Lina appeared to be content in

Albert's company, Caroline engaged herself fully in conversation with James. She learned that he had made several small-budget silent films which had been distributed across London and the Home Counties. He had secured funding to make a new film loosely based on Thomas Hardy's Mayor of Casterbridge and would be spending much of May in Dorset with his small company of actors. They talked about films and photography, and James was very interested to know where Caroline had gained her knowledge. She skirted around the subject, aware that it could raise some as yet undiscovered prejudice.

After dinner then went out on to the terrace and continued talking. Someone found a gramophone and played some scratchy records. James asked Caroline if she would like to dance, and she had to admit that she only knew the basics of a waltz. She did not disclose that Mrs Monger had taught her the steps just a few days earlier in their kitchen. James showed her where to place her hand on his shoulder, took her other hand in his and then gently moved her around in a circle as they swayed to the music from within the evening room. At the end of the song, he let her go, stood back a pace and bowed. Caroline smiles shyly and felt her cheeks glow.

Learning moderation after the night before, Caroline excused herself at eleven o'clock and went up to bed feeling a little more comfortable with the general proceedings than she had previously. She woke earlier on Monday and found James already in the morning room by himself when she went down to breakfast.

"Good morning, Caroline, the coffee is hot still if you would like a cup?"

"Good morning. I think I would rather have tea but thank you. And thank you for a very pleasant evening."

"It was very enjoyable on my part too, thank you. We'll make a dancer of you yet!"

Caroline helped herself to scrambled eggs and a slice of toast.

"I'll be leaving again this morning," James put down his cutlery and pushed his empty plate away, "but I wanted to ask you something. I could use someone with a knowledge of photography on set next month. It would mean joining us in Dorset, we've taken a house for four weeks all paid for, but I think you would be the perfect addition to our company. What do you say?"

Naturally, the question came just as Caroline took a bite of her toast. She rolled her eyes as she chewed, and James laughed and apologised. Having swallowed, Caroline asked, "You would like me to help you with your film? Truly?"

James nodded. "Not just help, there will be some money for your contribution. Not much, we're not talking Hollywood or anything like that, but a few pounds as long as we don't over run."

"Oh James, yes please! Oh, my goodness, this is so exciting!"

"Excellent! I'll write the address of the house when we're finished with breakfast and then I really must get going. I've got to be back in London this evening. Will you give me your address too, just in case our plans change at the last minute?"

Caroline enjoyed the following days at Milton Abbott. Visitors came and went, and when Lady Victoria went back to London, Caroline had Helen's almost full attention again. They explored the Swiss Chalet which stood on the side of the hill, backed by trees and overlooking the Tamar valley. They learned that the gardens had been laid out by the notable landscape architect Humphry Repton, with the house belonging to the Duke of Bedford as much of the land in west Devon did. Caroline wondered how Gordon had been able to afford the run of the place for a whole month, but Helen explained that the Duke spent most of his time in London and Gordon, being in the art business and an acquaintance of the Duke, had obtained a very favourable rent.

Days were filled with late breakfasts, then croquet until Lina and Albert appeared and took over the mallets. Afternoons of tennis, although Caroline had to borrow ill-fitting tennis shoes from a cupboard that Akers directed her to or reading on the terrace with a regular supply of tea. She used a joker from a pack of playing cards as a bookmark and had decided to keep it as a memento of her stay. Helen and Tommy played chess most afternoons, and one of the other guests brought paints, canvas and an easel and Caroline found herself the focus of his attention as she sat in the cane chairs in the sunshine.

Cocktails, Caroline discovered, were not mandatory. This pleased her as she really did not like the taste of gin no matter how it was disguised. She noted that almost all the other guests did and sank two or three each before dinner. On the fourth evening, when she declined the Singapore Sling that Tommy was mixing for the others, he winked and said that was quite alright because he had found a different cocktail recipe especially for her. After handing round the gin glasses, he returned and mixed brandy, orange liqueur and a squeeze of lemon juice, pouring it into a champagne glass for Caroline. She took a sip, letting the flavours roll over her tongue before warming all the way down her throat, and nodded and smiled at Tommy, thanking him for considering her. By the time dinner was announced the party were running low on the orange liqueur as everyone wanted to try 'Caro's Sidecar'.

Caroline made a single glass of wine last for the whole of dinner, and no one forced more on her to her relief. When dinner was over, and everyone had moved to the evening room she discovered the port that the men drank. After trying a little she decided it was by far her favourite alcoholic beverage. Helen preferred champagne, and when that was not available, she had a taste for gin or vodka. The gin was plentiful, and on two nights she had to be helped up to her room by Caroline and Lina, who did not drink alcohol at all.

On the final morning before Caroline and Helen were due to move on to the new house in Tavistock that afternoon, Caroline had written a short letter to her parents as agreed because she would be staying away from home for more than a week. She had been frugal with the details, sensing that her mother would disapprove of much of the antics of the guests. She ended sincerely, saying she was very much enjoying her stay. She truly was, the atmosphere of the house party was so relaxed, and even the formal dinners were jovial affairs. She had learned to play a decent hand of bridge, she had discovered cocktails, she had walked along the banks of the Tamar and lay on the lawns with Tommy and Helen watching shooting stars and making all kinds of outlandish wishes the evening before. She did not, however, mention James in her letter home. She wanted to keep that to herself for a little while longer, and she intended to write to him once she was home again, to confirm the details of where she should travel to in Dorset.

The weather had been splendid, and Caroline was about to walk to the village of Milton Abbot to post her letter when one of the young men who had arrived the day before called out to her.

"Are you going to the village?" Harry was wearing cricket whites and a sweater, which he had exclaimed at breakfast were the most comfortable clothes he owned.

"Yes, to post my letter. Akers gave me a stamp; he really is a magician!"

"Yes, top chap. I'll walk with you, if I may?"

They strolled along the driveway, past the gatehouse that Caroline had assumed was the actual Endsleigh Cottage when they had first arrived, and down to the village. The post box was set into a stone wall outside a tiny shop and post office combined. Harry said he would like a beer in the village pub, but when Caroline said she would walk back by herself, he shrugged and stayed with her. When they reached the gatehouse, Harry suggested walking down to the river and back to the house that way instead of straight up the drive. Caroline agreed, the ground was firm as there had been no rain for days and she wouldn't spoil her shoes.

The trees formed an arched tunnel over their heads and the birdsong mingled with the wind through the branches. It was picturesque, an English idyl, and Caroline stopped for a moment to close her eyes and breath in the warm blossom-filled air. And because her eyes were closed, she did not know just how close Harry was to her until he wrapped his arms around hers and kissed her roughly on the lips.

Caroline was shocked. She tried to take a step back, but Harry moved forward at the same time and they both lost their balance, falling to the grass with a thump. It did at least mean she could free her arms and try to push Harry off. He persisted with his kisses and attempted to grasp any other part of Caroline's anatomy she left unguarded.

She started to panic and found her voice, saying "No! Harry, no!" several times. He said nothing but focused his attention on pulling up her dress. Caroline's nails were not long, but she freed one hand and dug them into Harry's face as hard as she could, making him cry out in pain. He sat up and slapped her face hard, calling her a bitch. She had drawn blood, and he wiped the back of his hand across his face, looked at the smear, and quickly got up taking his handkerchief from his pocket and dabbing his cheek with it.

"You nearly had my eye, you stupid bitch!" he spat.

Caroline was frozen to the spot.

"No one will believe you if you say anything, so better not, eh?" Harry sneered, and brushing his knees with his hands, "just a bit of a tumble, no harm done."

He turned and walked briskly away back towards the gate-house.

Caroline lay quite still on the ground for several minutes after Harry had gone. She could taste blood, she thought she had bitten her tongue when Harry slapped her. The birds still sang, and the breeze still blew warm and soft over her skin. Eventually she sat up, pulling her dress down over her knees. She picked twigs from her hair, and discovered her elbow was grazed from the tumble to the ground. She took off her cardigan, gave it a shake to remove more small twigs and a holly leaf, and then put it back on again quickly as she felt cold. She got to her feet, perhaps a little too quickly as she had to put her hand out to a tree to steady herself. The side of her face felt hot and sore. The birds still sang. Slowly she followed Harry's steps back to the house.

Caroline managed to slip into the house and up to her room without seeing any of the other guests. She washed her face in cold water and changed into a sweater and one of her old longer skirts. She had already packed her things ready to leave after lunch; Tommy was going to drive her and Helen over to Tavistock in Gordon's car. She sat in front of the dressing table mirror studied the red mark on her face. How had it happened? One moment they had been walking and the next she was on the ground beneath him. There was a gentle knock at the door. Caroline's voice grated as she granted entry.

Akers came in, holding a tray with a sherry glass that did not look as if it contained sherry.

"Forgive the intrusion, ma'am. I heard one of the gentlemen talking and thought you might be in need of this." His grey eyes were kind, and his hand shook a little as he offered her the port.

"Thank you, Akers. I... I don't know..."

"No explanation necessary, ma'am. A tumble, I understand. The paths around this estate can be slippery. Would you like me to ask Miss Postgate to attend you?"

Caroline swallowed the rest of the port. "No thank you. Could you let her know that I have a headache and will be taking a nap to try and relieve it before we leave later? I shan't be wanting any lunch."

"Of course, ma'am. Shall I take your luggage downstairs?"

Caroline agreed, and when he closed the door behind him, she lay on the bed and covered herself with a blanket. She did not sleep.

The Colonel's new house was situated at the far end of Down Road in Tavistock, near to the entrance to the golf club. It was a bright white building, as its identical fellows that stood guard along the road were, all sporting names related to the trees and shrubs planted in the front gardens. Laurel View had five bedrooms and a bathroom on the first floor, with two reception rooms, a dining room and a kitchen on the ground floor, all generously proportioned. The houses had been built with the golf club clientele in mind; each had space for several motor cars on the curved driveway at the front of the house, and at the rear each had a small terrace with a set of French doors that overlooked Dartmoor beyond. They were equipped with the latest technology including telephones and electricity which heated the water from a large tank in the roof space. The Colonel had seen the purchase as a wise investment, and a place to entertain his friends from the club when his children were not using it.

William, as he had promised, was already there when Tommy drove the car into the driveway. Caroline had been silent for the whole journey, and Helen was not entirely sure it was because of a headache but did not pursue the matter.

"Well, this is a smart little castle!" Tommy exclaimed as he jumped out of the car and began to unload the luggage.

"Such a pretty house," mused Helen, "so far from anything of interest."

"But to have the golf course practically on your doorstep, isn't that a bonus, dear heart?"

"It is the only saving grace, Tommy. Tavistock is such a boring little town."

"Perhaps you'll have an escape, that will liven things up no doubt!"

"What do you mean, an escape?" Caroline asked. She took the case she had borrowed from Helen, and they all turned towards the front door.

"The prison. Oh yes, I know it's not exactly here in Tavistock, it's a few miles away in Princetown, but they do have escapees that cross the moor on moonlit nights. It's quite the outrage how many fellows break out of there, so I hear."

"Oh Tommy, stop it. When was the last escape? Three years ago? Four? Don't frighten dear Caro the minute she arrives." Helen took Caroline's arm, "He just loves a good horror story."

They went into the house. William was nowhere to be found, but he had left a note saying he was at the golf club and would see them at dinner. He also said he had engaged a woman to cook and clean on a daily basis, and a man to tend the garden, look after the cars and generally be useful. Helen wondered about the daily woman, but soon discovered that she was a well-rounded lady of forty-five who lived at the other end of Down Road when that woman appeared at the front door with a basket of provisions for their dinner.

Another strange room. Caroline sat on the bed and looked at the pretty wallpaper. It was a trellis design with yellow roses on a white background. The bedroom she had chosen was at the rear of the house in one gable end, and the window had an uninterrupted view across the moor. The difference between it and the view she had enjoyed at Endsleigh across the formal gardens could not have been starker. But she found that this view appealed to her more in that moment. The wildness, the way the clouds raced from one side of her vision to the other, and the range of hills in the distance that Helen had told her were called Tors. Helen had promised that William would take them for a drive across the moor while they were there. Caroline felt she wanted to walk off into the windswept heather and gorse and lose herself in the elements. She touched her face, which she hoped she had been able to adequately disguise with powder and pulling her hair forward under her hat. This time she lay down on the bed and slept until a knock on the door woke her for dinner.

It was a far less extravagant affair than the formal dinners at Endsleigh had been, and for that Caroline was relieved. Helen had told her not to bother dressing for dinner, as it would only be the three of them, Tommy having returned to the house party. The housekeeper Mrs Danks was an excellent cook and agreed to return the next morning with provisions for a picnic lunch as well as breakfast.

William was jovial, if somewhat of a fidget. He sensed that he was surplus to requirements that first evening and excused himself as soon after dinner as he could without seeming impolite to Caroline. The girls sat in the room with the French doors, though they were closed to keep out the wind which had picked up and grown chilly. There was a radio which played music quietly as Helen smoked and looked through a fashion magazine and Caroline continued to read her copy of *The Inimitable Jeeves* that she had purchased in Plymouth. At almost nine thirty Helen could not hold herself back any longer.

"Caro, what's wrong?"

Caroline looked up from her book and smiled a most un-convincing smile, "Nothing, nothing at all."

Helen tried again, "What happened to your face?"

Surprise, shock and finally defeat ran in waves across Caroline's features. "I... it was... oh Helen, it..." and she burst into tears.

Helen crossed the room and knelt at the side of Caroline's chair, pulling a handkerchief from her pocket and pressing it on to the girl.

"Caro, darling, I knew something had happened. Who was it? Did he... was he... did he force himself on you?"

Caroline, between sobs, recounted the episode as best she could but she found some parts were missing from her memory. Helen was furious. She got up and found a bottle of whiskey and two glasses in a sideboard. She insisted Caroline drink before speaking again. Meanwhile Helen paced the room with her glass.

"Damn that Henry Gregory! I never did like him or his brother. I shall make sure Gordon drops him like a hot stone."

"Helen, he said no one would believe me! Oh, what have I done, I should never have told you!" she started crying again.

Helen spun on her heel, "You have done nothing my dear, nothing at all! Have no fear, I won't give Gordon any more detail than I need to see him drop the Gregory brothers, and if he needs more then I shall say he assaulted me! But are you quite sure he... that he didn't...?"

Caroline wasn't entirely sure what could have happened, but she was as certain as she could be that Harry had not taken anything physically from her. Only her trust, she realised and shuddered. Helen knelt beside her again and put her arm around Caroline shoulders, feeling Caroline tense momentarily as she did so.

"I think an early night is called for, don't you darling? Will you be alright on your own in that end room? We can leave the landing light on if you want. I'll make sure William keeps out of the way until we need him to drive tomorrow. He won't mind, he'll probably go for a run first thing anyway. Caro, I'm so sorry that our lovely few days have been so ruined for you."

Caroline tried to smile at her friend though her nose was running, "It wasn't your fault, Helen. It was a lovely few days at

Endsleigh. Let's not talk about it anymore, please? I doubt I shall
ever see Harry again, and I'd like to forget all about him now."

"That's the spirit! Now, let's get you off to bed. I'll warm
some milk and bring it up to you."

Caroline fell in love with Dartmoor over the next three
days at Laurel View. The colours, and the way the shadows
of the clouds rippled across the endless land entranced her.
William drove the girls to Princetown where they gazed up at
the grim granite walls of the prison and heard the shouts and
wails of the occupants. Then on to Mortonhampstead for hot
chocolate in the saloon of a small public house. They picnicked
at Postbridge and crossed the stream back and forth over the
stone footbridge in the bright sunshine. Leaving the car at
Postbridge, they climbed the nearby Bellever Tor and gazed
out in all directions.

The next day Caroline persuaded Helen to walk down
the hill into Tavistock. Though Helen insisted on calling it
parochial and turning up her nose at its lack of sophistication,
Caroline enjoyed it immensely. They explored the abbey ruins,
the market and the shops along Brook Street. They had lunch in
the Bedford Hotel, and bought fudge and toffee, before making
the slow climb back up to Down Road above the town.

The final day of Caroline's stay at Laurel View was her
introduction to the art of swinging a golf club and attempting
to hit the very small ball a very long way. William had made
himself at home with the club secretary and other members,
and Helen and Caroline were lent clubs and appropriate shoes.
Helen's long arms were more suited to the distance strokes
than Caroline's, but Caroline found she had the greater skill
at putting when she eventually found the green. By the time
all nine holes had been completed they were all exhausted.

That final evening, Caroline presented Helen with a small
token of her gratitude, thanks and friendship for being such

an excellent host. It was a small brooch shaped like a peacock feather that Caroline had bought quietly in Tavistock the previous day. Helen accepted graciously, and they drank whiskey that evening in quiet, peaceful companionship.

6

JAMES

23 April 1925
King's Cross, London
Dear Caroline,

Hope this finds you well, and still up for the trip to Dorset as we discussed. We'll be filming around the coast at Portland, and it will mean long days, but I think you will enjoy it.

We've taken a place called Knapp House, between Swanage and Wareham. There will be 12 of us including you. The house has a pool so bring your bathing suit! We might be able to fit in a swim or two between takes. You won't need much else, just some practical clothes, we won't stand on ceremony.

I'll be driving down from London on Friday 1 May to make the house ready, and if you could be at Dorchester station on Saturday 2 May at midday, Julia and Elsie will be arriving there too and I'll collect you all at the same time.

Hope to see you soon!
James

After returning from Devon, Caroline found that she needed to spend time by herself. She needed to organise her thoughts from all she had experienced and find her feet again on metaphorical solid ground. Her father commented on how well she looked with 'all that Devonshire air', and Annie and Mrs Monger were very grateful for the toffee. Her mother did not acknowledge Caroline's trip. She hardly spoke to Caroline at all. Caroline suspected it was because of her hair cut, or perhaps the outfits she had returned with. Both were visible examples of Caroline operating outside of her mother's influence.

Caroline added the joker playing card and a golf tee to her keepsake box. She hesitated over the joker, it's contorted face staring up at her in mockery and reminding her of Harry. Should all her memories in the box be good ones? Not necessarily, she decided, but they should be instructional if they were not good. The joker card would remind her that some people pretended to be something they were not. She picked up the postcard with Elsa's face and held the two side by side. There was a balance and a symmetry that she found reassuring.

It took a few days to reacclimatise to the routine of 20 Glencairn Road but then Caroline was keen to be off again, and May could not arrive fast enough. She did have one dilemma however: a bathing suit.

Caroline had learned to swim at school. One of the benefits of growing up in a spa town, the girls had been taken twice weekly to the baths at Montpelier as well as having daily physical exercises outside. Cheltenham had quite the reputation for healthy activities, with golf, horse riding and several stables, swimming indoors and a proposed outdoor lido, along with the large municipal parks and the tree-lined streets. The College had a cricket ground, and there were two men's football teams and a women's team.

Caroline had not worn her bathing suit since she was fourteen, and naturally her shape and size had changed since then. She took it out of her chest of drawers and held it up against herself as she stood in front of the mirror on the door of her wardrobe. It would not do. Having been in the drawer for six years, the fabric felt brittle. Caroline decided not to try it on. In the drawer also was her swimming cap, a rubber item that was now badly perished. Caroline sighed. She had not expected to spend quite so much of this year shopping for outfits.

The following Sunday, Caroline attended the morning service at Saint Mark's. She was now considered part of the congregation and had quickly learned the most often sung hymns. She still sat with Annie's family, on the aisle end, but would now walk home by herself after talking for some minutes to Mary after the service had ended. Mary's morning sickness had passed, and she should have been blooming according to many in the congregation. Mary did not feel in bloom. She felt more tired than she had ever known and would sleep for most of the afternoon if Philip did not wake her, and still be ready for bed again by nine o'clock.

This Sunday Mary stayed seated as the congregation filed out and Caroline joined her on the front pew.

"You are looking well Mary."

"I do not feel it Miss Caroline, not as much as people tell me I should. How was your visit to Devon? We missed you for the Easter services. And your new hair style suits you very well."

"Thank you. Dartmoor was the most vast, wild place I have ever seen! I hope I shall be able to return there and see more of it. The locals say that in the winter the snow blocks most of the roads and sheep have to be dug out of drifts."

Mary shivered, "It does not sound like a place I would be happy to be in the winter. One day perhaps I will go to Trinidad and visit my relations. That would be warm." She smiled to herself and rubbed her growing stomach.

"Mary, do you feel able to accompany me to Cavendish House tomorrow? There are a couple of items that I need to purchase, and I really do not think my mother would want or be able to advise me."

"But she is your mother, why should she not?"

"I need to purchase a bathing suit," Caroline said with a frown, "and I think Mother would demand I have one with knickerbockers and long sleeves. That won't do at all."

Mary chuckled, "Yes, I will go with you. I will meet you at the tram stop on Gloucester Road, at ten o'clock, will that be acceptable?" She stood up, pushing herself with her hands on the arm of the pew and blowing hard through her mouth.

"Absolutely. Are you sure you'll be able to walk so far though?"

"I will be just fine, Miss Caroline. It will do me good to get outside for a while, and I will have more excuse to sleep in the afternoon!"

With Mary's help, and ignoring the manner of the assistant in Cavendish House, Caroline purchased a bathing suit consisting of some close-fitting jersey shorts in dark green that came to just above her knees, and a long-line vest top with a V-neck also in green that was almost as long as the shorts. A white rubber belt would stop the vest from riding upwards as she swam, and a new style rubber aviator hat finished the ensemble. She would wear her oldest stockings rolled down to just below her knees and a pair of canvas shoes in a bright yellow. The assistant had tried to convince Caroline to opt for a more flared and less fitted swim dress, but Caroline pointed out that those were better suited to a day at the beach rather than actual swimming in a pool which she intended to do.

The day before she was due to travel to Dorchester, Caroline was packing her case and carpet bag when her mother entered her room. They had barely spoken for two weeks, and yet Caroline found she was not as sorry as she might have been a year ago. She spent her time reading the newspaper, walking or painting in the garden with her small box of watercolours. She continued to collect the flowers on a Tuesday from Curzon's nursery but had begun to spend a little more time each week discussing the blooms with Mr Josiah Curzon and learning the various plant families and their characteristics. Mr Curzon told her he would deliver the flowers personally to St Mark's while Caroline was away. She felt as if she wanted to learn everything, to soak up as many new ideas as possible. She had a sense that there would come a time when she would be called upon to put her knowledge into practice and did not want to be found lacking.

"You are travelling tomorrow?" Elizabeth asked, her eyes taking in the array of clothing spread out on the bed and across the chair.

"Yes Mother, the nine-twenty train."

"And you are certain that there will be a number of people joining this house party?"

"Yes, there will be twelve of us James said. And no doubt a housekeeper."

"Are you sure it will be safe, Caroline? You hardly know these people."

Caroline paused in folding a sweater. Going away with Helen had not provoked this line of questioning, but Helen was of a respectable family. Caroline had evidently not been 'safe' at Endsleigh. But she had felt safe with James, when he had shown her the dance steps on the terrace. She hadn't known it at the time, because she had never felt unsafe with a man before, but she recognised it afterwards and was looking forward to seeing James again and learning more about making films.

"With twelve people Mother, I believe it will be safe."

"And you will be assisting them in producing a moving picture, is that correct?" Elizabeth couldn't entirely keep the acidic tone from her voice.

"Mother, you must not assume that every photographer or film maker is a bad influence. James has made several films; they have been distributed across London picture houses. It is quite the respectable profession."

"Perhaps, for a man. What is that?" she had spotted the bathing suit.

"The house has a pool and I want to go swimming, so I have bought a new bathing suit." She held her Mother's gaze more confidently than she felt.

"It looks far too small for you."

"It stretches to fit. And see here the belt stops it lifting up in the water. Quite ingenious I thought."

Elizabeth turned up her nose, "Quite indecent! How a young lady is supposed to preserve her modesty in such an outfit is beyond me."

Caroline tried to divert the looming lecture, "I might not have a chance to wear it, we might be too busy to go swimming. I wanted to have it just in case." But I will swim, she told herself; even if I am exhausted, I will swim at least once.

Knapp House stood exposed on the crest of a hill, looking out at the English Channel. It was constructed in an L shape with a small patio area at the rear in the shelter of the right angle. Lawns led away from the house down a gentle slope to a more level area where the pool and a small pavilion were located. The front of the house was in perpetual shade as it faced north, and most of the rooms had large windows on the opposite side of the building to make the most of the views and the sun. What the house lacked in a welcoming façade, the company that James had assembled more than made up for.

As there were only five bedrooms, everyone had to share. Luckily there were four girls who split into pairs. Caroline found herself sharing a small room containing two camp beds with Elsie. A year older than Caroline and with red hair in curls to her shoulders, Elsie was a Londoner with a harsh accent but an infectious laugh. Julia and Bella occupied the other 'girls' room next door although both were closer to thirty and could hardly be thought of as girls. Arrangements had been made for an older couple who lived at the farm a little further inland from Knapp House to do for the company while they stayed, preparing simple meals and provisions, taking in laundry and cleaning.

There was much to unpack and store on the first day, with the library being chosen as the most suitable location for the filming equipment. Baskets of props and costumes were unloaded from the large cars that three of the company had driven down in. James had brought his own car and his camera, with reels of film carefully stored in canisters. Caroline helped where she could, carrying and stacking items, but the company had mostly worked together before and seemed to slot into their own roles with ease. Caroline eventually left them to it, not wanting to get in their way. She went into the kitchen to get a glass of water from the pump that stood over the stone sink. Bella was sat at the table smoking and looking through a magazine.

"Can I get you a drink?" asked Caroline.

"No thank you, dear. I shall have a gin shortly," she looked up from her magazine, "known James long, have you?"

"No, not really. We met at a friend's weekend party last month," she took a sip of water, "but I've worked for a photographer and James thought I might be able to help."

"You're not here to act then?"

"Oh no. At least I don't think so. I never have before."

Bella tilted her head and looked at Caroline through the smoke she exhaled.

"You've got a good face. We might give it a try. I've no idea how we'll fill all the roles in any case, so you may have to!"

"Do you really think so? Oh, that would be too exciting!"

"Yes, well don't get too carried away dear, it's not all smiling into the lens. But you're the right size, and you've got a passable mouth. Have you seen the script?"

It was dark before Caroline found herself alone with James for the first time since she had arrived. She had been tucked away with Bella going over the script, which was not as much dialogue as a stream of written directions and explanations of each scene. James had typed out four copies for the company to share and his own had copious handwritten notes all over every page. Bella had encouraged Caroline to show her some poses and facial expressions, to see how well they conveyed meaning and seemed to be pleased with Caroline's style.

It had been agreed that meals would be set out in the kitchen and the company could help themselves as informally as they liked. This meant that some stayed around the kitchen table to eat while others found chairs, benches or low walls around the house to sit on while they ate. There were several loaves of bread, a large wheel of cheese and pats of butter on the cold shelf in the pantry, and baskets of fruit. They would not starve.

James was standing on the lawn smoking and looking across the bay. Caroline walked across the grass and not wanting to startle him, spoke while she was still a few feet away.

"What are those lights there?"

James turned and smiled, though his face was in shadow, and Caroline couldn't see it.

"Those on the right are Swanage, and on the left you can just see Poole. It's a pity we won't have time to explore, but we're not here for a holiday. How are you finding everyone?"

"Bella has been teaching me to act. She says I have a good face. And Elsie is a lot of fun. I haven't really spoken to Julia yet, but everyone seems to know each other already so I will just have to find my own place I suppose."

"You do have a good face," James said quietly. "We've all worked together before, though not everyone on the same film. John and Frank, I met when I worked the set of *Twice Two* for Minerva Films. Anthony, I think is the only chap I've worked every film with. He wrote the last one we made; it took us three weeks to shoot in Hampshire. I'm hoping this one will take about as long."

"Do we begin first thing in the morning? How do we start?"

"We'll spend the first two or three days working through the script here. Then we'll try some shots around the little hamlet we passed on the way here. I think it looks perfect with the ford and the cottages all around the green."

"And what do you need me to do?"

"I had rather hoped that you might be up for some acting. I know you understand composition and it will be good to have your ideas on that too, but I had you in mind for the part that is based on the Lucetta Templeman character in the original work. If you'd like to give it a try."

"Truly? Oh yes please, James!"

"Well, better get an early night then. We start at eight sharp."

They worked hard, long days. Caroline would never have believed that reading and talking could be so tiring, but she found no difficulty in falling asleep over almost every evening meal. They would run through scenes repeatedly, trying different movements to express the storyline, different combinations of actors and props. James directed, though often became involved in the action himself. Caroline hung back and watched how the others in the company held themselves and exaggerated their movements and facial expressions, trying to learn as much as she could as quickly as possible.

Elsie coached her as much as they had time for. Bella showed Caroline how to keep her hair under a wig, and how to apply the film make-up. The blue lipstick and eyeliner looked ridiculous, but Bella assured her that it stood out far better on film than any other colour. Caroline only fully believed her when she saw the men applying the same sticky blue paste to their own faces. She also quietly congratulated herself on getting her hair cut in Devon; having to coil it under a wig would have been most uncomfortable.

It was not all plain sailing. There were disagreements over who would be more suited to which part, and how scenes should be played. Julia flounced off after Elsie described her as an 'old wooden doll'. Anthony did not agree with some of the changes that the company wanted to make to his script. James became animated and shouted repeatedly that time was money. But on the whole, everyone rubbed along together knowing they were all necessary to create the finished, and hopefully financially profitable, film.

In Cheltenham, George and Elizabeth were in the parlour before dinner. Caroline's latest letter had arrived that day and George was reading aloud.

"… the blue lipstick is horrid, but it shows up perfectly on film, so we all wear it, even the men. Frank has shown me how to turn the camera handle at exactly sixteen revolutions per minute. That's the correct speed to prevent the film becoming either jumpy or slow. He says I have a knack for knowing how to do it. It's all very interesting, but I shall be glad to be home again as everyone is rather noisy and boisterous!"

Elizabeth frowned, "Blue lipstick indeed! I had been under the impression that she would be assisting with the costumes. And it is such a shame that she cut her hair while in Devon, I shall never truly get used to how she looks now. Have you noticed how her skirts are becoming shorter? And the bathing

suit she purchased, if it can be called that, I am surprised that
Cavendish House sell such items. George, we really must find
her a husband and put an end to this nonsense."

George replaced the letter into its envelope, "Elizabeth, you
must surely see that the more we encourage Caroline in one
direction, the more likely she is to run off down a completely
different path? And no doubt, a path that would be more
thrilling, but also more precarious and potentially dangerous.
She is only just twenty-one. Really, I see no need to hurry
things along just yet."

"I disagree. She is in need of a firm guiding hand that only
a husband can provide." Elizabeth's one annoyance with her
husband was his indulgence of their children. It had always
been the case.

"She has been spending considerable time with Mr Curzon.
That is something I feel we should encourage. I shall invite
him to tea when Caroline returns."

"My dear, I do not think…"

"What harm can an invitation to tea do?"

On the Tuesday of the third week, the company returned to
Knapp House at almost seven o'clock for dinner. A little black
car was parked outside the front door, which was wide open.
Everyone was curious to see who their visitors were despite
being asleep on their feet and ravenously hungry. They found
Helen and Tommy in the kitchen.

Helen stood up and gave Caroline and then James hugs,
saying loudly, "There you are! We were just about to move
on and find a hotel for the night. Tommy darling, let them sit
down, you all look like death!"

Helen and Tommy were on their way to London, on a whim
to gate-crash some debutant balls. Helen had never been quite
high enough on the social ladder to be a Deb herself, but the
temptation of champagne and all the right people was enough

for her to agree to Tommy's outrageous suggestion. They would stay with Lady Vic, who would be able to talk them into a number of parties in Belgravia.

Most of the company collected portable food and moved away to the other rooms. Caroline and James stayed in the kitchen with their visitors until Caroline found herself waking with a start after almost sliding off her chair. It caused much laughter, but also made it clear to Helen and Tommy that they really did need to find a hotel. Helen was insistent that Caroline and James should join them in London once the filming was completed. They said their goodbyes and headed off at breakneck speed along the country lanes in the direction of Wareham.

The following day at breakfast, James declared that the company was to have a day off. They were ahead of schedule, and all deserved a break from the concentration required for filming. Julia announced she would be going back to bed and asked that no one disturb her until at least midday. A couple of the men did the same, but the rest of the company were happy to relax around the house and pool. Caroline and Elsie were excited to finally have time to swim. Elsie's bathing suit was similar to Caroline's but in a navy blue. She had no hat, and so Caroline decided to leave hers off as well. Standards were definitely slipping while she stayed at Knapp House, she chuckled to herself as they sat on the edge of the pool with their feet in the cold water.

They lay on their towels on the grass for much of the afternoon, the men taking their turns to do lengths of the pool. The weather was glorious, and Caroline noticed that her skin was already turning a light brown after being outside in short sleeves for much of the previous three weeks. Bella loaned her a large straw hat to keep the sun from burning her face. No one wanted to put make-up on a peeling nose, she had explained.

Frank, who had slept until lunchtime and then taken a walk into the village, joined Caroline and Elsie on the grass. He had bought a newspaper and read out loud the headline story.

"Horror as eight killed in bus disaster!" he said dramatically. "Police investigations continue into a tragic accident that occurred at Rowley Bridge, seven miles from Derby last Monday. A thirty-seater coach carrying a party of members of the Derby Municipal Employees' Guild and their families on an outing to Bakewell from Derby suffered brake failure as it travelled down a 1:6 gradient to the bottom of the valley near Borden reservoir. It gained considerable speed and failing to negotiate the sharp bend at the bottom of the hill, crashed through the parapet of Rowley Bridge, landing on its roof. Many of the passengers were pinned beneath the vehicle, five being killed instantly, whilst two others died within half an hour and one later, while being transported to hospital. A number of other passengers were injured."

"Cor lummy, how awful!" whispered Elsie. "Imagine being crushed by a bus!"

Anthony had joined them while Frank was reading, drying himself on a towel.

"Sounds like an interesting subject for a script, I say."

"That's positively ghoulish!" Elsie exclaimed, "how could you?!"

"Very easily, I think. A real tragedy, not these made up, whimsical tales we work on."

"Well, I wouldn't work on it, far too gruesome for me. Would you Caroline?"

"I don't know, really, but I suppose if it could be written sensitively, not like the sensationalism of the newspapers…"

"Exactly!" Anthony broke in, "that's of course how it should be written, with a dashing hero pulling women and children to safety. I shall make a start as soon as we are finished here. Frank, don't use that paper for fire spills, there's a good chap, leave it on my bed when you've finished with it."

They completed the filming four days before the end of May. Anthony asked James to drive him to the station the next morning as he was keen to get back to London and make a start on his next script. When James got back to Knapp House, several of the others were ready to leave and were waiting to say their goodbyes. Elsie and Frank were planning to leave that afternoon together as they were both due to start in a provincial play in Andover in a few days.

"What next for you then?" Elsie asked Caroline as they washed and stacked plates in the kitchen.

"Home again, or on to London to stay with Helen and Tommy. Though I rather think I would like a few days at home first. There is much to be said for enjoying the company of others, but I find I do need some space in between times to be by myself."

"Oh no, I can't bear to be on my own for more than a few hours. Unless I'm asleep of course, or ill, but I rarely get ill." She dried her hands, "It's been lovely working with you Caroline. I hope we can get together again some time, and you will come and see us at Andover if you can? It's booked to run for six weeks, so there's plenty of time. Talking of which, I'd better go and give Frank a shake, or we'll miss our train!"

James almost bumped into Elsie as she left the kitchen, and they did a twirl together before she ran off giggling. James sat at the table and lit a cigarette.

"So, it'll just be us when Elsie and Frank have gone. Look here, Caroline, I have this place until the end of the month and I'm going to be staying on. How do you feel about staying with me? Nothing scandalous, I promise! I've already asked Mrs Judd to come and stay over and she's agreed so we can sleep at opposite ends of the house in complete propriety. What do you say?"

Caroline finished drying and stacking the plates and sat down opposite James across the scrubbed wooden table. She had been so caught up in the company that she had hardly

given any thought to what she would do next until Elsie had
asked her. The past month had been a universe away from her
life in Cheltenham, or even the weekend in Devon. She had
cooked, cleaned, made and mended costumes, and of all things,
acted. She had loved almost every minute of it, felt as if she
had found herself, and wanted it to continue. She also liked
James. She enjoyed their discussions on set; he listened to her
ideas and treated her as a valid member of the company even
though it was her first moving film experience. And because
he had, the rest of the company had too. She was sure of that.

"James, I have very much enjoyed being here with everyone,
with you, this month. I've learned so much, and accomplished
things I'd never dreamed of only a few months ago."

"I feel there is a 'but' coming…"

"No, well yes, but not the one you're expecting I think," she
smiled. "As you have taken the trouble to engage Mrs Judd as
chaperone, then I would very much like to stay here. Though
I'm going to move my things into Julia and Bella's room and
sleep in a real bed again!"

James laughed, "You have the run of the place!"

"But, and here it is James, I am not ready to become
'involved' with anyone. In any way. I'm only just getting to
know myself, and well, perhaps I'll tell you over the next few
days, but I want you to be under no illusions that I am looking
for a husband or … or a fling of some kind."

James looked at her serious face. She was so unlike the
women he usually socialised with, or any woman he had
known before. There was no pretence, no coyness, no vampish
allure. Caroline was open, and in many ways naive, but it
was refreshing. He felt more comfortable around her for it,
he recognised that at least. He was also aware that he could
take advantage of her easily, in so many ways. This thought
came unbidden, and he pushed it away as if it left a bad taste
in his mouth.

"I am not husband material. I have been told as much. And I am staying here simply because it is paid for and the weather is wonderful, and because I haven't had a break in almost two years. I would like your company Caroline, but I'm not asking you to spend every minute by my side. Come and go as you please. We might find we want to walk together or sit, or swim, or only be sociable at mealtimes. Please, do whatever you feel, but I would just enjoy knowing you were here." He surprised himself with the little speech, but it was the truth he realised. He just wanted to be around her.

Caroline was persuaded, "Then yes, I would like to stay on please. If you could run me to the station on Sunday morning, I would be grateful."

"I can do that. And I propose that we go out for dinner tonight, as a treat. We've both worked hard, and while Mrs Judd has been an absolute star, I am in need some something a little more substantial and a good claret. Will you come too?"

They ate that evening in the restaurant of the Grosvenor Hotel in Swanage. After almost a month of farmhouse cooked food, the menu seemed exotic and rich. After dinner they walked along the sea front as far as the bathing huts and back, the lights of the fishing boats twinkling around the harbour. The sea was calm and only an occasional gull stirred as it settled down to roost for the night.

Their final days at Knapp House were equally calm and quiet. Despite having James' car, they stayed close to the house. Both of them swam, alone and together. Caroline sketched, James read, and together they walked the cliff tops and sat and gazed out at the blue green water. Much of the time they were silent in each other's company, but over meals they talked.

James told her of the rooms he rented in London, at the top of an old house. He explained the circumstances of how he was told he was not husband material, and his failed engagement to a young woman who had broken things off to marry a pub landlord. He said he was prone to depressive episodes, of feeling his work was of poor quality and how he would never be recognised for his efforts. He spoke a little of his parents who had died within days of each other during the influenza of 1918 while James himself had been in France fighting the disease as well as the enemy.

Caroline described her life in Cheltenham as companion and support to her mother and how she had come to realise that there had to be more to her life than perpetual mourning for Freddie. She talked fondly of him, for he was her hero and truly no man would ever measure up to his ghost. Open as she was, she also explained the terms of her allowance as she had agreed them with her father, and how she still had no idea if she would be able to earn that amount of money in a year in order to fund another. She spoke of the people in her own life, of Midge and their school days together with Helen, of Annie and her plans for marriage with Jacob, and of Mary and the baby due later that year.

"I know I am not as experienced as other girls of my age," Caroline sipped her water as they ate dinner on their last evening in the kitchen, "but I am catching up. I want to say yes to as much as I can and live as much as I can. I know Freddie would have, so I'm doing it for him."

1

LADY VIC

Caroline arrived home late on the last Sunday in May, to a letter from Helen which included the address where they would be staying in London. Caroline lay on her bed in her old familiar room and read Helen's fluid handwriting. She closed her eyes and let the letter fall to the floor. Not yet, she thought to herself and drifted off into sleep.

Clothes needed to be washed and dried, letters replied to, a stub of blue lipstick added to her keepsake box, and Florence was at home next door and desperate to exchange news. Caroline also spent some time going over her finances. She had kept notes of the amounts she had been given by her father from her account, and of what she had spent the money on so far. Halfway through the year and despite adding the guineas she had earned from Elsa, she was down to thirty-three pounds, seven shillings and four pence. She had contributed to the meal kitty at Knapp House, and the bathing outfit had been an unexpected extravagance. Caroline sighed; not destitute, but she would need to be cautious while in London and would not stay more than three or four days.

Over breakfast, Elizabeth had informed Caroline that Mr Curzon would be taking tea with them on Thursday afternoon and that Caroline was expected to be present.

"Mr Curzon? Why on earth is he coming?" Caroline was surprised.

"He is a respectable businessman Caroline, there is no other reason required."

"I'll be seeing him in the morning to collect the flowers as usual."

"Indeed. He tells me you have been spending a considerable amount of time at the nurseries recently."

"Yes, he's been teaching me about the plants," she realised what Elizabeth was implying. "We only talk about the plants, Mother."

"A wholesome topic. He is a widower, I understand. And there is a possibility of his selling some of his land to the Council for the construction of dwelling houses." Elizabeth smiled sweetly, "A widower, though not an old man."

Caroline would not rise to the bait, "I will take tea with you and Mr Curzon. And on Friday I will be leaving for London. Helen has invited me to stay with her friend Lady Victoria for a few days."

"Lady Victoria? I am so pleased you are finding appropriate young people to socialise with!"

If only you knew, thought Caroline.

Collecting the flowers the following day, Caroline did not linger but made excuses that she was expected at ten o'clock at the church. The walk to St Mark's took Caroline around ten minutes; long enough for her to consider Josiah Curzon in a different light. She had known he was a widower; his wife having died only a few years after their wedding. Caroline thought him to be perhaps fifteen years older than her, which was not an unacceptable age difference. He was kind, softly spoken, generous with his time, and a successful businessman as her mother had pointed out. Did her mother know he was a Methodist? It made no difference to Caroline, though she resolved to make more of it if things became difficult. She liked Mr Curzon, but she did not want to be his wife.

On Thursday afternoon at four o'clock Annie showed Josiah Curzon into the parlour where Elizabeth and Caroline were seated. He had brough with him a large bouquet of pink roses and carnations, which Elizabeth instructed Annie to arrange on the dining room table. Caroline felt rather sorry for Mr Curzon as her mother interrogated him over his opinions on the deteriorating surface of the Queen's Road, the planting schemes in Montpellier Gardens and the price of coal. She seemed to ask him a question always just as he had taken a bite of cake or a sip of tea, and the delicate china wobbled precariously in his rough hands. Caroline said very little, but she listened attentively, warming to the familiar sound of Mr Curzon's voice. She learned that he originated from Wiltshire and had been apprenticed to a market gardener in Stroud before purchasing with a small inheritance what was to become his five-acre site of glasshouses for tender and exotic plants. At a quarter past five, he made his excuses, thanking Elizabeth profusely for the tea, and left.

Elizabeth was radiating an aura of satisfaction, "Such a very nice man. So … practical. Don't you think?"

"Yes Mother, he is nice. I think I shall sit in the garden with my book now if you don't mind?"

"Of course not, dear. Run along."

Still smiling, Elizabeth began planning an evening party for when Caroline returned from London.

Friday lunchtime Caroline stepped on to the platform at Paddington Station and walked in the general direction of

the other passengers towards, she hoped, the exit. The size
of the station took her breath away. She had thought Bristol
Temple Meads had been imposing, but she quickly realised
that everything in London would of course be on a much
grander scale. Just as she reached the exit, she heard her name
shouted across the concourse. Tommy and Helen were waving
and hurrying towards her excitedly.

Helen hugged her friend while Tommy took her luggage.
Helen explained that they were taking Caroline on the underground train to Green Park, and from there it was a short walk
to the serviced apartments in Bruton Street, just off Berkley
Square Gardens, where Lady Victoria lived. Caroline had expected to take a taxi, so this change of plan was very exciting.
Tommy told her they would not dream of allowing Caroline
to take the underground by herself, but that she would be
perfectly safe with him to escort the ladies. Caroline giggled
and thanked him for his chivalry.

When they were back at street level, Caroline was surprised
to see such a large green open space in the centre of London.

"Oh Caro, Green Park is one of the smaller parks! Hyde Park
is much larger. Perhaps we shall take a stroll there on Sunday.
You will stay until Monday, won't you?" Helen had linked her
arm through Caroline's as they walked.

"Well, yes, if it's alright with Vic, I should like to."

"Vic won't mind at all, darling!"

"I say, are you girls hungry?" Tommy asked, "I'm famished.
Let's dump Caroline's case and then go over to Frogmore's for
something to eat."

Caroline was relieved as she had been wondering if her
friends had already eaten. She discovered they hadn't eaten
breakfast or lunch, having rolled out of their separate beds just
half an hour before finding her at Paddington. It was one thing
that had caused her some discomfort while visiting people;
her own home's mealtimes were regular and if she had ever

been hungry in between she could usually find something to eat in the kitchen or pantry. She had liked the easy 'eat as you please' style adopted at Knapp House, but everywhere else she was at the whim of her hosts and had found herself almost feint with hunger two or three times when their meals had been later than she was used to. On this trip she had hidden a small packet of biscuits in greaseproof paper in her bag, just in case she should be presented with food she did not really like, or no food at all!

Frogmore's was a small café, serving teas, coffees, light lunches and pastries. Tommy announced that their order would go on his tab and that the girls could have whatever they pleased. Helen ordered poached egg on toast, Caroline had the same but added mushrooms and tomato, and Tommy went for the full English breakfast with a pot of tea for three. Over their meal, Helen explained the itinerary of the weekend in more detail. They were to visit a club that evening, the Ben Uri gallery in Bloomsbury and a party on Saturday at an exclusive address in Mayfair, and Sunday would be church in the morning, lunch at Vic's and then a stroll around one of the nearby parks. The gallery had only recently opened, and Tommy was very keen to view the exhibition, particularly the illustrations for the Book of Samuel by Enrico Glicenstein.

"You've brought the navy-blue dress with you?" Helen pushed her empty plate away on the table.

"Yes, I have, would it be suitable for the party? Or for the club this evening?"

"Darling, it will be suitable for church on Sunday. This is London, fashion is so advanced compared to the rest of the country. Tommy, Caroline and I will be calling at Swears and Wells this afternoon, be a darling and let Vic know we'll be back at the house around four, would you?"

Regent Street was busy with omnibuses and cars in both directions and Caroline was thankful for Helen's reassuring arm to cling to as they crossed the road. Swears and Wells had an impressively modern frontage, with mannequins in the large windows and a single model high above the entrance. Helen was obviously known to the assistants; she swept through to the ladieswear department. Caroline felt uncomfortable at Helen spending even more money on her outfits, but Helen waved her objections aside. It would go on to Vic's account and she would hardly notice, Helen assured her.

Caroline felt very exposed in the black beaded, dropped waist V-neck shift dress that Helen declared would be perfect for the club that evening. It was considerably shorter that Caroline had worn before. Stockings were purchased, a very fine denier, and a longer more sober dress in a claret colour that could be worn at the Mayfair party along with some elbow-length gloves. Caroline drew the line at more shoes, saying that her black pair would be perfectly adequate. After insisting that the clothes must be delivered to Bruton Street before six that evening, Helen and Caroline left the shop and wandered along under the awnings of Regent Street back towards Berkley Square.

When they arrived at Bruton Street, they found the clothes had already been delivered, and that Vic was waiting for them with Tommy in a large drawing room at the front of the apartment on the third floor. Lady Victoria kissed Caroline's cheek in greeting, with no different level of affection that she displayed when kissing Helen's cheek that Caroline could discern. Tommy was already drinking pink gin but got out of his chair and mixed Caroline a Sidecar. They stood at the window sipping their drinks as Vic and Helen talked in hushed tones on the other side of the room.

"It's a pretty view, isn't it?" said Caroline.

"Beats looking out onto a tanner's yard! Did you girls enjoy Regent Street?"

"It was so very busy; I was scared to cross the road. Tommy, Helen has been terribly generous towards me, but I feel rather uncomfortable that today's purchases were made on Vic's account. I don't know her at all well."

"Oh dash it, Caroline, Vic won't care. She is one of the richest women in London, maybe even in the country. And she inherits a bank vault more next year too. Honestly, don't give it another thought. I hope you like loud music, it's a jazz club we're going to tonight. The Clarion. They serve a passable dinner and then we'll dance the night away!"

Caroline considered the dinner served at the Clarion Club to be more than passable, but she understood the trend within her current social circle to denigrate anything that was good. They had arrived at almost nine o'clock and she had been careful not to drink too many Sidecars at Vic's. A small plate of canapes had appeared around half past seven which had seen off Caroline's rumbling stomach.

Helen had loaned her a fox fur wrap and a black headband with a small peacock feather, along with a long necklace of jet which she instructed Caroline to wear in the fashionable way. Caroline was still unused to the transformation she undertook when in Helen's company. It was similar to the experience of acting she had had at Knapp House, just with a different colour lipstick.

Around the dinner table, Lady Victoria was more sociable. Helen had told Caroline that Vic was extremely guarded around strangers who she felt only wanted to know her for her fortune. It seemed that Helen had been working behind the scenes to sooth Vic's concerns. Victoria was a striking young woman; tall and slender, with somewhat angular features and a face that naturally settled into a frown. Her blonde hair was short and cut with a longer curling fringe that continually fell over her right eye. That evening she wore a short leaf-green dress with sequins and beads in vertical lines like raindrops down a windowpane. They sparkled in the gas lights around the room and reflected off the many mirrors.

Caroline learned that Vic had been born in Scotland, had been schooled in Paris and London, and had travelled extensively. She had visited Egypt and had been there at the same time as Carter and Carnarvon had uncovered the tomb of Tutankhamen. This interested Caroline greatly, and they spent much of the dessert course discussing the finds and the possibility of more archaeology yet to be discovered. In turn, Vic asked Caroline about the film and wanted details of how it all came together. Caroline was happy to sing James' praises as director, and Vic nodded with a small smile.

As they ate, several people passed by their table to say hello. It was clear that Vic, Helen and Tommy were well known patrons. A large group of young men tried their best to entice Tommy to join them, and he agreed he would after he had finished his meal. The group moved on, swaying and tripping over chair legs and generally causing a ripple of annoyance amongst the other diners.

Helen had eaten very little and drunk a considerable amount. When they rose after their meal to move on to the ballroom, she knocked over her chair, and in the scrabble to pick it up she bumped into their table and sent a couple of glasses rolling to the floor with a crash. She abandoned the chair, stood up straight and held her head high, defying anyone to comment. Tommy set the chair right and shepherded the girls away from the broken glass while slipping the waiter a few coins as he arrived to clear up the glass on the floor. Caroline had reached out to help steady Helen; Vic turned smartly away and walked in the direction of the ballroom. She nodded to the doorman and was shown to her regular table where she waited for the other three to join her. Another waiter arrived with a tray of champagne in glasses and Vic took one. She watched the room over the rim of the glass, noting who was there and in what state of animation.

They had heard the music while they had been eating of course, but Caroline was surprised at how loud it was when they were in the same room as the band. Everyone around her seemed to be shouting, and the dancefloor was a hypnotic swirl of young people dancing vigorously by themselves and with each other. Helen had plucked a glass of champagne from a passing tray on her way into the ballroom and now placed it, empty, with exaggerated care on the table in front of Vic.

"I must dance!" she announced and grabbed Tommy as he was about to move off to join the crowd of young men. A look passed between Tommy and Vic, before he was dragged away.

Vic placed a cigarette into a silver holder and lit it. Without looking at Caroline, she said, "There will come a day when her behaviour becomes intolerable."

Caroline did not know how to respond. Helen had drunk too much on several evenings while at Milton Abbot, but apart from that Caroline had never been that close to an inebriated woman before. It simply did not happen in her world. She caught herself at that moment; what was her world now? Was it this place or places like it, endless travelling from one railway platform to another, from one extravagant gala to another? Or was it really Cheltenham with its familiar faces and routines, weekly visits to Curzon's and to Saint Mark's, and watching the years evaporate while she became more like her mother? Neither felt very homely just then.

Vic turned to her. She looked mournful.

"Isn't it strange how a person can be so many different things?"

"I suppose it is very much like acting," Caroline ventured.

"Yes, perhaps much of life is an act of some kind. We are all actors in this play. I so long to play another part, to write my own script. Much as you are."

"Oh no, I am simply trying to catch up with everyone else," Caroline said earnestly.

"Yet you make your decisions, do you not? You have an allowance. You come and go as you please. And you... are happy?"

"Yes, I am happy. Happier than I had been though I did not know it at the time."

"That is my burden, Caro. I am aware of my own unhappiness, and I am at a loss to make the necessary changes. I am not mistress of my role. Others write my directions. How does one change that?"

"But surely, forgive my bluntness, surely you have the means to go or do or be anywhere or anything you choose?"

Vic smiled, a genuine but sad smile Caroline thought.

"I have the financial means, though I lack the autonomy. I should have to run away with the gypsies and give up the one thing that makes everything else possible."

Caroline pondered the issue. "What is it that you want to do?" she asked.

Vic stubbed out the cigarette and removed the end from the holder. Her frown returned, as she considered Caroline's question. She found she had no answer. She only knew she did not want her life as it currently was. She looked around the room and saw that Helen was dancing with another woman, their arms waving above their heads in time to the music, their legs swivelling and kicking.

"I should like to go home. Caro, I don't wish to spoil your evening, please do stay if you are enjoying yourself. But you have encouraged me to think in ways I am not used to and am not able to in this atmosphere." She stood up, "I will tell Helen."

Caroline was uncertain how she should respond. Helen was her friend, but in her present state and with Tommy having disappeared, how would they find their way back to Vic's apartment? They would have to all leave together she decided and followed Vic across the ballroom floor, stepping between the dancers. Helen had stopped dancing but was swaying uncertainly as Vic was explaining that she was going home.

"We'll all go, Helen," Caroline shouted above the music.

"But we've only just started to have fun!" Helen wailed. Caroline half expected her to stamp her foot in protest.

"Stay if you wish. I was merely letting you know." Vic turned away.

"Come on, Helen, then we won't have to find a taxi later on."

Helen grabbed Vic's arm and spun her round so that they were face to face.

"Why will you never have fun?" she shouted.

People were now staring as they danced around the three women. Vic looked directly at Helen, removed Helen's hand from her arm and said sharply, "This is not fun, Helen." She turned again and walked to the exit.

"To hell with you then!" shouted Helen and turned away to resume dancing. Caroline stood for a moment in the centre of the moving bodies. Helen was wildly waving her arms around again. Caroline turned and went back to their table, apologising for getting in the dancers' way as she moved across the floor. She sat, not knowing what to do next. She noticed sympathetic glances from a few of the couples as they swayed past the table, and they made her feel uncomfortable. A waiter appeared and handed her a note. Vic had written:

> Caro
>
> The doorman will find you a taxi when Helen is ready to
> come home. I will see you tomorrow.
>
> Vic

Caroline sighed and folded the note, placing it into the ashtray on the table.

"Can I get you another drink, madam?"

"A Sidecar, please."

At quarter past one, Helen wobbled unsteadily to the table and collapsed into a chair. Caroline had spent the evening sipping Sidecars and talking occasionally to young men who stopped at the table. Several had asked her to dance but after the first, she had declined every other offer.

"I feel a little sick," Helen mumbled, fanning herself with her hand.

Caroline looked over Helen's head at the ballroom doorman who was approaching the table. "It's time we went home, Helen," she said.

Caroline lay in bed an hour later, having helped an almost insensible Helen undress and fall into her own at Vic's apartment. Her head throbbed but she was wide awake. She felt embarrassed for Helen, and for herself. She wished Tommy had stayed with them. She wondered if they would all still be going to the gallery tomorrow, and then realised it was today. She rolled over and closed her eyes. This was not fun, she thought as she fell into a restless sleep.

"Good morning. Would you like something to eat?" Vic was sitting in a lounge chair in the room that overlooked the square, wearing a silk dressing gown and looking through a magazine when Caroline appeared.

"Good morning. I hope we didn't disturb you when we came in last night, it was awfully late."

"Not at all, darling, I slept like the proverbial log, and this morning I have woken with what I can only describe as clarity. Now, toast and marmalade? Eggs?"

"If it's no trouble, toast and marmalade please, and tea. Do you have anything I could take for a headache?"

"I will call down immediately, and I am sure there are aspirin in the bathroom. Take a seat, do."

Vic returned a few moments later with two tablets and a glass of water. She sat next to Caroline at the table, and lit a cigarette, this time without a holder.

"I do not expect Helen to surface until much later. I also do not intend to waste such a beautiful day waiting here for her. I understand that you were to visit the Ben Uri gallery today?"

Caroline nodded, and then wished she had not as her head swam.

"Then that is what we shall do. I have no doubt Tommy will appear at some point; he has been raving about the exhibition for weeks. I assume he has some kind of natural calling to it."

Caroline's blank expression prompted Vic to explain, "An affinity. Jewish. Didn't you know? Oh, not that it matters one bit, not to me in any case though goodness knows it does to some people."

There was a knock at the door and a maid brought in toast, butter, marmalade and a pot of tea with two rattling teacups and a small milk jug on a rather large tray.

The young women set about the food together. Caroline was warming to Vic, the more time she spent with her. She found her deep and somewhat mysterious on the one hand, yet honest and frank on the other. If she had been asked at that moment whom she preferred, she would have chosen Vic over Helen. Lady Victoria left Caroline to finish eating while she dressed, and shortly afterwards they walked across Berkeley Square in the sunshine and found a taxi to take them north towards Hampstead.

Later, on their way back to the apartment, Vic turned to Caroline and placed her hand on Caroline's arm. "Thank you so much for an enjoyable day," she said.

Caroline glanced at Vic's hand, which Vic removed, "I have enjoyed it too. You know so much about art, I would never have understood as much of what we have seen today without you to help me."

"It has been a joy to have someone to discuss it all with! Now tell me, what would you usually do on a Saturday evening?"

Caroline was surprised at the question. "Well, it probably sounds terribly boring, but after dinner with Mother and Father, we normally retire to the parlour to read. If Mother goes to bed early, Father and I might play chess."

"Chess, I am rusty at that. Do you play Mahjong? Or bridge?"

"I played a lot of bridge when we stayed at Milton Abbott, though I am certainly no more than a beginner. But what is Mahjong?"

"Another strategy game, but one plays with tiles. I propose we have an evening of games! I will send an invitation to Claude and Evette and the kitchens can provide our dinner."

"I would like that. But would we be missed at the party?"

"Darling, we weren't really invited as such. I really feel an evening of games would be better for my equilibrium, and potentially better for Helen too."

"She may not agree."

"I am sure she will not."

She did not. Caroline tactfully retired to her bedroom shortly after Lady Victoria informed a severely hungover Helen of the change of plans for that evening. Helen was already cross that Vic and Caroline had gone to the gallery without her and had been attempting to cure herself with a hair of the dog when Caroline and Vic returned. Their voices rose to shouts, Helen's by far the louder, and soon after there was a slamming of doors. Caroline sat at the dressing table in her room and looked at her reflection in the mirror. She did not relish a repeat of Helen's behaviour from the previous night, but she was struggling to decide exactly whose guest she actually was in the apartment now.

She heard Tommy's voice in the hallway. She was about to go out and say hello when Helen's voice rang out with an "I don't care!" and more doors slammed. Caroline sighed. There was a knock on her door, and Vic opened it slightly.

"I believe we shall be a four this evening after all."

"You don't think Helen will return?"

"Not until much later, no. She disagrees with my position that a wild party every night becomes tiresome. No matter. We shall have an enjoyable dinner and evening with Claude and Evette, and we shall make you a Grand Master of Mahjong." she smiled with her mouth but not her eyes.

"Should I dress formally? I am still learning Vic," Caroline saw Vic's smile soften and reach her eyes eventually.

"Yes darling. It would be a shame to not wear such a beautiful outfit. Oh yes, Helen told me about her little treats for you, and I don't mind in the slightest. But I should like to see what I have paid for, if you don't mind. Now, don't hide yourself away in here, come through to the lounge and I'll take you through the rudiments of the game so that you are not a complete novice when we begin."

Claude and Evette were an older married couple who lived in an apartment in the building next door. They had fled France just before the Great War and made London their new home. Both spoke excellent English, though with noticeable accents that Caroline found endearing. They were mischievous, gently scolding each other over the food they ate, or left, the amount of wine they drank, and then the cigar that Claude smoked after dinner with his port. Caroline found herself laughing out loud to Claude's jokes, and even Vic joined in with enthusiasm.

The games were played with a level of seriousness, as both demanded concentration. At eleven o'clock Claude announced that it was approaching their bedtime and they would be taking their leave. There were profuse goodbyes on the landing outside Vic's apartment, and then the front door was closed, and Vic stood with her hands behind her back smiling the warmest smile Caroline had seen from her yet.

"That was delightful." She breathed.

"Wasn't it?! They are a lovely couple."

"I feel restored, Caro. Leave the debris, the maid will clear it away in the morning. Did you mention you were hoping to meet up with James while you were here?"

Caroline again was surprised at how Vic's mind held such small details. "Yes, but I made no firm arrangements."

"I will send him a message in the morning to attend us for a walk in Hyde Park tomorrow afternoon, if that is acceptable to you?"

"Of course, but…"

Vic closed her eyes, "It may be wise for you and James to be out enjoying yourselves tomorrow."

Caroline nodded. "Yes. Goodnight, Vic."

Caroline had not heard Helen return the night before. Breakfast had been tense, with Helen and Vic barely looking at each other. Afterwards, Helen had sat on Caroline's bed and apologised for her recent behaviour. There had been a few tears, though Caroline wasn't entirely convinced of their sincerity. She did accept Helen's apology, and suggested they have a quiet dinner somewhere that evening which Helen agreed would be a good idea.

With everything in London appearing bigger and more elaborate, Caroline had expected the church to be at least as large as Christ Church in Cheltenham. Though it bore the same name, Christ Church in Down Street, Mayfair reminded her more of Saint Mark's, if a little more ornate with its carved arched pillars. The congregation was a mix of races, colours, ages and classes, but the Vicar had a kindly tone and much to Helen's relief did not preach for more than half an hour. The hymns were familiar, and Caroline felt that she had some stability again after the turmoil of the previous forty-eight hours. Lady Victoria explained that the closest church to Bruton Street was a Roman Catholic establishment, so they had to make the pilgrimage to get almost to Hyde Park if they were serious about absolving their sins.

Lunch was a less frosty affair than breakfast had been, and the kitchens of the apartment block sent up roast beef, Yorkshire pudding and vegetables to Caroline's complete joy. She had just finished her lemon fool dessert and was feeling pleasantly full when James arrived. He had hoped that someone would let him know when Caroline would be in town and receiving the note that morning, he found he was very happy to be seeing her again. He scolded himself for such boyish enthusiasm; hadn't they both agreed that a relationship was out of the question? Still, the weather was holding and a walk around Hyde Park would be just the thing for a Sunday afternoon. He had been a little surprised to see the note was from Lady Victoria rather than Helen, but here he was, nonetheless.

Caroline excused herself from the lunch table to get ready while James chatted to Helen and Vic. Once they were down in the lobby, James convinced Caroline they should get a taxi the short distance to the park. He pointed out that she had walked almost the whole distance twice that day already, and they would be walking again once they arrived, and so Caroline agreed.

Hyde Park was full of the middle and upper classes in their Sunday finery. The sun beat down and the distant sheep, introduced to keep the grass trimmed, shimmered in the heat. Caroline wore her favourite summer dress, a peach sleeveless drop-waisted frock finishing around six inches from the ground, with an overlay of peach lace. She was careful to cover her shoulders with a cream lace wrap, though she noticed that many of the younger women were dressed in similar styles to those she had seen at the Clarion. Some had parasols, some had large straw sunhats.

James and Caroline walked sedately along the straight paths and talked of Helen and how the editing of the film was progressing. James bought a small bag of seed and Caroline fed the ducks on the lake. A while later they bought flavoured ices and sat on a bench to eat them.

"Vic says you were going to have a quiet dinner somewhere this evening. Would you like to do something a little more exciting? Although not as exciting as the Clarion perhaps."

"What did you have in mind?" Caroline held her handkerchief under her ice to catch any drips.

"I have tickets to a small production of *The Pearl Fishers*, if you'd like to come along. Well, when I say I have tickets, what I mean is I know a few of the company and they always keep a few seats back for friends. But perhaps you don't enjoy opera?"

"I have never been to a performance of an entire opera before, only to recitals. I'm not familiar with the title."

"It's Bizet. The chap did *Carmen*, you're probably familiar with that one."

"I have heard of it, yes," she finished her ice and dabbed her mouth with the handkerchief. "Yes, I'd like to see the performance please James. I don't think Helen and Vic's truce will last for very long and I'd rather not be hiding in the bedroom when it breaks!"

"I don't know what's got into Helen recently. She never used to drink as much as she does now. Anyway, let's not bother with them. Would you mind awfully if I collect you at seven thirty? The show starts at eight, and I don't mean to be tight but if we try for dinner somewhere as well, we're bound to miss the start."

"That's quite all right, Vic says the kitchens will send up food whenever it's requested so I can manage with a cheese sandwich and some fruit. We had such a large lunch after all!"

James left Caroline on the apartment steps, with a promise to return in a taxi at seven thirty sharp. As she went inside, the concierge handed her a key and explained that Lady Victoria had gone out, but that Caroline was to let herself in and make herself at home. This she did, requesting her light supper and enjoying the peace of the empty apartment before changing for her evening out. She decided that a serviced apartment was a very practical solution to a young woman's need to find somewhere to live, although she doubted that she could ever afford to live in London. For all its entertainments, London was not the place for her, she knew.

Lady Victoria and Helen had still not returned by seven fifteen. Caroline scribbled a short note, propped it up against the vase on the cocktail cabinet and went down to meet James.

After a brief explanation of the story, Caroline found the opera simple to follow and she enjoyed the melodies immensely. The theatre was small, seating only six hundred patrons, and the performers would never make it to Covent Garden. However, their enthusiasm was infectious and the audience appreciative with a standing ovation at the end for a good five minutes. In the taxi back to Bruton Street, James asked when Caroline was returning to Cheltenham.

"Tomorrow morning. I am rather looking forward to being home again if I am honest. London is just too much for me," Caroline smiled.

"Then I am glad that we have had time together this evening. Do you still have no real plans for the rest of the summer?"

"I must find some employment. I can't imagine it will be as enjoyable as making films, but if I am to retain my allowance, I really must secure something. It's so ridiculous that I am forbidden from working with Elsa again, but I suppose Mother and Father have my best interests at heart. I shall call on her when I am home again, but it's employment I need."

"Would you consider staying in London if employment could be found?" James asked hopefully.

"Oh no, I don't think so. I should like to explore more of London one day, but even with the parks, the buildings are so tall and loom over one, and the cars, the underground and omnibuses give me quite a fright."

James smiled to himself. She was so straight forward, and so unassuming, why did he think she might guess that he would want her to stay? He would not spell it out for her, he understood that she was still determined to find her own place in the world. Perhaps, in the end, that might suit them both; he was, as he had said, not husband material, but they could be friends at least.

"If I were to spend a few days in Cheltenham, perhaps later this year, would you be at home to show me the sights?"

"Oh, James that would be lovely! Of course, you must let me know if you come down. We're stopping, I think we are at Vic's... yes, we are. Thank you so much for a wonderful evening, and please do write and tell me if you are planning on a visit."

The driver opened the door and Caroline got out, waved quickly and then trotted up the steps. James waved back. It was a funny thing, he thought as the car pulled away again and headed towards his home, the more he told himself he was not husband material, the more he wanted to be so.

8

JOSIAH

When Caroline left on the nine-fifteen train from Paddington
the following morning, everything seemed to be right again
between Lady Victoria and Helen. They both saw her off from
the platform with hugs and kisses and Helen promised to say
goodbye to Tommy from Caroline once he surfaced again. She
said she had a fair idea where he had been staying and would
root him out in a day or so to take her home to Devon.

The train was not full, and for most of the journey Caroline
had a compartment to herself. She let her mind flow back over
the weekend's events and wondered again how long Vic and
Helen's relationship would continue. She had very much enjoyed seeing James again, but would he really visit Cheltenham?
She had the impression that he was always very busy with his
films, and she decided not to place too much store on what
was probably a throw away remark after all.

Back home in her room, Caroline unpacked her luggage
and spread the detritus of her trip out on her bed to select an
item for her keepsake box. As she picked out the gallery leaflet,

Annie brought in a jug of warm water for Caroline to wash her face. She caught sight of the short black dress laid out on the bed and took a sharp intake of breath.

"Oh Miss, that is beautiful!"

"Isn't it? I have no idea when I will have an opportunity to wear it again."

"Shall I take it down for cleaning?"

"Yes, it smells of smoke. In fact, everything does. I had hoped that hanging it all outside would air it, but I really think they will need to be washed."

"It'll need a gentle soak, all those beads'll come off if it's rubbed too hard."

Caroline held the dress up again. "It's not entirely practical, is it?" she smiled at Annie.

"No Miss, but it is lovely. If we get it freshened up, you could wear it for the dinner party next week."

"What party?"

"Mrs Munhead says she's to have a dinner party Thursday week. Given me a long list of dishes, and Mrs Monger is going to stay on late for it."

"Do you know who is invited?"

"Dr Riley, Mr and Mrs Paul, Mr Curzon, old Mrs Joyce. I think that's it. With you and your parents it will be eight round the table. I'm glad it's not more, I'm that nervous about serving strangers!"

"You'll be perfectly alright, Annie. Mr Curzon, you say. How interesting."

When Caroline collected the flowers for Saint Mark's the following morning, she noticed Josiah Curzon's hands lacked their usual crust of soil.

"Mother says you will be joining us for dinner next week."

"I have been invited, yes. I was happy to accept, I go out rarely in the evenings."

"There will be eight of us. Annie is most nervous about serving so many." Caroline wanted to make it clear that he was not to expect a cosy meal for four.

"Eight you say. Well, it will be a pleasant evening, I am sure."

He watched Caroline as she left through the glasshouse door. A pretty girl, and the short hair suited her, but not a patch on his Emma. Still, should he remain a widower for the rest of his days? And who would carry on the business after him? He and Emma never had a chance at a family, so perhaps a younger wife would be a good idea. But only if Caroline were interested, he told himself, and she had not given any indication so far that she was.

12 June 1925
Plymouth
Dearest Caro,

Once again, I must apologise for my behaviour in London. It must have been too awful for you to hear Vic and I arguing as we did, and it was a shocking way to treat a guest. But I can tell you that the same tableau will not occur again. Vic and I are no longer, whatever we had been. She informed me the day after you had left that she intends to return to Egypt and does not expect to see England again for some time. Our plans so oft spoken to find a small corner of the world where we could be together appear to have been nothing more than a mirage. Naturally I did not take this news with the decorum expected of a young woman. I debased myself yet again, I begged and pleaded, promised never to touch another sip of alcohol, but to no avail. Reading this back to myself, I seem to be taking it rather well. Yet you do not see my tears, dearest Caro, or hear the insults I shouted that even I was not aware I knew until that moment.

I fled to Tommy's rooms, which of course do not belong to Tommy but to a dashing young beau from Warsaw who studies

*at an art school. My promise not to touch alcohol again was
short lived, as Janek had several bottles of vodka available
which I learned to drink in the Polish style with a glass of
water for each glass of vodka consumed. Indeed, I think I now
prefer it to champagne. At some point my belongings arrived,
I know not how. Janek grew tired of having us under his feet,
and so Tommy has delivered me again to Devon where I now
contemplate life in a nunnery.*

*I jest, dear one, but how can a heart bear more than one
such rejection in a lifetime?*

*Write to me here. Tell me you had a wonderful time with
James again. Tell me of your plans for the rest of the summer.
I shall live vicariously through you until I am able to control
my excesses and allow myself out into company again. I am
an embarrassment, and I shall be cured.*

Your friend in need,
Helen

Caroline felt a pang of guilt. Could she have precipitated
the dissolution of the affair by encouraging Vic to discuss
Egypt with her? Surely not, the seeds of unhappiness had
appeared to be already germinating before that conversation.
Poor Helen. A nunnery though, on reflection, might not be
the ideal place for her and besides Helen had never shown
much religious zeal. She needed a hobby. Something to sink
her passions into. She had shown a talent for golf, perhaps
that would be the thing. Caroline would suggest it when
she replied.

Caroline did not see Josiah the next Tuesday as he was busy
with a client from Bristol. She did, however, see a notice on the
gate of the Sunningend engineering works that stood opposite
the railway station.

OPPORTUNITY
WOMEN WITH NEEDLEWORK SKILLS ARE
INVITED TO APPLY WITHIN.
DAY AND NIGHT SHIFTS AVAILABLE.
ENQUIRIES TO MR CAMBRIDGE, MGR.

At the kitchen table later that day, Caroline asked Annie if she knew anyone who worked there.

"Yes Miss. Mrs Everett across the street worked there last year and there's plenty of men from Rowanfield who work there. They don't employ as many as they did during the War, but it's better pay than labouring."

"I am thinking of enquiring for a day shift."

"That would be twelve hours, Miss, six days a week," Annie said with a 'really, are you sure?' tone.

"Then I would have to get used to it. I must do something Annie, and I can sew far better than I can cook."

Caroline enquired the following day and was shown into a waiting room outside of Mr Cambridge's small office. There was a peculiar smell, akin to rubber, that was rather unpleasant. After fifteen minutes, Mr Cambridge appeared and ushered her into his office where she took a seat in front of his desk. After a few perfunctory questions, Mr Cambridge looked up from his papers directly at Caroline.

"Forgive me, miss, but this is hard work we are talking about here. Not just a bit of linen stitching."

"I understand that Mr Cambridge. I am willing to work hard, and I feel I am far more suited to practical tasks than theoretical ones."

"Well then let's go down to the sewing room and see the girls."

The sewing room was a long rectangular building with high windows along one side that could be opened with poles.

Caroline was introduced to the Supervisor, Mrs Chandler, who explained the activities that her girls performed. Wooden frames that eventually became the wings, tails or fuselage pieces of small aeroplanes were brought into the room; a sheet of canvas was held against the frame and two women would take turns threading a large sewing needle back and forth to secure the canvas. Once it was sewn into place, the frame proceeded to the doping room where a special paint was applied to give the canvas strength and rigidity. The girls in the doping room had an allowance of half a pint of milk a day to help combat the fumes of the paint and were inspected by a doctor every two weeks for signs of illness. Mrs Chandler was proud of how well her girls were treated.

Mr Cambridge showed Caroline back to his office where she sat down again.

"Do you still think you could manage the work, Miss Munhead?"

"Yes, yes I do."

"And you can start on Monday? It will be six til six for the day shift, six days a week, with a half hour for lunch at midday. We have no canteen here, so you'll need to bring your own. You'll be provided with an overall which will be deducted from your first two week's pay, so you'll start on two pounds and four shillings, rising to two pounds and ten shillings."

Caroline tried hard to conceal her eagerness. "That will be acceptable, Mr Cambridge. I will be at the gate at ten minutes to six on Monday morning."

She practically ran home to tell Annie but swore her to secrecy for the time being.

Thursday evening Caroline dressed with care. It was not an occasion for the short black dress, and the long navy-blue evening gown was rather too grand for the company which would be assembling in the parlour shortly. She chose the royal blue peacock dress that she had worn on her first evening at Milton Abbott. She carefully applied lipstick and a little rouge, which she immediately scrubbed off again, and reapplied the lipstick and blotted it with an old handkerchief. It was a warm evening and the fire in the parlour would be lit so there was no need for a shawl. She made a mental note to purchase a small fan like the ones she had seen women use in London the next time she was in Cavendish House.

Deliberately Caroline waited until she had heard the front doorbell ring four times before she went down to join the adults, as she thought of them. Annie was looking uncomfortably hot as she passed Caroline a tiny glass of sherry, and then hurried back to the kitchen. A few minutes later, George announced to his guests that dinner was about to be served and would they please make their way to the dining room. Elizabeth took Josiah's arm, leaving George to escort Caroline.

"You look stunning, my dear." He whispered as they led the way.

Caroline found she had been seated between Josiah (with her mother on his other side) and Dr Riley (who had Mrs Paul on his far side). The elderly Mrs Joyce, a widow of many years, clad in layers of black lace, often shared a pew with the Munheads at Christ Church. Mr Paul was George's tailor and owned a small outfitters shop in the lower High Street. His wife was a tiny woman of four feet nine, who had produced three sons all standing over six feet tall in their socks.

Over the main course of roasted goose, Elizabeth leaned towards Josiah and said a little too loudly, "Mr Curzon, what is your opinion of these 'Bright Young Things' we hear about in London?"

Caroline and George exchanged glances.

"Well, Mrs Munhead, having never met any of them, I can't say for certain. I believe they mostly have more money than sense, though I could be wrong."

"Money is the root of all evil!" declared Mrs Joyce, forgetting for a moment that George's employment depended on it.

"Indeed, Mrs Joyce," agreed Elizabeth. "It could be said that young people need a steadying hand when it comes to finance. Too many are able to spend as if there will be no tomorrow."

"It has been my experience with my employees, that to limit wages limits a man's ability to be frivolous. They learn the value of their wage and how to make it last the week, with a little put by for emergencies." Josiah took a very Methodist view to unnecessary possessions, despite his trade in unnecessary plants and flowers.

Mr Paul nodded his agreement.

"One of my tailors asked me for a raise just last week. I sat him down and asked him to show me where his current payments are spent. We were able to find savings in several areas, and no further talk of extra remuneration has been forthcoming."

"An admirable approach, Mr Paul. I do think, Mrs Munhead, that it is a pity so many young women feel the need to take employment. A man's wage should at least cover his family outgoings, and there do seem to be fewer opportunities these days with double the workforce, if you understand my meaning."

"Oh, I do Mr Curzon, I do."

Caroline put her knife and fork down and dabbed her mouth with her napkin.

"And for those young women who have no husband's wage to rely on Mr Curzon, how should they sustain themselves?"

"Well, Miss Caroline, I should say they must find a husband as quickly as possible or learn to live within their parent's means," Josiah said seriously. "And after all, a young lady would be taking a job for only a short time before children come along, in the normal scheme of things."

"It must be a great sadness to you Mr Curzon, that you and your late wife had no children," Mrs Paul was relieved to find a subject she could comment on with some understanding.

"Indeed, it was, madam. But," he glanced at Caroline, "I am not yet past my prime. I may take another wife yet if God sees fit."

"An admirable and optimistic outlook, Mr Curzon. Do have some more potatoes." Elizabeth suggested, seeing they were on Caroline's far side and she would need to pass the dish across to Josiah.

Mrs Paul, quite oblivious to the sub-conversation, pursued her interest, "Are there wedding bells on the horizon for you, Caroline?"

Caroline took a sip of water. "I don't think so Mrs Paul. You see I shall be starting a new position at the Sunningend works on Monday morning."

There was a pause. Doctor Riley stepped into the breach, "I heard they were looking for someone to work in the General Manager's office."

"Oh no Doctor, I shall be sewing canvas wings under Mrs Chandler's supervision."

George disguised his smile by taking another mouthful of food and ignored his wife's silent horrified stare.

"Betty Chandler? Admirable woman," said the Doctor.

Elizabeth regained her composure.

"Mr Curzon, do advise me, which is the most suitable shrub for autumn colour?"

After dinner in the parlour, Josiah gradually made his way to Caroline's side with a glass of port for them both.

"I had not realised that you were looking for a position. I'm sure I would have been able to oblige with a few hours administrative duties each week had I known."

"Thank you, Mr Curzon. I very much enjoy your instruction on the various plants I collect for the church each week, but I am most keen to broaden my experiences at present. Unfortunately, I shall no longer be able to visit on Tuesday mornings as I have been."

"Well, that's a great shame. Of course, I will make arrangements to deliver the flowers as we had before. I know the lads appreciate seeing their hard work decorate the church of a Sunday. Perhaps you'll find occasion to visit us still. It would be a pleasure to pick out a bouquet for your dining table."

Caroline was expecting an argument with her mother the following morning. Instead, Elizabeth took breakfast in her room and then after dressing she went out to Christ Church without saying a word to Caroline. When her father returned home from work, Caroline went to speak to him in his study.

"Father, will you deposit my wages for me into my account each week please? I do not think I shall need to keep the money here, and my only day off will be Sunday."

"Of course, my dear. Are you sure it is an occupation you will be able to sustain? Tell me a little more about what you will be doing."

Caroline explained the sewing of the canvas. "I don't know if I can manage it, Father, but I will try. I thought it would be a respectable position."

"I have no doubt about that. Sunningend is indeed a respectable employer, and they take good care of their employees. They had some difficulty last year, but I believe they have secured new orders for some of the aviation companies both here and internationally. However, your mother feels you behaved inappropriately at dinner last night, particularly in front of Mr Curzon."

"Because I said I had secured a job?"

"Without telling us in advance, yes. It came as a shock; you must understand that."

"I'm sorry, Father."

"Well. Do not be surprised if Mr Curzon dines with us again at some point. Your mother seems to have taken a shine to him, presumably on your behalf. Should she pursue this avenue of activity?"

"Father, I have no desire to become a wife at the moment. I want to work for as long as I can, perhaps two or three months, so that my allowance is topped up. If I enjoy it, I may stay on." She sat on the edge of a chair, "I have enjoyed my trips away so far this year. I am seeing different ways of living from our own here – not that there is anything wrong with how we live of course. It is becoming clear to me that as a young woman, there are opportunities available to me that Mother would never have had, and perhaps does not understand now. In London I saw women police officers, and women managing shops, clubs and galleries. Women who do not see their natural progression as being to marriage and children.

"There is a whole world to explore. Midge is contemplating missionary work in Africa or South America when she has completed her teacher training course. Lady Victoria, who I stayed with in London, is to travel back to Egypt. I would love to travel and see new things, but I know that will require an income, and unless I were to marry someone who travelled for their job, it would be impossible for me to do so. As I see it, I need to work to earn some money now, so that I may travel if only a little way, before any thoughts of marriage take hold."

George nodded. His daughter had become a sensible young woman, and he was loath to clip her wings. Freddie had yearned to travel; it had been the lure for him to join the army. Caroline was right, Elizabeth did not understand how the world had moved on, while she had stood still, looking backwards.

"If you are to travel, you will require a passport. I believe the passage itself to America costs in the region of forty to fifty pounds. To France it would naturally be less, although flying would I expect be more. Travel is an expensive pastime, Caroline. But as you say, there is the possibility of finding a husband who travels, someone in government, or the army perhaps. And to find him, you will no doubt need to spread your wings a little further than Cheltenham. I understand this. Just please, try not to antagonise your mother. She will become used to your working eventually. What time do you start your first day?"

"Six in the morning. I need to be at the gate just before then."

"Then you will need to rise when Annie does. Make sure you ask her to wake you."

9

LOTTIE

Caroline stood at the gates of the Sunningend works at five forty-five on the Monday morning, a cheese sandwich wrapped in old newspaper and an apple in a string bag for her lunch. Mrs Chandler arrived a few minutes later and took Caroline to a small cloakroom just off the sewing room where she could leave her coat and bag. Then she looked Caroline up and down, and opened a cupboard where overalls were hung on pegs. She rummaged for a moment, then pulled out one she thought would fit Caroline, which it did. It was made from cotton ticking and had a large patch pocket on the front. Caroline overlapped the front around herself and tied the belt to keep it closed.

The morning went by quickly. It was not so much the amount of information that Caroline needed to learn, but the ability to handle the needle, which was almost a foot long, and tie the knots in the thick thread, at the same speed as the woman she was working with. They had to become like a machine, both in step with each other, working smoothly. The frames were light but difficult to keep upright. The canvas had to be pulled taut as it was sewn. There were seven other young women in the sewing room, and five who worked in the dope room. Mrs Chandler oversaw both rooms for the day shift and was senior supervisor above the night shift supervisor, Mrs Vickers.

At midday everyone took their lunch on a patch of sloping grass outside the sewing room. A large bucket of water was provided for the girls to dip enamel mugs in to for drinking. After the relative quiet of the sewing room, where talking was strictly limited to the work at hand, Caroline listened intently to the chatter of the girls as they ate their lunch. She had been paired with an older woman called Eileen that morning, who had hung back to speak with Mrs Chandler when they had stopped for lunch. Now Eileen sat between Caroline and another younger girl called Gwen and explained that she and Gwen would be swapping for the afternoon. Gwen looked at Eileen with a blank expression. Eileen sighed and turned to Caroline.

"She's a bit simple, this one. Gwen will be taking over from me on the frame we've been working on this morning. Alright?"

Caroline nodded and smiled at Gwen who looked at her but kept on eating her slice of cold pie.

By five minutes to six that evening, the sewing room was hot and stuffy despite the windows all being open as wide as they would go. Mrs Chandler approached Gwen and Caroline to inspect their work. Caroline could feel the sweat trickling down her back. She thought she had improved during the afternoon and between them they had completed three large tail frames that day. Mrs Chandler picked at the knots with her fingernails.

"All tight, that's good. Need to pick your speed up though. If you're on tails, you need to be finishing at least five a day. Gwen can go faster, so don't worry about her. Pick this one up again in the morning to get the last bit done. The night shift will be on wings tonight." She turned to inspect another pair's work.

Caroline smiled at Gwen over the top of the frame. "Thank you, Gwen."

Gwen studied her with pale blue eyes and no expression on her face. Then she turned and walked to the cloakroom.

One of the other girls saw Caroline's smile drop and went over to her.

"Don't worry about Gwen, she doesn't talk to anyone. Don't think she can. You done well today for your first try. My name's Lottie."

"Thank you, Lottie. I've enjoyed it, though I am tired, and my feet are throbbing."

A horn sounded out across the works to signal the shift change, and the door to the cloakroom opened to allow the next group of young women to take the day shift's place.

After two days, Caroline developed blisters where the needle rested and rubbed between her thumb and fore finger. She refused the bandage offered by Mrs Chandler, not wanting to appear soft in front of the other girls. Lottie inspected her hand at lunchtime and agreed it would be best to let the skin harden by itself. Caroline noticed Lottie's hand was scarred in a similar place. A little goose fat dabbed on the blister and left overnight, Lottie suggested, would help it heal. It did not seem to matter how fast Caroline worked, Gwen kept pace with her, even on occasion seeming to impatiently want the needle on her side of the canvas.

By the end of the week, Mrs Chandler pronounced Caroline's probation complete and said she would be recommending to Mr Cambridge that she be kept on. While Caroline was thrilled, she noticed some of the other girls who had moved a little way off from her at lunchtime exchange glances. Lottie was happy to hear the news and the two of them walked together to the gates at the end of the Saturday shift, their pay packets carried safely in their bags.

"Lottie, the other girls don't like me much, do they?"

"Never mind them. They don't like me much either. They say I only got the job because Mrs Chandler is my aunt Betty. No matter that I can work twice as fast as anyone on day shift! Except perhaps Gwen."

"But I don't want people to be unhappy to work with me."

Lottie covered a yawn with her hand and then said, "You know what brings people round? A cake. Bring us a cake in on Monday and everyone will be your friend. See you!"

Caroline's first Sunday afternoon off was conducted under the instruction of Mrs Monger. Caroline had suggested a jam sponge but was quickly told that was far too ambitious and prone to disaster for a novice baker. Instead, Mrs Monger's fool-proof ginger parkin was decided on. Though it emerged a little too brown on top, she commended Caroline for her efforts (mostly weighing the ingredients and watching the butter melt) and found a tin large enough for Caroline to carry the sticky squares to work the next day.

As Lottie predicted, most of the girls were unable to resist the cake and the ice was truly broken between them. Even Gwen managed a faint smile after taking a large bite from one of the sticky squares. Only one girl still held back during lunch time. Hannah was a few years older than Caroline at twenty-seven and was married to a man who had lost part of his right leg during the war. Some days later, Hannah was talking to Lottie in the cloakroom as Caroline arrived. Hesitating behind the door when she heard the conversation, Caroline stood quietly, listening.

"…all I'm saying is, she don't need to work. She's taking a job from someone like my Jim."

"But your Jim couldn't do our work Han, you know that. He can't stand all day or move up and down the frames like we have to."

"That's not the point, she just don't need a job. Her family is well provided for, and here I am having to cover all our bills by myself. I'm tired of it, Lottie."

Gwen appeared and glancing at Caroline, barged the door open and walked in, calling a halt to the conversation. When Caroline arrived home that evening, a fresh bouquet of roses and carnations stood in a vase on the dining table. Annie informed her they had arrived from Mr Curzon that afternoon with his best wishes. Caroline had an idea.

The first Sunday of each month, Caroline attended Christ Church with her parents. On the way home afterwards, Caroline excused herself and disappeared into the Nursery entrance. Elizabeth smiled at George.

"You see," she said, "the seed germinates!"

Caroline found Josiah at home; his cottage set behind the glasshouses. Surprised to have a visitor, particularly on a Sunday, he apologised for his appearance and unkempt parlour. His bible lay open on the table and a pair of spectacles rested between the pages.

"Thank you for the flowers you sent Mr Curzon, they were beautiful."

"No trouble at all Miss Caroline. I thought perhaps if you had a preference on colour, I could send another some time."

"Mother likes yellow roses, thank you. Mr Curzon, I have something to ask you. It is irregular, and I fear I may be overstepping some invisible line somewhere, but I should very much like your help."

"Anything I can do, just ask. Would you take a seat?"

"Oh, no thank you, our luncheon will be ready at home. But I was wondering if you might have any positions available in your glasshouses?"

Josiah's surprise was clear, "But I thought you'd started at the works?"

"I have, yes, but the position would not be for me. It is a particular type of position that is required, one with no lifting or carrying, but I believe the gentleman is quick with his hands and quite intelligent." Though she didn't know if that was true, Caroline felt it was the right thing to say.

"No lifting or carrying you say? Well, that's most of what the lads here do as you know. I was thinking I could do with someone to help with the orders and paperwork and such. Sending out invoices, that kind of thing. Who is it that you are asking for?"

"A young man, the husband of one of the girls at work," Caroline hoped she was doing the right thing. "He was a soldier, but lost his leg, or part of it at least. She supports them both. His name is Jim," what was Hannah's last name…. "Jim Cox."

"Well now, if you tell him to come round next week and ask for me, I shall see him. I can't say more than that."

"Thank you so much Mr Curzon! And thank you again for the flowers. Now I really must dash!" Caroline fled before Josiah could say any more.

Caroline wanted to tell Hannah about the job as soon as she got to work but held her tongue until lunchtime. The July sun was as relentless as June's and the girls sat in a line on the dry grass with their backs to the hedge in the small amount of shade it provided. Caroline saw a space next to Hannah and sat down with Lottie on her other side.

"I meant to say, Lottie, I heard of a job yesterday."

Lottie was intrigued. She knew she wasn't looking for another position and didn't think that Caroline was either.

"What doing?" she asked.

Caroline spoke as clearly as she could without actually turning to face Hannah.

"It's at Curzon's Nursery, managing the invoices and orders, the paperwork. It would suit someone who needed to sit down a lot," she felt Hannah grow still beside her, "I was told if someone were to visit this week and ask to see Mr Curzon, he would be willing to interview them." She risked a glance at Hannah, and found she was staring at Caroline mid-chew.

"What's the wages to be?" Lottie asked, understanding the reason for the conversation.

"Oh, I didn't ask. I should have. But it's a position of re-sponsibility, so I'm sure they will be reasonable."

Lottie winked at Caroline, out of sight of Hannah, and took another bite of her apple.

Hannah practically ran out of the sewing room as the shift horn sounded that evening. Caroline was knotting the last piece of canvas on a wing frame and didn't notice Mrs Chandler come up behind her.

"I heard what you said about the job at lunchtime," she said, as Caroline jumped and almost dropped the frame.

"The job, yes, I was told about it at church, after church," Caroline felt she ought to be truthful with Mrs Chandler.

"It's been a while since Jim worked anywhere. Do him good to get out of their house, give him a bit of pride back."

"The position hasn't been advertised anywhere, so perhaps if he can pay Mr Curzon a visit soon, he will have no other competition for it. Oh, but do they live close by? Will it be too far for him to go?"

"They have one of the railway houses at St George's. He can take the tram. It was a kind thing for you to do."

Caroline smiled, "I don't want anyone to think badly of me Mrs Chandler."

"I don't believe anyone here does, but times are getting tough, there are fewer jobs and more men looking for them. Young women working upsets some people, yes even now it still does. I remember when the war started and I came here, the things people said to me about taking a man's job! Didn't make a jot of difference that the men weren't here. I suppose it made them think again about women, about what we can do.

I remember hearing Christabel Pankhurst speak in London, I was there when she came out of prison and she said how if women were paying taxes and government were making decisions on housing and children's health, then women should be able to elect their own representatives. So, it wasn't just women taking men's jobs that people were upset about."

Caroline was amazed, "You were a Suffragette? You knew Miss Pankhurst?"

"Not knew her to speak to as such, but I was in London with a group of girls, and we went to welcome her out of the prison. We were active in our own way. We marched, we posted leaflets. It was important, but not everyone thought so. And with all the young men coming home with legs, arms and goodness knows half their heads sometimes missing, a lot of women who didn't want to work have found they have to just to make ends meet. And there's the difference Caroline, some women want to work like you do, and others, perhaps many, do not want to but have to. Most men want to work, and they see women doing what they themselves used to, it makes them feel useless. I can see it from both sides."

"I hadn't thought of it like that. I suppose I don't need to work, but I do want to. I have a small allowance. But all the sewers here are girls, women. Would men do this work?"

"Not now, not for the pay offered. But if things get more desperate, then I'm sure men would want to take the jobs from you girls just to keep their children fed and a roof over their heads. Whether they would be as nimble with their fingers is another matter altogether. They would certainly want my job. You won't find many women supervisors in any engineering works; I am lucky to have my position here. If it wasn't for... well, never mind about that."

The night shift girls were taking up their positions around the room and a girl came over to carry the wing Caroline had been working on through to the dope room.

"Mrs Chandler, did I do the right thing about that job for Jim Cox?"

"I don't think you did any harm by it. It's still for Jim to secure the position, that much is on him."

Lottie was waiting for Caroline in the cloakroom.

"I was starting to think you were going to do the night shift as well!"

"Oh no. I'm too tired. Lottie, did you know Mrs Chandler was a Suffragette in London?" Caroline hung her overall on a peg and the girls walked out to the works gate together.

"Yes, I told you, she's my aunt. She was arrested for it. Force fed in prison, so I've heard. That was before she got married to Mr Chandler. He was in the army, died early on in Turkey I think, has a funny name, starts with G.."

"Gallipoli?"

"Might be, I don't know. They were only married a few months. I never met him, but I've seen a photograph and he was a handsome chap. Very tall, with a moustache. When he died, my father had Aunt Betty come and stay with us for a while and then she got the job here and moved into a little house over near the Bath Road. She started in the dope room, and she was the one who said the girls should have their milk. I think Mr Cambridge has a soft spot for her."

This was a lot more information than Caroline had expected to learn about her supervisor. She parted from Lottie at the gates, Lottie making her way towards the gas works where she lived in a side street with her parents and brothers, one older and one younger. Caroline walked across the railway bridge and turned into Glencairn Road, digesting this new knowledge about Mrs Chandler.

Caroline was impressed, particularly at how Mrs Chandler had played down her involvement in one of the most important movements of the century. She had known one of the Pankhursts! And now, she was a single woman, holding a responsible position in what was on the whole a male-domi-nated engineering works. Caroline presumed she would be in receipt of a small widow's pension from the army on behalf of her late husband, but that would not be enough by itself to cover her rent and other expenses. Mrs Chandler would be in the 'need to work' group she had spoken of.

Caroline also wondered about Lottie's comment that Mr Cambridge had a soft spot for Mrs Chandler. She realised it was often difficult to know if a man was married or not, because all men were referred to as 'Mister'. Yet a woman was always Miss until she was married, regardless of her age. Caroline frowned to herself. She was still pondering this when she almost crashed into Annie who was emptying some ashes into the bin near the front door of number 20.

10

ANGELICA

The summer grew in heat as August approached, peppered with thunderous downpours that caught many without umbrellas by surprise. When it was too wet to sit on the grass for their lunch, the girls of the sewing room ate their sandwiches, pies or cheese and fruit in the cloakroom. Lottie chattered away happily. She seemed to know everything that was going on around the town, and eventually Caroline learned that Lottie's father was a supervisor at the gas works, while her mother worked at the recently opened telephone exchange in the centre of the town. Gwen remained mute but had begun to smile occasionally at Caroline when they worked together on a frame. Even Hannah had begun to thaw, and Caroline understood it was because Jim had been engaged by Mr Curzon as his Office Clerk.

Caroline continued to deposit her weekly pay with her father, and with working so many hours she hardly had an opportunity to spend any of her money at all. Florence was briefly at home again next door, and she and Caroline went to the Daffodil Cinema one Saturday evening to see the new Charlie Chaplain film *The Gold Rush*. Caroline sat enthralled through the performance, laughing out loud at Chaplain's antics. Florence was planning a trip to the South of France accompanying her elderly great aunt in September, and Caroline listened closely to Florence's description of her efforts to obtain her passport and arranging the tickets for the boat train and the crossing to France. Florence was fond of her great aunt but was not enthusiastic about spending a whole month with her. She was hoping to be able to leave the elderly woman on a sunny hotel terrace and spend her own time on the beach and in the hotel bar.

Mary Rose's baby was due at the beginning of August. She had been plagued with pains in her hips for the past six weeks and had been instructed by Dr Riley to rest for at least two hours every afternoon. Philip Rose had been taking on more of the parish visits from the Vicar and was often seen gliding along the streets on his black bicycle with his trousers neatly clasped to his ankles with gleaming clips. Caroline spent at least three Sundays each month in the congregation of St Mark's and had started to help Mary back to their house after the service while Philip chatted to the parishioners.

This particular Sunday, Mary seemed hotter than usual. A light sheen of sweat covered her face, and her hands were clammy. She took Caroline's arm as they walked across the grass to Mary's front door. It was a small, neat redbrick house, built for the railway but rented by the Church for their officiant.

"Will you come in for a minute?" Mary asked as she turned the key in the lock.

The house was as neat inside as it was outside. A narrow hallway with stairs at one end and a door leading to the front room as well as one to the kitchen at the back of the house. Two bedrooms upstairs of roughly equal size. The bedroom at the rear looked out across the farmland of Arle with a small, neat garden, half vegetable plot, half flowers, beneath the window. The two women went through to the kitchen.

"Are you sure you are alright?" Caroline steered Mary towards a chair by the range.

"To tell you the truth, no I don't think I am," Mary frowned, her Bristol accent with its hint of Trinidad sounding more pronounced as she grimaced.

"Shall I fetch Philip?"

"No, he'll be along presently. Could you fill the kettle? Perhaps a cup of tea will help."

Caroline did as she was asked while Mary closed her eyes and sat with her legs stretched out in front of her and her hands clasped across her round stomach. Caroline was quietly looking for cups and saucers in a cupboard on the wall when Mary gasped. Caroline turned to see Mary looking in dismay at the puddle forming on the floor around her.

"Mary? Whatever..."

"The baby is coming."

"What now? Oh goodness, what do you need me to do?"

"Miss Caroline, I need you to stay calm. If you can help me up to our bedroom and then perhaps bring the tea up. It will be a while yet, I'm sure."

"But how can you be sure? I mean if that..." Caroline gestured to the amniotic fluid on the brick floor.

"It shows things are getting started. Come on now, you've seen babies born before, haven't you?"

Caroline blushed, "No. I don't really understand how it all happens. One hears stories of course, but I don't have any younger brothers or sisters or even cousins, so no."

"Good time to learn then."

Mary eased herself up from the chair and reached out to Caroline who took her hand and tried not to stare at the extra trickle of fluid that had escaped.

"Which room is yours?" The stairs were narrow and impossible to walk side by side, so Caroline went first but backwards, holding Mary's hand as she climbed.

"The front. Now, there is a rubber sheet under the towels on that chair, see it? Pull the blanket and top sheet off the bed and spread out the rubber sheet, then put that old one on top, the one with the seam."

Caroline did as she was instructed while Mary took off her shoes, stockings and knickers and wrapped them in one of Philip's shirts that was hanging on the wardrobe door.

"Could you take these down to the kitchen, there is an old bathtub just outside the door for clothes to be washed. I expect the kettle is boiling now."

When Caroline returned with the tea things on a tin tray, Mary had changed into a thin cotton nightdress and was sitting up in the middle of the bed with a couple of pillows tucked behind her back. Caroline noticed as she handed Mary a cup of tea that she paused for a moment before taking the cup and saucer.

"I think I need to time these now," Mary said after taking a sip from her cup.

"Time what?"

"The contractions. You really know nothing about having babies? My body is trying to push the baby out, everything gets tight for a moment and then relaxes again. I've had a few this morning, but now they are getting stronger, so I need to see how long between each one. I know Philip will want Dr Riley here straight away but there really is no need until the contractions are only a few minutes apart."

"Do they hurt?" Caroline was morbidly fascinated.

"Not yet, but they will."

They heard Philip come in through the front door go through to the kitchen and then call up the stairs.

"We are up here!" replied Mary. Philip bounded up the stairs and into the bedroom.

"Is every ... Oh! Mary are you alright? Shall I get the Doctor?"

Mary chuckled, "You see?" She smiled at her husband, "No, it's too early for the doctor yet. Go and make something to eat for yourself and Miss Caroline, if you'll stay?"

Caroline nodded.

"Well, alright, but then I will ride over and fetch Dr Riley. And no arguments!"

He bent over and kissed his wife's head, almost stumbled over Caroline as he stood up again, and retreated gratefully from the room.

"Is there anything I can get for you?" Caroline asked again.

"You could open the window, it's hot in here. Thank you for staying. Philip will be a wreck here by himself, and if I cannot have my mother here then I would like you in her stead."

Caroline felt honoured. She didn't know how she could be of any use, but she would stay for as long as Mary wanted her there.

Dr Riley arrived an hour later, having sent Philip home again with instructions to time the contractions. The doctor was sure there would be no complications with the birth, but Mary had been in pain with her hips and if the baby was large then some assistance could be required. He examined Mary as soon as he arrived, while Caroline took the tea tray down to the kitchen. When she returned to the bedroom, she found Mary on her hands and knees on the bed, with her head resting against the headboard.

The doctor saw Caroline's expression of concern.

"All is well Miss Munhead. Mary was feeling some pressure on her hips, so we are trying a different position. All perfectly normal. Did you know many women give birth squatting or sitting in birthing chairs? No? Oh yes, most common in indigenous communities. Gravity helps the baby, you see."

Dr Riley had spent part of his early years as a practitioner in South Africa and was a rare enthusiast for letting the woman lead the way in childbirth. Mary groaned briefly as another contraction came, and then relaxed as it ebbed away. The doctor looked at his watch.

"Two minutes, Mary. I should think baby will be here within the hour so I will stay."

Two hours later and Mary was still having evenly spaced contractions but there was no sign of the baby. Philip was pacing the kitchen and Caroline was kept busy going up and down the stairs for water, biscuits and raw carrots for Mary.

"Can you walk a little?" the doctor asked Mary.

"I think so, just around the room."

"Yes, good, Let's get you up then. Caroline, take her other arm. We'll go at your pace, Mary."

They walked around the bed slowly, out on to the landing and into the rear bedroom, then returned to the front. The next contraction came, and Mary remained standing, leaning her head against the wall with her supporters on either side. As it passed, she looked at the doctor.

"I think that felt different," she took a deep breath. "I think another one is coming."

At ten minutes past five that Sunday afternoon, Caroline witnessed her first birth. Standing ready with a towel to the side of Doctor Riley, and with one of Mary's feet resting on her shoulder, she was in awe of how it all happened. The doctor wrapped the baby quickly in the towel after checking its mouth and handed Mary the bundle while he pressed gently on her stomach to assist the afterbirth. Caroline was confused, didn't new babies cry? Why was this one silent?

She looked at Mary, who was gazing in adoration at the two dark eyes gazing back at her. After a moment the baby screwed up its face and began to cry, summoning her father from his seat on the edge of the bed in the back bedroom. The doctor swiftly covered Mary's legs with a sheet and removed the bloodied towels, clearing his throat to get Caroline's attention as he left the room. She followed him, ignored completely by the new little family.

"Put the kettle back on the stove, we'll have some tea before I get off home."

He disappeared into the garden for a few minutes and returned as the kettle started to boil. The two sat on either side of the small kitchen table and drank their tea in the quiet of the early Sunday evening.

"How are you finding it at the works?" Dr Riley asked.

"I enjoy it a great deal. My hands have toughened up now, and I'm used to standing for most of the day. I really enjoy working with the other girls. I think I've missed that since leaving school, I haven't really been in that environment for such a long time."

"And your parents approve?"

"Oh, Mother will never approve. She wants to marry me off as I am sure you know, Doctor. Father is very interested in how the canvases are attached to the frames. I wonder if he should have been an engineer rather than a banker."

"Your Father has many interests, he's a most intelligent man. I did wonder at the more regular appearance of Mr Curzon at your parent's dinner parties recently. He's a good, solid man Caroline."

"Indeed, he is, and at least ten years older than me and already widowed! I have no interest in marriage Dr Riley, not yet anyway."

The doctor smiled. He was about to say more when Philip appeared in the doorway.

"Mary would very much like you to come up Caroline. Doctor, please do stay a few moments more, I shall be back down."

Caroline followed Philip up to the bedroom, now with curtains drawn and a small lamp lit on the bedside table. Mary smiled a big, emotional smile as Caroline perched on the bed beside her.

Mary looked up at Philip who nodded, and then at Caroline and said, "Miss Caroline, we would like to introduce you to Miss Angelica Caroline Rose."

Caroline burst into happy tears and gave her friend a hug while trying not to squash the baby sleeping in her arms.

The interest of the parish in the new baby was barely concealed. Everyone was curious to see what colour skin the mite had, what sort of hair, eyes, etc. Philip had anticipated this much and had suggested that the church fete be held as close to the expected birth date as possible so as to provide a means for the people he was coming to think of as his flock to view his beautiful child. Mary had agreed on the principle that one long busy day would be preferable to a steady stream of well-wishers at their door and in their front room. She even suggested that the Christening might take place on the same morning, to have everything done on the same day. That was to be a small affair, and as things turned out with just a week between the birth and the fete, everything fell neatly into place.

Celestine was invited, with money sent to pay for taxis and her train fare. Mary was nervous as to whether her mother would make the trip from Bristol by herself, but she telephoned the Vicar on the Friday and shouted loudly into the receiver that she would be on the ten fifteen train from Temple Meads the following day. She would stay with Mary and Philip and little Angelica over the weekend and return home again on the Monday. Caroline had been spending an hour with Mary every evening straight after finishing her shift at work before walking home and eating a cold dinner, and then falling exhausted into bed. She was greeted exuberantly by Celestine on the Saturday evening, who had taken to singing gospel songs loudly while rocking Angelica in her arms.

Mary and Philip had asked Caroline to be one of Angelica's Godparents, along with the Vicar and the Rose's next door neighbour Mrs Brooks, a widow with two teenage sons. Caroline had been hesitant at first, seeing it as a great responsibility. She talked to her father about it, who pointed out that Caroline's Godparents were all now dead and had he thought more sensibly at the time he would have liked to choose someone a little younger who could play an active part in her life. It had been a cause of concern for George over the years, for Caroline and to some extent for Freddie, that neither he nor Elizabeth had siblings and so there were no aunts, uncles or cousins for the children to mix with while growing up. It was one of the reasons he had decided Caroline should attend school as a weekly border, despite living so nearby. It was not for the education, so much as for the socialisation of his little girl.

Sunday morning Caroline wore her peach lace frock and a straw hat as the sun was strong even before nine o'clock. It had been a whirlwind of a week, with preparations for the fete and the Christening all coming together. More than once, Caroline had caught herself wishing she did not have to spend twelve hours a day in the sewing room, and then pulled herself up sharply. Other women managed to raise entire families and work the same hours, and she did after all have the choice. Some of the girls at the works would be attending the fete in the vicarage gardens in the afternoon and Lottie was very excited for Caroline to meet her parents and her brother who said he would drop in for a while.

Saint Mark's church was fuller than it had been in a very long time. People squeezed into the pews, squashed against the stone pillars and stood three deep at the rear of the church clutching hats and handbags in sweaty hands. The Vicar started the service, handing over to Philip when it was time to perform the Christening. Caroline had taken her usual place next to Annie with her family but could hardly see the Vicar for Celestine's amazing head-ware with its copious plumage. Celestine had become almost as much the focus of attention as Angelica amongst the congregation, and she was enjoying every minute of it. Caroline went forward when Philip called for the Godparents to assemble and heard Celestine whisper loudly.

"She is a good girl, that Miss Caroline."

Mary brought Angelica to the font. The baby was dressed in a long white robe with tiny yellow flowers stitched onto the yolk. Her dark arms and face standing out against the fabric. Caroline was delighted to see Angelica wore the bonnet she had bought as a gift. With the promises made by each Godparent, Philip dripped some water onto Angelica's forehead and on cue the little girl began to cry. There was much nodding and smiling from the women at the front of the church, as if this confirmed Angelica's place in their community.

After the service as Philip and Mary said goodbye to the well-wishers, Caroline hung back with Annie in the cool of the church. Everyone would be going home for lunch and then most would return at two-thirty for the opening of the fete.

Annie sighed, "That'll be me one day." she said wistfully.

"Where is Jacob today? I thought he'd be here."

"No, he's making a few calls on people who haven't paid their bills this morning. He said he'd be more likely to find them at home as these particular people don't often go to church. He's taking on more responsibility now; his father's arthritis is getting worse."

Harry Jenks did very little of the lifting and carrying in the coal yard these days, more often sitting on an old wooden bench outside the office waiting for the cart to be loaded and then taking the reins himself with one of his younger sons riding with him.

"I suppose it will become Jacob's business eventually," Caroline mused.

"Yes, in a few years, though I expect his father will never leave the yard completely. I can't see him putting his feet up on anything other than the wagon footplate. Jacob is going to ask Father for my hand next weekend."

"Oh Annie, that's wonderful! Congratulations!"

"Well," Annie blushed and looked down, "Father hasn't said yes yet."

"But he will, of course he will! Oh Annie, I'm so happy for you. But will that mean you'll be leaving us? When you're married, I mean?"

"Not straight away, unless Mrs Munhead wants me gone. I was hoping to stay on until the first baby comes. Give us a chance to get some savings together and make the house nice. Jacob says he's going to apply to the Housing Committee for one of the new ones they are building up the way," she waved her hand in the general direction north of the church. "We might be able to get married before Christmas. He says if we're still living apart, it will go better with the Housing Committee and that's why I was hoping I could stay on with you. I only go home to Father's house on Saturdays, so it won't be such a big change for me."

"You don't want to live with the Jenks?"

"Oh no! Next to the coal yard?! I don't know how Gloria keeps her linen clean with the coal dust and smuts from the trains all day long. It's bad enough where you are, though the wind doesn't always carry the smuts to your side of the tracks."

No, thought Caroline, there is a definite difference between this side of the railway and the one where I live.

They went out into the sunshine and parted as Caroline went back to the Rose's to help Mary and Celestine with lunch.

There was again quite a crowd at the Vicarage waiting for the gates to open. The Vicar's garden was around a third of an acre and was his pride and joy, if vicars were permitted pride, he would joke. It had been decided to have free entry, to encourage as many visitors as possible, but to provide charged-for refreshments alongside the assorted tables of items for sale and games to be played. Someone had suggested guessing the weight of Angelica, but that was quickly dismissed as Philip had been telling everyone he met how she weighed 'a healthy five pounds four-and-three-quarter ounces'. Instead, they opted to guess the weight of a firm round cheese donated by the Coates Dairy and guess the number of Barratt's Blackjack chews in a stout glass jar that had previously held pickled onions.

Caroline had offered to help with a plant stall, hoping it would allow her some time to sit down. She looked out across the lawn as Celestine carefully carried two cups of tea on saucers towards Mary who was sat on a chair under a beech tree with Angelica in the pram next to her. People moved around the stalls in a roughly clockwise direction, with children running across the lawn in the middle of the tables. It was a comforting scene, Caroline thought. Everything in its place, the sun bathing everything in a honey glow, everyone having a lovely time.

Her revelry was broken by a shout from Celestine and a piercing cry from Angelica, quite unusual for the little girl. Celestine had a young boy by the ear as Mary scooped Angelica up into her arms and tried to sooth her. Philip raced over to see what had happened, managed to release the boy from Celestine's grip but kept a firm hand on his shoulder. A small crowd gathered around them including Lottie who had waved to Caroline as she had just arrived with her family. Caroline peered across the lawn but did not want to leave the plants or the saucer of pennies unattended.

After a few moments the crowd dispersed, and Philip marched the young lad towards the gate. Lottie came straight over to Caroline, a look of shock and concern on her face.

"Well! Some people should have better control of their children, that's all I can say!"

"What on earth happened?"

"That boy pinched the baby! Can you believe it?! Pinched her hard and then said it didn't matter because his father said coloured people don't feel pain like we do." Lottie looked like she would burst with righteous indignation.

"How dreadful! Is Angelica alright?"

"Yes, a pinch won't do a lot of harm, but still, you just don't do that sort of thing. I expected better from the children down here. Mr Rose is taking him home, going to have a talk to his father."

"Oh dear, Philip will be very upset. Lottie I'm so glad you came, but I'm rather stuck here until half past three I'm afraid when Mrs Dewer is meant to be relieving me."

"That's alright, I'll take mother and father round the stalls and see if Robert can win us something on the dart board."

"Do bring them here and introduce me, won't you?"

"Of course, they all want to meet you!"

Robert Lewis did indeed manage to win the family something on the dart board. He had the highest score with nine darts and became the proud owner of a young sheep that had been tethered to one of the trees in the shade. It would be taken away to be butchered and Robert could collect the meat later that week. His father was beaming at his son's accuracy, and not unhappy about a full menu of mutton dishes for the next couple of weeks.

At four-thirty the last of the prizes were given out and the vicarage garden emptied of its visitors. Caroline offered to stay and help clear the debris, but Phillip insisted that she should go home and thanked her profusely for everything she had done over the past week. She went to find Mary to say her goodbyes and found her tucking a sleeping Angelica into the pram while Celestine nursed a box of chocolates that she had won on the tombola, and which Caroline suspected were melting in the heat inside their box.

"Everything alright now?" Caroline asked, peering into the pram.

"Yes, we are all well again now," Mary said softly.

"Wicked child!" grumbled Celestine.

"Yes, Mother. But nothing that we have not heard before."

"Really? How could anyone believe such rubbish?" Caroline felt upset on her friend's behalf.

"You may not have noticed, Miss Caroline, but we are not the same and people still wonder at how humans could be so different. They think just because our skin is different that we must also be different on the inside."

"But that's quite ridiculous. Oh Mary, I'm so sorry that you've had to bear this today. It was meant to be such a happy occasion."

"It has been. I will not let a small ignorant boy or his family spoil my daughter's Christening party. And you have been such a good friend Caroline, I cannot thank you enough for helping us."

"Philip has already. I don't know who was more embarrassed at the end, me or him! He's told me to go home and not worry about clearing up, so that's what I am going to do. But I will see you in the week, perhaps Wednesday after I finish work? And Celestine it has been lovely to see you again too!"

Celestine reached out and gave Caroline a bone crushing hug, almost knocking her feathered hat off.

"You are a beautiful young woman, Miss Caroline! Just the right friend for my daughter, and now the right Godparent for my granddaughter. I drink your good health when I am home again!"

11

BOB

The following week, the night shift of the sewing and dope rooms were asked to stay on at the end of their work, while the day shift arrived. All of the girls gathered in the sewing room, with much whispering about what was to be announced. Mr Cambridge entered the room with Mrs Chandler a pace or two behind him. She stood next to Mrs Vickers the night supervisor. Mr Cambridge carried a wooden crate which he set down on the floor and stood on so that he could see to the far end of the room over the heads of the assembled women and girls. A hush quickly descended. He cleared his throat.

"Now, you'll all know that we came to the end of a large order last week. Your work has been exemplary, and I want to thank you all for that. Unfortunately, that large order is likely to be one of the last of that size. We have work on the books, but not enough to sustain the current working pattern that you are all engaged under. The managers have decided that we will continue with a day shift and a night shift, and that you will all remain employed. However, we will be stopping the operation of the sewing and dope room from the end of the Friday day shift to the beginning of the Monday day shift."

There was a murmur as the women digested this information. One raised her hand and Mr Cambridge nodded in her direction.

"So, us night girls will lose more hours than the day girls, is that right?"

"Unfortunately, yes. It is what the managers have decided, in order to maintain employment for everyone some economies have to be made. It will in fact bring the overall wages of the night shift into line with the day shift, as you are paid more per hour at present. As I say, this arrangement will begin when the day shift ends this Friday."

He got down off the crate, glanced at Betty Chandler, and walked out.

The night shift women slowly left the sewing room, a feeling of dismay and unjustness radiating from them as they talked together while taking off their overalls. Caroline had to work hard to conceal her happiness; she would have two days holiday each week instead of one and the loss of a day's pay mattered very little to her at that moment. When the night shift had left, Mrs Chandler called the day girls around her.

"Is there anyone here who will need to find other employment in light of this new arrangement? I'm asking you all now, because I shall need to inform the managers, but also because I want to give you as much assistance as I can to find another position," she looked at the mostly unhappy faces in front of her. "I am aware that there are one or two possible vacancies at the telephone exchange that might be suitable, and also Coates Dairy is opening a new creamery, so they'll be needing people. You might need a day or so to consider it all, I understand that, but I don't want to see any of you struggling. You are all good workers, and I will be happy to write references for any of you that might require one."

There was silence in the room, apart from the bird song through the open windows.

"Well, think about it, and come to me at once if you need to."

At lunchtime, Hannah sat down next to Caroline on the grass. They could not be said to be friends, but Caroline no longer felt deliberately excluded from Hannah's circle. Lottie sat on Caroline's opposite side and munched her apple, waiting for Hannah to speak.

"Our Jim is doing well at the nursery. I shan't miss a day's pay as much as I would have this time last year."

Caroline swallowed a piece of pork pie, "I'm glad to hear that, Hannah. It's a shame about the night girls, but at least we do all still have jobs."

"Yes, well, I just wanted to say thank you for what you did. It was kinder than I deserved," she got to her feet again and went to sit with another group further along the grass.

"An apology, lummy!" said Lottie mischievously, once Hannah was out of earshot.

"Lottie don't be mean. She didn't have to say anything at all about it, so we should be charitable towards her for it."

"Alright, I know." She threw her apple core to the side for a waiting blackbird, "You won't be missing a day's pay either I expect."

"No, I shall be glad of another day of not working, but I do understand it will make things difficult for some of the girls. What about you?"

"I think I shall be alright. I knew about this last night, Aunt Betty came over and spoke to mother about it, that's how she knew about the positions at the exchange. You need quick fingers there too, so it would suit some of the girls here. Not Gwen though."

"Will she be alright, do you think?"

"What Gwen? Yes, I expect so. Her mother has a war pension, and they own their house so no rent to pay on it, it was her family home."

"How do you know so much about everyone Lottie? It's as if you're a little bird sitting at everyone's open windows listening in on them!"

Lottie blushed, "I do listen. Mother and Father know a lot of people around Cheltenham. People are always coming in and out of our house, and with Robert's friends too. I know I shouldn't say everything that I do, but I can't help myself, it comes out of my mouth before I know what I'm saying sometimes. And you're a good listener too, if you weren't I wouldn't say half as much."

Caroline laughed, "Are you saying it's my fault for listening to you?"

"Yes, I am," laughed Lottie. "There's one thing I'm going to tell you now that I probably shouldn't. Our Robert hasn't stopped talking about you since the fete."

"Robert? But I hardly even said hello to him!"

"That must have been enough. Quite taken with you, he is."

"Lummy!" said Caroline, and they both burst into laughter.

14 August 1925
King's Cross, London
Dear Caroline,

A thousand apologies for not writing sooner, but I have been very busy with a couple of projects that could be very good for my career. I know I said I would visit Cheltenham if I could, and I do still want to as it sounds such a pretty town from your descriptions, but it may not be this summer. You see, I've landed a job directing a play here in London and it's due to open shortly and run for six weeks. It's not film, but I do so enjoy the thrill of directing and seeing the performance appear as I imagine it.

*I wanted to let you know that it is going to be at least
September before I'll have a chance to call on your hospitality.
I imagine I will be quite in need of it by then, London is an
awful place to spend the summer!*

*I heard that Helen and Vic were no longer an item. It's
terribly sad for them both, but society simply wouldn't have
tolerated it for much longer. Tommy has been back in town, but
without his pal Helen, he seems diminished. As if she were the
one who encouraged him, though we know he needs none of
that. We had dinner last week and he said he would be going
back down to Devonshire to try and cheer Helen up. Goodness
knows what he had in mind for the old girl!*

*Caroline, I will come and see you, I give you my word. And
I will write before then, as I cannot presume to just turn up at
your door and expect you to drop whatever you are doing on
my behalf. I have often thought of our walks along the coast
path at Knapp House, and our quiet pleasant evenings in the
library. Peace is something of a rare commodity here. And before
I forget, I'm enclosing with this letter a cheque for your part
in the film. They only came through on it last week, so please
don't think I've been holding on to it.*

*I hope you are well and enjoying this heatwave as best
you can!*

*Yours fondly
James*

Folded up inside the envelope, Caroline discovered a cheque
for seventeen pounds and six shillings. She wondered where the
film might be shown. Would she be recognised in the street?
She doubted it, given the wigs she had worn and the layers of
make-up. She remembered James saying something about the
distributor being German, so it was possible it would not be
seen in England at all. Caroline took the cheque to her father
and wrote the details in her notebook of accounts. She was

now in the black, as her father had called it, with a balance of fifty-six pounds, seven shillings and three pence. Could she stay that way for the rest of the year?

As for James, she had hardly thought of him over the past few weeks with all the excitement about Angelica and then the fete and Christening. Now with his letter in her hand, she felt a strange lightness and she smiled. A silly infatuation, no doubt. She was happy for him that he had found a play to direct, and a little sad not to be seeing him again quiet as soon as she'd anticipated. Just when she was about to gain another free day each week too. Caroline had already decided how she would spend her first Saturday off.

After breakfast with her parents, where she had to explain again to her mother why she was not rushing out to work, Caroline took the tram in to the centre of town. The streets were dusty and the flower beds in much need of rain. The Promenade was busy with shoppers and young people riding bicycles. Caroline made her way past Cavendish House and entered the premises next to it with a jangle of the bell above the door.

A young man, hardly out of school and short trousers Caroline thought, looked at her over his spectacles. "Can I be of service, ma'am?"

"Is Miss House available?"

"If you would like to take a seat, I will enquire. Who shall I say wishes to speak with her?"

Caroline smiled, "A friend." She wanted to surprise Elsa. Though she had sent two letters while she had been at Knapp House, she had not received a reply. She heard footsteps descending the stairs and stood up.

Elsa followed her young assistant into the shop and looked at Caroline for a moment before she realised who was before her.

"My God! Caroline! How wonderful to see you, come through to the back, please. My goodness, this is such a surprise!"

she was quite overwhelmed. "Peter, we are not to be disturbed is that understood? The proofs for the Johnstons are under the counter there, just take their money or write them an invoice if they come in. Caroline, we must have some coffee…"

They went through to the rear of the shop and Elsa closed the door behind them.

Caroline noticed immediately the piles of unwashed crockery, the overflowing ashtray and the various items of clothing draped over anything that would support them. She sat on the only empty chair and took off her hat while Elsa made coffee for them both. Elsa chattered away about how Peter was reliable but nervous around everyone and she might need to poke her head around the door if the Johnstons did call in. Then she turned and moved a pile of newspapers from another chair before sitting down.

"So, tell me all of your news! You've cut your hair too; it looks perfect on you."

"Thank you. Where do I start? It seems an age since I last heard from you."

"I wrote to your house to answer your letters from Dorset. I wasn't sure how long you would be down there and didn't want the letters to get lost."

"To the house? My parents'?"

"Yes, twice."

"I never… Oh, no. Do you think Mother would have taken them? I never received them, Elsa."

"But how would she know who they were from? Surely you receive letters from your friends regularly?"

"Yes, but they don't have a Cheltenham postmark. Oh, for goodness' sake, this really is too much!" Caroline made to stand up, but Elsa put her hand on Caroline's arm.

"Leave it for now dear. Tell me how the film making went. I laughed when you said about the blue lipstick, that's an old photography trick you know."

For the next hour Caroline relayed her adventures since May. She found herself saying James' name rather a lot and felt self-conscious about it. She hoped Elsa wouldn't be upset by it and she tried to make more of the events at the night club in London than her day in Hyde Park. But most of her conversation was filled with the engineering works sewing room girls, and the birth and christening of Angelica Rose.

"And they named her after you? How wonderful."

"Yes, it was quite a surprise after the whole thing had happened right in front of me, and I was so tired. Doctor Riley walked me home and I'm sure I was almost sleep walking for most of it! She is such a sweet little thing though; Angelica is the perfect name for her."

"How long do you think you will stay at the works? I heard they are laying people off."

"I really don't know. The night shift has lost some hours, and some of the men have been let go – that's the right expression, isn't it? – so perhaps it won't be my decision how long I am there for."

The bell above the main door jangled to announce the arrival of a customer, the Johnstons by the voices the two women could hear. Caroline stood up.

"Well, my dear, I really must be getting along, I don't want to hold up your work."

"You'll keep in touch, won't you? Drop in any time. And I'll make sure I send any future letters from Winchcombe or Tewkesbury!"

Caroline laughed as they embraced. She was still cross with her mother, but that would keep for now.

Stepping out into the sunshine again from the darkness of the shop, Caroline needed a moment to adjust her eyes. She was hungry and it was lunchtime. She decided to walk along the High Street and find a tea shop to have something to eat. It was the first time she had been into Cheltenham in the day since she had bought her swimming costume. Caroline felt as if she was seeing the town with new eyes; she felt herself walking taller, looking around her at the townspeople going about their business. She felt older and it surprised her. She wondered how other people saw her, if they recognised her as one of their own, or thought of her perhaps as a visitor, a tourist in her hometown.

Caroline found a café and ordered a cheese omelette and a pot of tea. While she waited for her lunch, she continued her train of thought. That year she had visited several new places and hadn't really considered them against each other for more than brief moments. Eventually, she understood, she would strike out on her own, or at least without her parents, and would have a home of her own. Perhaps with a husband, although that idea was pushed firmly to one side as she could not imagine becoming irrevocably joined to any man just then. So, a home of her own, but where?

The omelette and tea arrived. Would any of the places she had been to so far be suitable? She considered them in turn. Pangbourne, sleepy and muddy, but close to Reading if she required entertainment. Bristol was lively, colourful, noisy. It had possibilities. Milton Abbott – no, she would not care to return there or linger on its associations. Tavistock was similar to Cheltenham, although she imagined all that grey granite could become oppressive over a long winter on the moor, much like *Wuthering Heights*. Plymouth had not particularly impressed her, perhaps because she had already seen Bristol, but then she had really only seen a fraction of the city. She wondered if Helen might have her to stay for a few days so she could explore more of it.

She was pouring a second cup of tea and thinking of Swanage and the little villages of the Purbeck Peninsular when she realised a figure was standing on the opposite side of the table and had just cleared his throat. She looked up, but as the figure was standing between her and the café window, all she could see was a dark shape.

"I'm terribly sorry, I can't see with the window behind you."

"I'm sorry Miss, I just thought I'd say hello," the shape moved to the right and Caroline realised it was Lottie's brother Robert.

"Robert! Oh hello. Would you like to sit down? I think there is enough tea here for another cup."

"Thank you, Miss," he caught the eye of a waitress and asked for a cup and saucer, before sitting to the side of Caroline so that she could see him more clearly. "I don't think I've seen you in here before."

Robert seemed a little large for the chair, Caroline thought. He was dressed as if he had been working, though he was clean enough to enter a café. His stout boots were scuffed and well worn. He had on rough jacket and trousers, with a collarless shirt and a red thin scarf tied around his neck despite, or because of, the heat.

The waitress brought the cup and saucer, and Caroline poured the last of the tea.

"No, I haven't been this side of the High Street for quite a while," she said. "Is it a favourite place of yours?"

"I come in for my lunch on Saturdays such as this, and then often I go over to Fairview to watch the football match. If Cheltenham Town are playing at home that is. I have a half day on Saturdays."

"As I'm sure Lottie has told you, we are no longer required to work on Saturdays, so I am enjoying my freedom today." Caroline smiled at Robert in an attempt to ease his obvious shyness. "Is there a match on today?"

"No, they're away at Droitwich today. It'll be a tough match. Perhaps… you might like to come and see a game one Saturday, now you're not working?"

"That would be exciting, yes I would like to Robert."

"Call me Bob, most people do."

"Very well, Bob. Will you tell Lottie when the next home game is? She might like to come along too as neither of us are working."

Robert looked somewhat crestfallen at the thought of his little sister tagging along but accepted the compromise.

"I will do that. Well, I should be getting along now. Thank you for the tea, most kind of you."

"You are very welcome, Bob. Good to see you again."

When Robert had left the waitress approached and asked if Caroline wanted anything else. She ordered a slice of almond tart, and instead of contemplating Swanage as she had been, she contemplated Bob.

Lottie had told her that Bob worked at the gas works with their father. She had been vague about his actual role there, but it appeared to be something to do with monitoring a lot of dials and gauges and making sure there was enough gas for everyone to use. Bob was three years older than Lottie, two years older than Caroline at twenty-three. He was almost six feet tall and towered over most of his workmates. His hair was short at the back with a longer fringe, his eyes a light brown with flecks of gold around the centres. Caroline caught herself; had she looked that closely? She must have, and she hoped it hadn't been too obvious. Bob had an honest, serious face, she concluded with the last bite of her tart. It would be fun to attend a football match, the men at Knapp House had talked animatedly about their favourite teams. It seemed to inspire a passion in some people.

Caroline chose to walk home, up to Montpellier and then through Lansdown. Now her thoughts returned to Swanage. She had very much enjoyed the time she spent at Knapp House, with the company and afterwards when it had just been James and her. The air was invigorating, and the pool was such a luxury! She wondered what it would be like to live on the coast in the winter.

Finally, as she turned into Glencairn Road, she thought
about London. Far bigger and busier than Bristol, and if she were
being honest, not somewhere she could ever see herself living.
Certainly not in the very centre. Lady Victoria's apartment was
immaculate and beautifully furnished, but Caroline was under
no illusion that she would ever be able to afford more than one
or two rooms in a significantly smaller house and probably in
a far inferior part of the city.

She pushed her key into the lock and let herself in. The
house was quiet except for the clock ticking softly in her father's
study. She remembered her parents were attending a garden
party in aid of the Hospital that afternoon. Caroline breathed
in the familiar smell of polish and fresh bread. This would be
home for a while longer, she decided, but she would tell Annie
to make sure any letters addressed to her were placed in her
room and not left on the hallway table from now on.

The first Saturday in September Cheltenham Town were to
play Coventry City at home. Caroline had arranged with Lottie
that she would meet her and Bob outside Pittville Gates at two
o'clock and they would all walk together the short distance to
the football ground. Caroline had not expected such a swell of
people as greeted her as she stepped off the tram. It seemed as if
the whole town was moving *en mass* in the same direction. She
spotted Bob standing by the ornamental gates and pushed her
way towards him. Lottie came into view by his side and the three
of them joined the flow of humanity away from the town centre.

There were a significant number of women in the crowd.
The town had enjoyed a modicum of success with their wom-
en's team until the Football Association banned all women's
teams from playing at their association grounds in 1921. Since
then, a few teams still played around Gloucestershire but most
of the attention had returned to the men's game. Lottie, Caroline and Bob found space on the gently sloping grass where

all three could just about see the pitch. Bob explained that he would normally watch from the wooden stands opposite, but if they stayed where they were they would find it easier to go home if the girls found it too much of a crush.

Caroline noticed that many of the spectators wore red and white scarfs and rosettes. Bob explained that the team were known as the Robins because they played in a red and white outfit. The noise of the crowd indicated that the teams were out on the pitch, and Bob kept up a commentary so that Caroline could follow the twists and turns of the game. Lottie had been to see football matches a few times before with her brother and understood the rudiments of it. She couldn't see very much being the smallest of the three, so Bob's narration helped. Caroline was entranced by the way the crowd responded to fouls, shots at goal, and goals themselves with a spontaneous roar. Generous applause followed missed shots and fair play alike. It was unlike the constant roar of the horse racing crowd which lasted the whole of each race. This was a mesmerising experience and she felt as if she were part of some long-lost tribe on a singular mission to be victorious over its foe.

Unfortunately, Cheltenham were not victorious on that occasion. Coventry City won 3-2, and more generous applause followed the final whistle. The crowd began to move away almost instantly, many to the pubs nearest to the ground. Bob would very much have liked to join them, but he did not think a pub was a suitable place to take either of his companions on a match day, so they walked slowly back towards Pittville. Lottie and Bob saw Caroline safely on to her tram.

As they waved her on her way, Lottie said to her brother, "If you want to go back and have a pint with your pals, I can get home."

Bob looked wistfully back towards the Duke of York with its crowd of men standing around the door, "You'll go straight home? I'll only have one, tell mother I'll be home for dinner."

Lottie punched his arm playfully, "I'll tell her, brother, so you'd better be. And what should I tell Caroline?"

"Don't you go saying anything. I'll do this in my own time. Go on, get off home."

Josiah Curzon had, as Dr Riley commented, become a regular visitor to the Munhead's dinner table over the summer months. On alternate Thursday evenings he would scrub his hands with coal tar soap and a nail brush, change into clean clothes and make his way along the short distance from Queens Road home to Glencairn Road. Often, he would catch up with Mrs Joyce and escort her the final few yards to number 20. She was his senior by a good thirty years but enjoyed the fresh air and could often be seen walking around Lansdown admiring the gardens of her neighbours. They shared an interest in plants, and this was the usual topic of their conversations on the way to, and sometimes during, dinner.

Elizabeth was growing concerned that her attempts to bring Josiah and Caroline together appeared to have stalled. Caroline chatted amicably with Josiah, but he spoke just as much to Mrs Joyce and any other guests as he did to Caroline. Elizabeth had even raised the subject of marriage in general on a couple of occasions, quite without shame, yet still the two did not seem to be any closer. She was also aware of Bob Lewis' arrival in Caroline's circle, and she was determined that that particular acquaintance would not progress further. A gas worker indeed. She refused to allow Caroline to slip into the working classes simply because she insisted on her crusade to experience their occupations.

George had warned his wife more than once about pressing too far with her match-making. He was vicariously enjoying his daughter's adventures and knew that she was in no hurry to bring them to a close and settle down to wedded bliss. He had been making his own enquiries as to obtaining a passport on

Caroline's behalf, so that he might be able to advise her if she found she needed one. He was encouraged by her determination to make her allowance last the year (he had feared she might blow it all by Easter) and to even recoup it so as to hold him to their deal.

On Florence's return from France, George suggested that they add her to their party the following Thursday. Elizabeth was at first hesitant, but Caroline took her father's side as usual and between them they convinced her. Florence made an entertaining distraction. She chattered about her travels, and in particular the fashions of the South of France that year. Caroline had heard much of it already but was relieved to not be the centre of attention for once. She also noticed that Josiah paid Florence rather more attention than was perhaps appropriate for a guest to. Was that jealousy she felt rise in her throat?

At their lunch the next day, Caroline told Lottie how Josiah had almost ignored her all evening.

"But I thought you weren't interested in him. What does it matter if he makes cow eyes at someone else?"

"It matters because he is our guest. I might not want him to make cow eyes at me, as you so delicately put it, but that doesn't mean I want him to make them at anyone else either."

"Sounds like you want to have your cake and eat it too. Anyway, here's something that'll cheer you up. Bob says would you care to accompany him to the picture house tomorrow for a matinee show? I said I'd ask and let him know what you said tonight."

Caroline didn't hesitate, "Please tell him I would be delighted! I think the matinee starts at two-thirty at the Daffodil, so I will be at Montpelier Rotunda at two if he would meet me there."

"I'm sure he will," smiled Lottie.

The matinee was a triple bill. A short romance, followed by some news reels, and then the feature film, which was *The Man Without Desire*, a re-showing of a box office smash from a couple of years earlier. Caroline wondered if Bob had known it would be a romantic programme, she didn't think that it would be his natural preference. She enjoyed the film, particularly the young Ivor Novello, despite having seen it on an earlier run at the cinema with Florence before she had left for France. If someone with that much presence came into her life, how could she resist their charms? All of her resolve to remain single would crumble, she had no doubt.

They emerged into the cloudy evening and Bob suggested they take a walk around Montpelier gardens. There had been a shower of rain while they had sat inside the cinema and now puddles dotted the cobbles and rivulets gurgled into the drains at the side of the road. They came to a large puddle and though Bob crossed it in a single stride, Caroline hesitated. He held out his hand to steady her, a look of concern on his face. She smiled, grasped his hand, and made the short leap across the puddle landing neatly at his side. There was a moment when they both stood a little too close and smiled a little too warmly, before Caroline let go and they continued with their walk.

As they completed their circuit of the gardens and Caroline's tram came into view, Bob cleared his throat.

"Would you consider taking a walk with me next weekend?"

"Where did you have in mind?"

"I was thinking perhaps around Pittville Park, we could take a boat on the lake or listen to the band play. Maybe take tea in the Pump Rooms. Whatever you fancy."

Caroline thought for a moment. "Would you mind awfully if we went the weekend after next? Only I have some letters to write, and I barely have time to eat in the evenings before I fall asleep."

"The weekend after on the Saturday?" Cheltenham Town would be playing a home game, but he could miss it. He nodded, "Yes. Will you tell Lottie what time and I'll meet you at Pittville Gates like we did before?"

"Oh, is Lottie coming too?"

"No, I was thinking just you and me."

Caroline stepped towards the tram, "Yes, I'll tell her. Goodbye Bob!"

21 September 1925
King's Cross, London
Dear Caroline,

Just a quick note. I shall be able to visit next weekend on the 26th, I'll be on my way to Bristol, and can stop for one night in Cheltenham if you are available. Is there a hotel you can recommend? I will aim to be on the 2.15 from Paddington so hope to be in Cheltenham St James for around 5pm. We could have dinner somewhere perhaps?

Yours, James

Caroline was excited to receive James' note, but it would be the same Saturday that she had agreed to meet Bob again. She decided to recommend the Queens Hotel and sent off an equally short reply saying she would be at St James' station to meet him from his train. The hotel was only a short walk from the town centre and their restaurant was reputable. She thought perhaps they could go to the Daffodil afterwards and see a film.

She dropped her reply to James, along with letters to Midge and Helen into the bright red letterbox at the junction of Queens Road and Christ Church Road. On her way back, Caroline noticed Florence going into Curzon's Exotic Nursery. Caroline waved but Florence did not see her.

Caroline dressed carefully for her appointment with Bob. She would not have time to return home before meeting James at the station, so her clothes would need to be suitable to carry her through to the evening. The weather was cool with a stubborn westerly wind that herded dark clouds across the sky. At the last minute, Caroline decided to wear a coat, and almost missed the tram that was waiting on Gloucester Road.

Bob was anxious. There were crowds again making their way to the football ground and he hoped that Caroline would not have any difficulty in crossing town. He liked Caroline a lot. He wasn't sure if it was love but it was definitely affection; she was just so interesting and so pretty, the prettiest girl he had known though he accepted that Cheltenham was not perhaps full of pretty girls being a small town in the Cotswolds. The trouble was, he didn't really know what to do next. The men at the gas works who had been married over the past few years all seemed to spend a year or two courting their sweethearts before proposing. A year seemed a long time to Bob. Could he keep Caroline's interest with football matches and the cinema and afternoon teas for a whole year?

He was ready to settle down, he knew that much. The family home felt much smaller now than when he, Lottie and their little brother Charles had been young children. He shared a bedroom with Charlie, which wasn't unusual, but the boy was fascinated with aeroplanes and had models of them all over the room. Bob had to be careful not to knock one over or tread on one and that was difficult when he came home late at night. He had saved his wages, minus the housekeeping he gave his mother weekly from his pay packet and knew he could afford a small house somewhere in St Paul's around the gas works. But he didn't relish moving out to live by himself; could he convince Caroline to share a home with him?

He saw her walking towards him, her plum-coloured cloche hat pulled firmly down on her head to stop the wind carrying it off. She smiled and he tried to smile back. It was not something he did very often, he was mostly a serious young man.

"You didn't tell me there was another football match today!"

"Would you rather go along and see it?" Bob asked hopefully.

"Oh no, I've been looking forward to a stroll around the park and a cup of tea," Caroline put her hand on her hat as another gust of wind threatened to steal it. "Shall we go?"

They walked along Park Gate and paid their penny to enter Pittville Gardens at the small green hut where the park keeper sat on a deckchair, an old tabby cat on his lap. The cat was not his, but it arrived every morning just after he did to open the park and happily kept him company for most of the day if he provided a saucer of milk. The trees swayed in the wind, still mostly in leaf though the colours were beginning to turn from green to yellow. They walked around the lake and over the little bridge, stopping to watch the ducks being fed by a small child with a handful of bread crusts. They continued up the short sloping path to the Pump Rooms. It was a grand regency building of Cotswold stone that looked out over the park with an ornate drinking fountain and cups that were chained to it on one side of the ballroom inside.

They took seats at a table by one of the long vertical windows so that they would have a view of the park. A brass band had been playing for the entertainment of the public in the little bandstand just outside the Pump Rooms, but they were now packing away their instruments. A waitress came and took their order, and Caroline undid her coat and took her gloves and hat off and placed them on the table in front of her.

"You look smart," Bob said. He had rehearsed a few things to say the night before with Lottie's help.

"Thank you. I am meeting a friend off the train at five, and with this weather I really wasn't sure what to wear."

"I think we've seen the end of summer. I like to watch the leaves change colour in the autumn. Do you?" Remember to ask questions he told himself.

"Oh yes. And gathering conkers and chestnuts when they start to fall. Our apple tree has been particularly productive this year."

"We only have a yard, no room for anything much to grow. We had chickens a few years ago, but when they stopped laying, we ate them and never got any more."

The waitress brought their tea.

"Tell me more about your job. Lottie was rather vague when I asked her."

Caroline watched him over the rim of her teacup as she sipped her tea and he talked at some length about his position and how the gas had to be regulated and the correct pressure maintained. It was the most she had heard him say in one go, and she was pleasantly lulled by his voice. She nodded encouragement a couple of times as he glanced at her to see if she was still listening. He was a good man, she decided. A stable and responsible man. Intelligent enough, though somewhat lacking in worldly experience. She smiled to herself; a year ago she too was lacking in that area.

Bob saw her smile and frowned, not knowing what he had said to cause amusement. Caroline quickly realised.

"I was just thinking how responsible your job sounds, it must give you a sense of satisfaction to know the safety of the town is in your hands."

"Well, it's an important job, yes. Some days it can be a bit dull, but that's a good thing when you're dealing with gas."

A woman walked past the window pushing a pram with one hand and holding the hand of a small child with the other. The child was trying to turn away and watch the bandsmen.

"You have a younger brother?" Caroline tried to rescue the conversation.

"Charles. He's thirteen. Wants to be a pilot."

"Thirteen? That's quite an age gap between Lottie and him."

"Yes, there were two others, Kenneth and Sarah, but they both died with the influenza. Mother had it bad too, we nearly lost her."

"I'm sorry. We were lucky. So many families suffered. But a pilot sounds a fascinating occupation. How does one become a pilot?"

"He's keen to secure an apprenticeship down at Filton. He tried at Bicester, but they didn't have any places. We've got models of planes all over the house at home that he's built."

"That's wonderful that he has an interest."

"It is. Father doesn't want him to come to the gas works, he says there will be more opportunities for him with aircraft. I can't see it myself, and I wouldn't want to go up in one. Would you?"

"Oh yes! That would be terribly thrilling!"

"I'm not so good with heights. Prefer to keep my feet on the ground you might say."

Yes, thought Caroline, I can see that.

"What do you want to do, Bob? With your life I mean. How do you see yourself in five years, ten years maybe?"

Bob poured a drop more tea into his cup and stirred it thoughtfully.

"I can't say it's something I think much about if I'm honest. My own home I suppose, perhaps out towards Prestbury way, not in town like we are now. With a garden. I'd like to have some more chickens and grow some vegetables and fruit trees. The soil is good in Prestbury, that's why the market gardens are there. A family, in time. A car. Just to be comfortable," he was struggling to express how different this all sounded from his current living arrangements without giving Caroline the impression that he was a pauper.

"And I'm sure I'll get there soon enough," he added with an optimistic smile, "I've got a bit saved up. What do you want from your life, Caroline?"

Caroline couldn't deny that Bob's description of his hoped-for future was appealing, even desirable. To have the security of one's own home, watching your garden and family grow... but she wanted more.

"I want to explore. I want to learn things, see how things work. I feel as if I have so much catching up to do with other girls of my age. At least I did with my school friends. The girls at work perhaps not so much. But I know there is so much to see and do away from Cheltenham and I want to experience it, or as much of it as I can. My friend Midge is training to become a teacher and might even go to Africa when she is qualified. Have you ever been out of Cheltenham?"

"I've been to Gloucester. And to Evesham once."

"Don't you want to see other places? Even Bristol is very different to Cheltenham. If Charles gets his apprenticeship, you could visit him there. And the sea! Oh Bob, you must see the sea!" Her face lit up when she spoke of it, her mind flying back to the sunny days above Swanage.

"It's not that I don't want those things, Caroline. They all sound interesting. I suppose I just don't think of them that often. My mind is usually thinking about work, sometimes football. I read the newspaper, I know what goes on up country and in London, and I see the newsreels at the cinema. I like films, that one we saw the other week was good. Security is important though Caroline, that's all I can say."

They finished their tea. Bob paid the bill, and they left the Pump Rooms walking past the bandstand and back down the sloping path towards the lake.

"We could take a boat out, if you like? I don't mind water."

Caroline checked her watch. "I don't think there is time today, Bob, it's almost four and I do have to meet James at five."

"James?"

Yes, my friend James, I told you, he's arriving by train."

Bob stopped walking, "When you said a friend, I thought, well I thought you meant a girl."

"But James is a friend. He's the one who made the film I took part in, and he showed me around Hyde Park when I went to London."

Bob looked at his shoes. He hadn't expected this kind of competition on top of Caroline's travel plans and he wasn't sure he would be up to the challenge. But Caroline should have said something about this James before letting him splash out on the cinema and pots of tea.

"Then perhaps we shouldn't be seeing each other like this."

"Whyever not? Honestly Bob, I don't understand. Surely you have other friends? People you go to watch football with?"

"Not girls though. And if I was walking out with a girl, then I wouldn't take another out. That's just not done."

He looked directly at her now, a deep frown on his brow. He thrust his hands into the pockets of his jacket.

Caroline didn't know what to do. It hadn't occurred to her that there would be anything wrong in seeing James again, or seeing Bob, or both. She considered them both friends, though very different in their own ways. To her it was no more than sitting with Lottie for lunch and then visiting Mary after work on a Wednesday. She could see that Bob was annoyed and realised he had placed more importance on this excursion than she had.

"Bob, I... I thought we were friends. I like you, I've enjoyed today, but I am truly not looking for a more involved relationship, not now, not yet at least. There is so much that I still want to see and do in the world. Could we keep walking? This wind is rather chilly."

Bob nodded his head and began walking again, though slowly as if he was struggling to think and walk at the same time. He felt foolish. Of course, this young woman was too good for him, too curious, too bright. How could he hope to keep her interested in his small world when there was so much more out there for her.

"Can we still be friends, Bob? Are you angry with me?"

"Not angry no, never that," he still couldn't look at her. "I'd just hoped we might be... well, a bit more formal is all."

"But Bob, we've only known each other a few weeks," Caroline said as gently as she could.

"I know. It doesn't feel like it to me though, and does that matter so much anyway? If you like someone a lot, I mean?"

"I would like us to keep on being friends for now. If we can?"

Bob took a long breath in. Did he really have any choice? What he hadn't told Caroline was that since he first saw her, she had been on his mind far more than work or any football game. He wanted to be around her as much as possible. She was like a bright light with her enthusiasm and freshness. He had a feeling that to constrain or limit her would put out that light.

"Yes, we can be friends."

Caroline turned down Bob's offer to accompany her all the way to St James' station. He was relieved; he didn't want to meet this friend and find himself more inadequate that he was already feeling. They parted on the High Street and Caroline made her way along to the station and bought a platform ticket. It was twenty to five and she bought a newspaper to read while she waited. She was engrossed in a review of a recently released film *A Romance of Mayfair* about an heir who fell in love with an actress when a porter put his head around the waiting room door and announced the Paddington train was approaching.

Caroline had a strange sense of déjà vu, despite up to now it being her that was met on a platform by someone. The train's eight carriages were mostly full, and several passengers got off before James appeared with a kit bag over his shoulder. He smiled warmly and kissed her cheek as they came together.

"Hellish journey, eight people in the compartment and two snoring their heads off since Oxford! How are you Caro?"

"I am well, thank you. Why didn't you drive down?"

"Ahh, yes, a little accident in the motor. Not my fault I hasten to add, damned idiot shot across a junction straight into me."

"Gracious! Were you hurt?"

"Only my pride. No, the car took the full force on the front bumper, so she's in the garage being straightened out and costing me far more money than I expect she's now worth. So, I'm back to the old iron horse for now. I say, are you hungry? I am famished, didn't have time to grab any lunch before I caught the train. Is there somewhere we can eat?"

"The restaurant at the Queens is rather good I'm told. If you take a room, there we could eat something and then perhaps go to the cinema? The Daffodil is only a short walk from the hotel."

"That sounds perfect. So, this is Cheltenham, eh? What should I know about it, apart from it being your hometown?"

Caroline had decided to forego the tram up to Montpelier and led James on a walk back into the town centre and along the Promenade with the trees rustling their yellowed leaves overhead. The Queens Hotel came into view as they walked past the Neptune fountain at the end of the Promenade and started the slight climb up towards Montpelier with Imperial gardens on their left. The trams rumbled by as they walked and talked, and James was appreciative of the regency buildings that lined the streets and enclosed the green squares of the town.

When they reached the hotel, Caroline waited in the lounge while James went up to his room and washed his face. It gave her time to inspect the clientele from a comfortable seat, and order two coffees as the dining room would not be open until six. The hotel was considered a jewel in Cheltenham's somewhat rusting crown, having accommodated King George III for five weeks while he took the waters in the building's previous incarnation as Sherbourne Spa. Its wallpaper, designed by Pugin, was florid. There was much gold leaf and polished wood and brass on display. In the lounge a fire burned all year round and the leather upholstery was soft and cracked in places where it had been worn by countless bodies. The concierge wore a top hat of grey to match his grey suit, his moustache trimmed and waxed with precision. He had raised an eyebrow when they had arrived, knowing Caroline's father personally and Caroline by sight, but said nothing.

In the lounge Caroline observed a number of older men, some in tail suits and high collars, reading newspapers or quietly dozing in the warmth of the fire. There were two elderly women, seated separately at opposite ends of the lounge. Caroline wondered why they had not sat together for company. One knitted, her needles keeping a steady rhythm and her hand a metronomic swirl of grey yarn for each stitch made. The other was reading a book, a small glass of what Caroline assumed was sherry or Madeira wine on the table beside her chair. It occurred to Caroline that she was by far the youngest person she had seen at the hotel since she arrived with James, and she had an alarming premonition of herself many years in the future in some dusty hotel lounge ending her days and unable to leave. She shuddered as James appeared in the doorway and came to sit in the armchair next to her.

Unlike the conversation with Bob earlier that day, Caroline found it easy to talk to James. They were genuinely interested in each other and the world around them. They discussed Helen and Tommy, the play that had been a success, the appointment that James had on the following Monday at the Old Vic in Bristol, and his thoughts on trying his luck in America or Italy. It was, he said, where the real money was for film making. Caroline talked of Angelica, the sewing room girls, and Florence's entrancement of Josiah Curzon much to Elizabeth's annoyance.

After dinner they strolled around to the Daffodil and saw a short programme of a newsreel and a mediocre (in James' opinion) adventure film from America called *The Sea Hawk*, directed by Frank Lloyd and starring Milton Sills. Caroline enjoyed the film but was keen to understand James' critique of the director's style as they walked back to the hotel.

"Will you be alright going home by yourself? I'd be happy to go with you."

"No, it's perfectly alright, the tram stops almost at the end of the road where I live."

"Well, I'm sure you know your town far better than I do. I've had a wonderful time tonight, Caro, I hope you have too?"

"Yes, absolutely! I can't tell you how refreshing it is to have someone to really talk to about … well, about anything and everything!"

"Yes, I agree, I feel the same. Is that your tram now?"

"Yes, it is. Well, goodnight, James. Who knows, I might find myself in London again before Christmas, but if not, please do let me know if you are passing through again won't you."

They were standing close to each other, the wind again threatening to take Caroline's hat. James leaned forward and kissed her cheek again. "I will. Of course, I will," he said.

12

TOMMY

Cheltenham in October 1925 was wet and windy, but unusually mild. The townsfolk grumbled about being too hot in their mackintoshes and shook their fists at the wind as it blew their umbrellas inside out for the umpteenth time. Fires were lit in homes in an attempt to dry clothing, yet everything felt damp and clammy. The sewing room was hot, and Caroline copied the other girls in removing her blouse to air and dry out while she worked in her vest and overall. They had to keep the windows closed when it rained so that the canvas didn't become damp before it was stretched over the frames.

There was a rumour of further order losses at the engineering works. The night shift girls were sullen and quiet when they passed the day shift in the changing room. There was talk of unrest and agitation amongst the mineworkers across the country, and when Caroline asked Annie if the Jenks' business had been affected, Annie would only say that Jacob and his father were concerned. The men at the engineering works talked in hushed tones of joining a union or even forming their own. The supervisors relayed this back to the managers who posted notices around the buildings to say that anyone found to belong to a union would be dismissed without notice. The management considered themselves to be good employers and would continue to support their workers as best they could while maintaining productivity and the competitiveness of the company.

Caroline continued to call on Mary on Wednesday evenings after work. It had become part of her routine and Mary was not only glad of the company while Philip took the evening service, but also happy to provide Caroline with a meal. Angelica was filling out into an alert and contented baby, putting on weight to the satisfaction of the district nurse who called weekly and would do so until Angelica was six months old. Mary looked tired and said Angelica would still wake two or three times in the night. Mary had been sleeping in the back bedroom with the baby so as to not wake Philip, but she was finding it difficult to get enough sleep. Caroline had so rarely heard Angelica cry, the thought of her being disruptive at night seemed unthinkable to her.

Mary had agreed to teach Caroline to knit, on the pretext of making Angelica some outfits. Caroline had been shown several times at school, but usually dropped so many stitches she had been permitted to work at her sewing skills instead. Fortunately, she was now able to put those to use in her employment, but she wanted to be able to create something as a gift to her Goddaughter and was determined now to complete the little matinee jacket Mary had suggested.

As the month blew and dripped to a close, Caroline and Bob along with Lottie and a workmate of Bob's called Eric attended a tea dance at the town hall in aid of a new wing extension to the general hospital. Caroline had given some thought to Bob's reaction to James' visit and declined several offers to dance from other young men. She accepted one from

Doctor Riley, which she felt Bob could not object to, and also swapped partners with Lottie so that she danced with Eric and Lottie danced with Bob. Caroline had worn her beaded black dress and noticed the looks she received from the other young women, and men, when she handed her coat to the cloakroom attendant. Her dress was noticeably shorter than those still in fashion in the Cotswolds. Bob thought she looked stunning and overcame his own reluctance to dance so that they hardly sat down while the music played.

3 November 1925
Plymouth
Dearest Caro

I am racing this note off to you and hope it reaches you in time. Tommy and I are driving up to Blackpool to view the electrical illuminations next week and would love for you to come with us. We'll be passing through Cheltenham on Friday afternoon, God willing, and aim to be in Blackpool some time on Saturday evening to stay for two or three nights. Do say you'll come! I really feel I need to make it up to you for my awful behaviour in London. Tommy has been a thoroughly good egg about it all and is trying his hardest to make me jolly again. I am sure Blackpool will be full of old men and whippets and have told him it is a ridiculous excursion, but he is insisting. I need you to keep me company while he dallies with the locals.

Look for us around 3pm on Friday the 6th
Yours intrepidly
Helen

Caroline chuckled to herself when she read Helen's scrawled note. Helen and Tommy were such a comical pair when they were on form, and he had been so kind to her in Devon, she was very fond of him. Now she had not one but two dilemmas: she would need to take some time off work, which of course would be unpaid, and she would need to tell her parents that she would not be at home for the anniversary of Freddie's death. It would be the first time since he had been killed that they would not be together as a family, but Caroline was relieved to have this excuse to be somewhere else. She had a strong feeling now that she was living her life in a way Freddie would have approved of, perhaps even encouraged. She knew her father would be unlikely to raise any objections, but her mother was another thing entirely.

However, Elizabeth had been troubled by a cough which was becoming worse and had been finding it difficult and tiresome to eat very much. She had lost some weight and the day Helen's letter arrived, Elizabeth went early to bed without any dinner. Caroline told her father of her plans, and as expected he did not try to dissuade her from going. He said he would tell Elizabeth when she was feeling better.

Caroline was more worried about asking Mrs Chandler for the time off work. She waited until lunchtime the following day and then hung back when the other girls had gone to collect their food. Mrs Chandler looked up from the tail piece she was inspecting as Caroline approached.

"Mrs Chandler, I was wondering if I might have a few days off."

"How many days exactly?"

Caroline had already decided to err on the side of caution, "This Friday and all of next week please. I know it's more than a week, but some friends have asked me to go away with them. If you don't think you can hold my position open for me, I quite understand."

Betty Chandler shook her head and put the tail piece down, "It's not so much that I can't hold it open for you, it's more that it might make you a candidate if we need to let any more girls go."

"I rather thought I would be in any case."

"Not necessarily. Your work is neat and quick. But it would be difficult for me to justify keeping you on having so recently taken time off. Other girls have had no holiday at all this year."

"Would it be better if I resigned? You could fill my place properly then."

"No. No I can hold your position. For now. Understand?"

Lottie was rather less enthusiastic about Caroline's trip. She had grown fond of their lunches together and chats as they left the works each evening.

"Your aunt says I can come back, so it'll only be for a few days."

"Do you want me to tell Robert?" she was used to being the messenger now.

"Would you? Make sure he understands that I'm going with Helen and that Tommy is absolutely not a rival."

Friday was bright and crisp, though the air was cool. Elizabeth was still in bed when George left for work that morning. He told Caroline not to worry, to enjoy her trip and that he would ask Dr Riley to call that evening to give her mother a tonic. Caroline couldn't help but be concerned; her mother hadn't had any significant illness since Freddie's death. She hoped it wasn't a ploy to make her think twice about going away again.

Annie presented Caroline with a sandwich wrapped in brown paper to take on her journey,

"Just in case it gets late before you have your dinner," she said.

Caroline tucked it into her bag and placed her bag on top of her case which stood waiting in the hallway. It was almost three o'clock and she put on her coat to wait for her friends. Twenty minutes later there was a blast of a horn outside.

Tommy's current car was large with red leather sprung seats and a top that could be lowered on sunny days. This was not one of those days, and Caroline was thankful to be provided with a plaid travelling blanket as she sat in the rear. Helen was looking refined in a navy woollen suit and navy fur-trimmed coat. Tommy sported a tweed jacket and yellow waistcoat, his hair slicked back with pomade under his cap.

They had gone as far as Worcester when Tommy asked the girls if they could hear anything odd. They could not, but both were less than familiar with the natural sounds of the internal combustion engine. Tommy's frown grew as they approached Birmingham and they agreed that he should drop the girls off at the Grand Hotel where they had arranged rooms and try to find a garage to look at the car. The hotel was on a more opulent scale that Caroline had imagined, despite its name. Marble staircases and tall mirrors on every wall made her think of the palaces she had read about in the 1001 Arabian Nights as a young girl. Helen of course was used to the surroundings and to the staff, and quickly took charge of their reservations having their luggage taken to their rooms and ordering dinner for the three of them.

Helen and Caroline were to share a room, with Tommy taking a smaller room along the landing. The girls had been changing for dinner and were about to go down to the dining room when Tommy knocked on their door.

"Just caught a chap as he was locking up. He'll take a look at our chariot first thing in the morning but thinks it's in need of an oil change."

"It won't hold us up for too long, will it?"

"If it's just the oil we should be back on the road by the after-noon. You gals can amuse yourselves in the morning no doubt?"

They went down to dinner together, and Caroline noticed that Helen drank only water with a squeeze of lemon juice in.

As they waited for their main course, Caroline asked if Tommy had been to Blackpool before.

"Oh yes, I spent most of my summers there as a boy. My uncle has a house just outside the town," he exchanged glances with Helen. Caroline didn't notice.

"I'm sure the lights will be wonderful. This is the first year since the war that they have turned them on, isn't it?"

Helen looked at Tommy, "I think we should tell Caro now."

"Tell me what?"

Tommy nodded. Helen took a sip of her water.

"We are not only going to Blackpool to see the lights. Tommy and I are going to be married."

Caroline's eyes opened wide, and her mouth gaped. "How? I mean, Helen you don't like… Tommy is… you are…" she struggled to form her thoughts.

Helen smiled, she had expected this reaction and had deliberately waited until they were between courses so that Caroline had no danger of choaking on her food.

"Darling, yes and yes, but don't you see, it's the perfect resolution to both our situations? My parents will be happy to have me out of their hair, and Tommy's father has been trying to persuade him to find a nice young girl for years. This way, everyone gets what they want."

Caroline dropped her voice, "But I don't understand how you two can get married. You don't love each other, not in the way a husband and wife ought to. And don't you have to be resident for weeks before you can be married?"

"That's the beauty of it all," said Tommy. "Uncle knows the Registrar in Blackpool and is willing to say I've been resident for the 15 days they require. No one is going to question it. So, Helen and I become man and wife, and then we plan to rent a little house somewhere. We thought Exeter or Exmouth."

"I'm sorry, I still don't understand."

"I think Caro means the sex," said Helen, rather too loudly for Caroline's liking. "If I were to marry anyone else, there would be such awkwardness should I wish to entertain a special friend. And Tommy simply courts controversy, and quite frankly the law, if he brings a friend home. But together, don't you see, we shall be sharing a house but not living in each other's pockets. I can be absent visiting a sick relative, and Tommy can be working away, and no one will question either of us. It's absolutely perfect."

The waiter brought the main course and no more was said on the subject until the girls were back in their room. Caroline had had time to consider the subject from all angles.

"You know, the more I feel I should condemn your plan, the more I can see why it is possibly the most sensible thing I've ever known you to do."

Helen laughed as she removed her make-up in front of the dressing table mirror.

"Sensible? Good lord, perhaps I should tell Tommy the whole thing is off!"

"The only fly in the ointment I can see, is if either of you fall in love with someone else."

"Well, they can either move in with us, or one of us will move out. Legally it won't make any difference. Neither of us will ever be able to marry someone we truly love, you know that. This way we preserve what little respectability we can salvage and keep our families happy at the same time."

"Will you be happy though Helen?" Caroline asked gently. She knew Helen had been deeply wounded by Lady Victoria's rejection.

Helen looked at Caroline's reflection in the large mirror.

"She is engaged to be married now too you know. Some archaeology or history professor she has met out in Egypt. Plans to stay out there with him."

"Oh Helen, I'm sorry."

"Don't be darling. I shall be perfectly alright with Tommy by my side. If you'll be our witness, we'll just need to find one other person to see us through."

The next morning after an extravagant breakfast of eggs, salmon, toast and several pots of coffee, Tommy went off to the garage and Caroline and Helen went to explore Birmingham's famous jewellery quarter. Caroline had never seen so many jewellers' shops so close together and the craftsmanship of the pieces was exquisite. Despite Caroline's insistence that Helen should not spend any more money on her and that an apology was not required to be accompanied by a gift, Helen still purchased a silver bracelet for Caroline along with a sapphire and diamond ring for herself. An engagement ring, she explained.

They amused themselves in the city art gallery for an hour, and then began to make their way back to the hotel where they hoped Tommy would be waiting with the car. As they took a circuitous route across Victoria Square to stroll along New Street, they noticed a crowd gathered around a speaker waving a handful of leaflets in the air. The girls moved closer, both curious to hear what was being said.

They found a gap in the crowd that they could see through without getting too close. There were several large, serious-looking men in long black overcoats and black leather gloves who appeared to be watching the crowd, and in front and centre of them a small woman with wild dark hair was aggressively challenging the onlookers. She wore men's clothes and no make-up. She also had a strong accent, and it was difficult for many to make out exactly what she was saying though they nodded in general agreement. Helen recognised the woman and after a few moments, tugged gently at Caroline's sleeve and indicated that they should go. As they turned to leave, two policemen approached and those at the edge of the crowd dispersed while the people closer to the woman remained. Caroline had only made out a few words, such as 'Jewish menace', 'monarchy' and 'communism'. Helen made sure they were well out of earshot before she slowed down and explained to Caroline who she thought the woman was.

"Her name is Maud; I've seen her around London. She is no more Italian than I am, but she adopts the accent because her hero is Mr Mussolini."

"The Italian? I was having trouble following what she said, I wish we had taken a pamphlet."

"No! No, we want nothing to do with women like Maud. Oh yes, it's all very well saying she was a Suffragette, just like Christabel Pankhurst, but you know today they want nothing to do with emancipation for women? They openly criticise Lady Astor and want to tear down the political establishment for goodness knows what ends. Really Caro, we are better off staying out of their way."

Caroline was surprised. Helen was not normally given to insightful political discourse, but she spoke with such strong conviction about the woman they had just seen that Caroline felt she should trust Helen's judgement.

"But why would one fight for something, only to achieve it and then turn against it?"

"I presume because they must have a cause to fight for. They are unsatisfied, and perhaps the grass was not greener for them after all. They have a particular dislike of the Jews for whatever reason and are fiercely against any further rights for women. One understands that they demand absolute obedience to their creed, and I suspect that is what caused them to step away from traditional conservatism. Father won't have them mentioned in his hearing. William got onto the subject a while ago and Papa almost exploded. He said he had fought one war against that kind of thing, and it should be the last war on the subject. He has been rather gloomy recently, he is convinced there will be another war, that too many ends were left untied."

"Surely not. Surely the world would not go down that path again? So many men lost and injured, and the cost of it all."

"Papa seems to think so. I really don't know Caro, but with women like Maud whipping up trouble perhaps Papa is right."

They took tea in the hotel lounge while they waited for Tommy to return. He bounded in just as they were emptying the pot and informed them that the chariot was running perfectly, and they should get off as soon as possible. It would take them around five hours to reach Blackpool by which time it would be dark. Tommy had a good idea of where he was heading but he still preferred to drive during daylight hours so that he could spot landmarks along the way. Caroline wondered if they would be staying with Tommy's uncle, but Helen said they had reservations at the Clifton Hotel.

Although Caroline had fallen asleep in the back of Tommy's car, she felt inexplicably tired when they arrived in Blackpool. The illuminations could be clearly seen and stretched for six miles along the seafront of the town. The hotel was less extravagant than the Grand in Birmingham and smaller in scale. The arched windows on the ground floor appealed to Caroline, and she was pleased to find that it looked out partially towards the sea. This time they each had a separate room and after dinner Caroline was relieved to excuse herself and go straight to bed, leaving Helen and Tommy in the hotel bar.

Sunday morning Caroline woke feeling refreshed. She dressed and put on her coat and hat and went out to walk northwards along the Promenade before breakfast. The wind buffeted her, and she had to keep her hand on her hat to stop it being blown into the sea. In the daylight she could see the wires and lightbulbs that made up the illuminations, along with the comical and sometimes grotesque tableau which were also lit up at intervals along the Promenade. She decided it all looked a lot more attractive in the dark. On reaching Blackpool's own Grand Hotel, she turned back. Caroline scanned the roof tops in search of a church spire or tower and spotted one which she thought was quite close to the Clifton Hotel. Not yet hungry, she detoured into the town and found the red stone and flint panelled exterior of Christ Church looming in front of her. She chuckled to herself that she had found the namesake of her own family church and went inside.

It was cold and dark inside the building. It smelled of hymn books and polish. Caroline sat tentatively on a pew near the door and looked up towards the altar. The stillness was oppressive. She had not expected to feel uncomfortable in a church, but she did at that moment. Caroline wondered if it was because of Helen and Tommy's plans. Could her knowledge of those be the reason her soul felt as if it were being inspected so minutely in that place. She knew the lifestyles of her friends went against the teachings of the Church. Did it matter? Was God truly a forgiving God, or a vengeful one? If he cared so much for humanity, and she had pondered this many times before, why would he allow humanity to fight itself with wars? Why did he take Freddie in the prime of his life? Tears prickled her eyes, and she took out her handkerchief and dabbed them.

Caroline enjoyed the companionship she felt at Saint Mark's. She respected the familiar routines at her own Christ Church. Was either of those things a belief in God? She shivered. There in the gloom, the silence and the cold, she felt there was no spiritual presence whatsoever. She got up to leave and stopped at the table near the entrance where the visitor book and various leaflets were laid out alongside a donation box. Caroline placed sixpence into the box, took a small raffia cross, and walked out into the daylight needing the company of others again.

She found Helen and Tommy in the dining room eating breakfast and the three of them soon planned their activities for the day. Tommy would visit his uncle, and Helen and Caroline

would walk out along the North Pier. They would all return to
the hotel for the afternoon and sit in the glass-roofed lounge
relaxing. Even in a busy seaside town there would be very little
in the way of entertainment on a Sunday.

Tommy was buoyant when they gathered again that afternoon. He had had a good lunch with his uncle and confirmed
the arrangements for the wedding which was due to take place
at ten o'clock on Tuesday. For the sum of three pounds and
five shillings their respectability could be assured. Tommy had
agreed to take Helen to meet his uncle once the wedding had
been concluded, with a suspicion that a considerable financial
wedding gift could be on the cards.

He was in such good spirits, he chattered on without
prompting to Caroline as Helen went outside into the courtyard
to smoke. Caroline learned that Tommy had been born in
Sheffield and had an older sister who sadly drowned on a family
holiday. His mother had taken her own life shortly afterwards
being unable to bear the grief. Tommy's father was a wealthy
businessman with interests in steel production and wireless
manufacturing. He was content to fund Tommy's interests as
long as he kept himself out of the newspapers and courts, and
the two rarely had any contact.

Tommy had been raised principally by a nanny after his
mother's death, until his father sent him to board at Salcombe
College in Devon. It was a Methodist school, though eclectic
in its educational outlook, and helpfully willing to overlook
Tommy's Jewish heritage. He had met Helen one Christmas
while staying with a friend in Plymouth and the two had
hit it off immediately. Tommy was interested in modern art,
particularly sculpture, and was keen to create a studio where
he could indulge his novice enthusiasm. It had been his idea to
try and find a home somewhere between Exeter and Exmouth.
He felt the light there was particularly good. Helen had been

indifferent to it until they visited during the summer; then she had loved the estuary and the view across to Dartmouth. While she adored London's social scene, her heart was in the Devonshire countryside.

"So, you will become an artist. What will Helen do, do you think?"

"I rather think she will find some local political cause to get behind. She is such a good organiser, and she instinctively knows what needs to be done."

"She'll spend all of your money, you know."

Tommy laughed. "She's welcome to every penny! What is money for if not to spend? You're shocked? I want to settle down Caroline, I'm tired of all the escapades and the brief encounters. Oh, I know I'm only twenty-five, but I feel I've already lived a hundred years and forgotten most of them. There is so much pressure in town to be this, do that, know everyone and hate most of them. To be seen in the right places – and right for whom I ask you? There is no substance, no honesty, I can't stand it. I feel a freedom when I paint, and I want to get that freedom back again."

"Is London truly that bad?"

"You don't know the half of it. Everyone is false, everyone spends their entire time pretending. Have you read any of G. K. Chesterton's Father Brown stories?"

Caroline shook her head. Her literary tastes were eclectic, and she had enjoyed Mrs Christie's recent novels alongside P. G. Wodehouse's Jeeves and Bertie Wooster. She had brought a copy of Virginia Woolf's *Night and Day* to read while in Blackpool and had just finished *The Mark of Zoro*, but Father Brown had so far passed her by.

"I'm not familiar with them."

Tommy looked across the room as Helen returned. "I think every generation believes the ones before them had it best. There is a comfort in reading about bygone days where things were clear and right. If I could live in Father Brown's world, I would jump at the chance."

Helen sat down, "Whose world, darling?"

"Father Brown."

"But he's a Catholic, Tommy. You'd be doubly damned in his world. Are we dreaming of living in novels?"

Tommy shook his head, "The stories were serialised in the *Evening Standard*. I suppose they might appear as novels one day."

"Which novel would you live in if you could?" Caroline was keen for Helen to go next as she was struggling to think of her own answer.

"I think more than one novel. I have always liked the Claudine stories; I could live in the last century in France I believe."

"Mine would have to be the communities that Thomas Hardy wrote about, I think. Perhaps Little Hintock in the *Woodlanders*. Somewhere like that. I don't think I would like to live anywhere too busy; one likes some quiet to return to."

"Yes," agreed Tommy, "some quiet to return to. I like that."

On Monday at breakfast Helen announced that she would require a new outfit to be married in. Caroline and Tommy exchanged rolling of eyes, but then Caroline decided to play the matron of honour dutifully and suggested that some flowers might also be in order. Tommy exclaimed that he hadn't bought a ring, to which Helen thrust her hand forward.

"I have!" she said, turning the ring so that the light caught the sapphire.

"No, that's not a wedding band dear heart. You shall have a respectable gold curtain ring tomorrow. I'm sure I can sniff out a jeweller's here."

"Let's go shopping this morning then and meet for lunch at the Centre Pier," Caroline suggested and the others agreed.

There was no large department store in the town, but the girls found a small women's outfitters that had some fashionably dressed mannequins in the window. The matronly assistant at first tried to suggest that Helen have something made for her, but once the urgency was explained she brought out several dresses for Helen to try on.

"Do you know, I really don't feel I can wear white," Helen was looking over her shoulder at her reflection in a long mirror while trying on the third dress in that colour.

"Madam did say she was to be a bride."

"Yes, but it is also November. Something smart in claret or mustard would be better, with a matching jacket. Do you have such a thing?"

While the assistant was retrieving what she hoped would clinch the sale, Caroline whispered to her friend, "Claret? Are you sure?"

"Why not?"

"I thought you were aiming for respectability."

"So, nothing backless then," Helen grinned mischievously.

Twenty minutes later they emerged from the shop having given instructions for the outfit to be delivered to the hotel later that day.

"An absolute bargain, I should have purchased two!" teased Helen as she linked her arm through Caroline's, and they headed towards the sea.

That evening after an earlier dinner, the three friends strolled south along the seafront joining the considerable crowds who still thronged the streets during the winter evenings. They watched the gayly lit 'gondola' tram as it trundled up and down, passengerless but with a driver and two conductors aboard. Tommy bought a swirl of candyfloss on a stick to share, and they watched a variety show at the end of the pier which included some Pierrot clowns. As part of their act, they walked through the first few rows of the audience handing out paper flowers to some of the ladies.

Caroline received one, with the clown pretending to swoon in her presence which made her giggle. As they walked back to the hotel, they took turns to mime an action suggested by the other two with Tommy exaggerating his actions so wildly that he almost knocked an elderly gentleman over the railings and into the sea.

There was still one thing to organise as Helen dressed and applied her make-up and Tommy shaved and tied his bow tie on their wedding morning: the second witness. Tommy had been strangely reserved and almost disinterested in the subject when Caroline had raised it the evening before. He simply waved her concerns away and said that someone would turn up. The girls breakfasted in the hotel, but Tommy had said he would be eating elsewhere as it would be bad luck to see his bride before the ceremony.

Helen admitted to nerves. She paced, smoked, and fidgeted until Caroline suggested another walk along the seafront. Helen shook her head.

"I will have a gin. My last day as Miss Postgate, I think I am permitted," she announced.

Caroline was keenly observing her friend. She had experienced a birth, christening and now a wedding that year but thankfully no funeral. It had exceeded any expectations she may have had when she had resolved to ask her father for an allowance twelve months ago. Caroline had learned a lot about the intricacies of human interaction, and while she still felt she was catching up, she had at least joined the race.

As they put their coats on to leave, Caroline suddenly remembered an old saying.

"Do you have something old, new, borrowed and blue?"

Helen thought for a moment, "Old shoes, new dress, blue ring, but nothing borrowed."

"Here, borrow this," Caroline delved into her case and pulled out a clean handkerchief, "now you can get married."

They arrived at the Registrar's office with five minutes to spare. There was no sign of Tommy, so they took seats in the corridor outside the office door. Helen glanced at her watch and tapped her fingers on her handbag while Caroline held the posy they had chosen on the way. Then they heard footsteps running up the stairs and onto the landing came Tommy, followed by James.

The girls got to their feet.

"I thought you were going to stand me up!" scolded Helen, brushing invisible hairs from Tommy's lapels.

"Whatever are you doing here?!" Caroline was too stunned to object to James kissing her cheek.

"Got the train up last night," he tried to get his breath back, "Tommy telegrammed. Said he'd explain when I got here. Met me at my hotel this morning. Glad I wore a decent suit. Got to go back this afternoon."

"You're not staying? Oh, that's a shame. But it's a lovely surprise to see you again."

The office door opened, and the Registrar ushered them inside. A few minutes later, Mr and Mrs Gersen-Fisch reappeared in the corridor followed by James and Caroline. Helen turned to Caroline as they reached the top of the stairs.

"I believe the done thing is to throw one's bouquet for the bridesmaids to squabble over. But as there is only you darling, I shan't spoil it by throwing it," she passed the flowers to Caroline, looked at James for a moment, and descended the stairs.

Caroline held them, feeling acutely aware that James was standing next to her.

"Not husband material, remember?" he whispered as he placed his hand gently on her back and they followed their friends out into the street.

The wedding breakfast was tea, coffee and cream buns in a Lyon's café. Tommy insisted on telling everyone that he had just got married until Helen said she would divorce him if he didn't shut up. It seemed no time at all before James looked at his watch and got up to catch his train back to London. Caroline followed him to the door as Tommy paid the bill.

"Have you decided yet if you will go to America?" she asked.

He rubbed his chin with his hand and looked off towards the sea as if he could see the New York skyline on the horizon, "I'm still trying to decide between there and Europe. I have contacts in both, it will all depend on who comes through first."

"It's been lovely to see you again," Caroline didn't know what else to say, despite having told James twice already.

He smiled, "You too Caroline. I hope it's not too long before the next time."

Again, he kissed her cheek as Tommy and Helen joined them outside the café.

And then he was gone. Caroline followed Helen and Tommy along the path towards the Winter Gardens where they had agreed to spend the afternoon. They chattered on about mutual friends, but Caroline wasn't paying attention. She could still feel James' lips brush her cheek and smell the coffee on his breath. She had wanted to go with him. Not necessarily back to London, but to be wherever he was. The moment had passed so quickly, she had no opportunity to organise her thoughts and ask if she might travel with him perhaps as far as Birmingham. A few more hours in his company, even if they were mute the entire journey. It was impossible. He had no time to devote to her, he was pursuing his career and that would take him from theatre to film studio around the world. She wanted to travel, but not to follow in someone else's wake. She wanted his attention, not to be sitting in a lonely room waiting for his return.

They entered the Winter Gardens and strolled amongst the tree ferns and other semi-tropical plants. They marvelled at the birds that lived in the glasshouses and then stepped outside again to take a turn on the big wheel. Caroline was very nervous as she climbed into the gently rocking gondola capsule, one of thirty on the ride, and as it moved off it began to sway more determinedly. Tommy and Helen seemed unafraid and peered out of the glass pointing out various landmarks. Caroline sat as far back on the bench seat as she could and closed her eyes tight as the gondola swung even more as it crested the wheel and began its descent. When she felt herself on the downward section again Caroline opened her eyes and hoped the other two had no noticed her fear. If she were ever to travel on an aeroplane, she would need to be braver that that!

Back on firm ground, Caroline suggested that she could return to Cheltenham the following day by train and allow Tommy and Helen to remain in Blackpool as long as they wished. They both protested that she was not being a gooseberry, but Caroline stood her ground. She was enjoying the town, and her friend's company, but James' appearance had unsettled her, and she had a nagging concern about her mother's health. She wanted to go home. They eventually accepted Caroline's proposal but all three of them agreed that for their final night in the town, and Tommy and Helen's first night of marriage, they would return to the Winter Gardens to the Empress Ballroom to dance the night away.

Alone in her room at the hotel before dinner, Caroline considered writing to James. She wanted to encourage him to follow his desire wherever it took him, and to simply write to her on occasion with news of his progress and achievements. She had no illusion that he would wait for her, or that he would expect her to wait for him, but she did not want him to disappear from her life completely. She sat on her bed and wondered how she might take the news of his finding love elsewhere. It was bound to happen eventually. She would not throw herself on the floor and have a tantrum, nor take to her bed for weeks on end. She shook her head; she would continue with her own life. If their paths crossed again, she would take pleasure in his company for those fleeting moments until fate took him away again. She would be satisfied with that. She did not write to him.

James spent almost the entire train journey back to London remembering Caroline's smile and the touch of her cheek, over and over again.

Helen slept in late the next morning having said copious goodbyes to Caroline the evening before. Caroline's first train left Blackpool at eight fifteen and she would have several changes before she arrived back in Cheltenham. Tommy accompanied her to the station, carrying her case onto the platform.

"Thank you again for being our witness, Caro. I'm sorry we had to behave in such a clandestine way, but Helen so wanted you to be here she didn't want to risk you saying no."

"I think I would have agreed had I known in advance. I care a great deal for Helen, Tommy, I would hate to see her as upset as she was in London."

"Message received and understood. I truly think we'll be alright. As soon as we get back to Devon, we shall start looking for a house. You'll come and see us again when we've found one, won't you?"

"Of course. I think this is my train," she picked up her case and they kissed each other's cheeks. "Goodbye Tommy, and good luck!"

13

FLORENCE

The house was in darkness when Caroline arrived home. She found Annie in the kitchen darning a sock and the girl jumped with a start as Caroline appeared in the doorway.

"Lord! Miss Caroline, I didn't hear you come in! We weren't expecting you until Friday. Let me put the kettle on for some tea, you must be hungry?"

"Annie, why are all the lights off? Where are my parents?" She sat on the wooden chair and watched Annie bustle around the room.

"The fire is lit in the parlour, but Sir said not to bother with the lights until he gets home. He's visiting your mother at the hospital and said he'd be home around nine."

"The hospital?" Caroline felt her concerns had been accurate.

"Doctor Riley came Saturday evening, and then came back with the ambulance on Sunday morning. Caused a right stir in the street it did, Mrs Arthur at number twelve was hanging over her gate like a ghoul!"

"What was Doctor Riley's diagnosis? Annie, I have no interest in Mrs Arthur, tell me what you know of my mother please."

Annie placed a cup and saucer on the table in front of Caroline, "I think it might be best for your father to tell you. He knows the details."

"Tell me what you know, Annie."

Annie bit her lip. Given the closeness of their ages, it sometimes put her in a difficult position. She looked at the young woman in front of her, smuts on her face from her multiple train rides that day and tiredness as well as concern in her eyes.

"Your mother has a lump on her side. She hadn't told anyone. Even your father didn't know. The Doctor said it's causing her cough, and he's got her into the hospital so he can try some special treatment. I don't know what it is, but it has to be done there."

Caroline swallowed. Lumps were cancer, she knew that. Cancer killed people. Not always straight away but surviving a year would be optimistic.

"Thank you for telling me," she said quietly. She drank her tea in silence and then took a sandwich in to the parlour to wait for her father. Annie mentioned that there were letters waiting for her in her room, but she was in no hurry to read them. She asked Annie to see to her case and sat next to the fire listening to the crack and hiss of the coal and beech wood as they burned.

At a quarter to nine her father arrived.

"Annie, I thought I said not to bother with the lights tonight," he called out and went straight into the parlour to turn them off. Caroline rose to her feet when she heard his voice and went to him. She felt as if she were fourteen again and learning of her brother's death. George took her into his arms and stroked her hair.

"Dear girl. We weren't expecting you. Is everything alright?"

Caroline looked up at him, "Yes, but it's not alright here is it."

"No. Rather the opposite I'm afraid. Has Annie explained?"

"She said mother has a lump. What is the treatment doctor Riley wants to try?"

"Some form of radiation therapy. It is very new and somewhat experimental as I understand it. Your mother had the first dose yesterday. Doctor Riley warns that she might feel much worse before she feels better, and today she has been rather poorly."

"But she will feel better?"

They both felt they knew the answer. George gently disentangled himself from his daughter.

"We very much hope so. But tell me, how are you here again so soon? Are you sure nothing is wrong?"

They sat, either side of the fire, and Caroline retold her long weekend. George listened attentively, asking for more details now and again. He too had heard of Maud and the concerns of some of the activists who felt the workers were gaining more than their station allowed. He laughed and then stopped himself as Caroline explained the marriage rationale. He cared little how people lived their lives in the privacy of their own homes and felt strongly that the law overreached itself in those matters. He paid attention when Caroline spoke of James' brief appearance. The way her face softened, and her voice became lighter. He nodded when she said that she just had a feeling she should be at home and thanked her for acting on her feelings.

"I am glad to have you back again my dear and I am sure your mother would very much like to see you tomorrow. You could visit after lunch, or we could go together; I will go directly to the hospital from the office so I could meet you there."

"Can I decide in the morning? I think I should like to go to bed now. It's been a very long day."

The letters remained unopened until the following morning at breakfast.

5 November 1925
Pangbourne
Dear Caroline,

 I thought, as you are having such an exciting year, I should get this invitation to you as quickly as possible! Mother says you are most welcome to spend the weekend before Christmas with us again this year if you have nothing else in your diary.

 It's been all change here again too. Matthew has taken a cottage on the estate and he and Kate will be married in February. Luke passed his finals and is now Doctor Frampton. He's working at the Royal Berkshire Hospital in Reading at the moment, and we hardly see him as he is sharing a house with three other young medics. He says it's easier when he has to work nights.

 Did I tell you Mark was thinking of doing some missionary work? He has applied for a post in Tanganyika which is Africa in case your geography is rusty. If he goes, I'm thinking of joining him out there when I finish my teaching course. I think that would give you a run for your money in the excitement stakes! Mark's post would be for two years, but I am considering six months. Long enough to decide whether I am suited to the climate.

 I won't say anything more. If you can come and stay, we'll have lots to discuss. Do let me know what you decide as soon as possible. Term here finishes a couple of days before that weekend, so I'll be able to meet you from the train again.

 Au revoir
 Midge

The second letter, Caroline noticed as she opened it, was postmarked Winchcombe.

8 November 1925
Cheltenham
Dear Caroline

As we agreed, I have trekked across the Cotswold hills in the hope that this arrives safely in your hands!

I have been in discussion with Oscar Gerrard, the owner as you might know of Gerrard's Department Store in Gloucester. He is putting on a fashion show in the evening of Saturday 12 December as a charity event for the Royal British Legion and I've been engaged to take the publicity photographs. There is a chance that a national newspaper will take them up, so it will be good for business on both our parts. I am telling you this my dear because models are required to wear the clothes and I rather hoped that you might like the opportunity. Did you also mention to me once that your neighbour is as tall as you? Would she be interested too do you think? You would both be recompensed for your time, and there is the possibility of a new outfit or two. What do you say?

I need to let Gerrard know by Friday 27 November, so if you have time on Saturday please call in to the shop.

Yours

Elsa

George had been watching Caroline's expression while she read and as she folded away the second letter he asked if it were good news.

"Midge has invited me to stay again just before Christmas. I'd like to go, but if Mother is still sick then…"

"If you want to go, then go. Your mother is in the best hands, and we two can do nothing more to aid her recovery."

"Well then yes, I should like to go. Midge is such a brick, and she says she might be joining her brother in Africa next year so I might not have a chance to see her again for a while."

"Then you must go. And the second letter?"

"Father, I know you and mother said I shouldn't associate with Elsa House, but she is my friend, and I cannot cut her off completely because of something in the past that I had nothing to do with."

"If I remember correctly, we asked you to terminate your employment with her. Your mother may indulge in some social engineering, but I will not tell you who you can or cannot be friends with Caroline. You are of age now and can make those decisions for yourself – whatever the outcome."

Caroline explained Elsa's proposition. George finished his eggs and drank the last of his tea. The clock on the mantle told him he would have to leave for work in no more than ten minutes. He might be senior accountant but that did not mean he could arrive late to the office.

"I think if you can persuade Florence to accompany you, it would make for an interesting evening. We should all support the Royal British Legion, it's a most suitable charitable cause. I can see we shall have to purchase a new wardrobe for all of the clothes you are accumulating," he smiled at his daughter, and she laughed, happy to have his blessing.

Caroline called on Florence later that morning. Florence had always been ambitious. Caroline often wondered if it sprung from a desire to keep up with the girls Florence had been schooled with. Her great aunt's funding of schooling and travel had been designed to enable Florence to attract the most desirable suitors that her teacher parents could not hope to find by themselves. Caroline also suspected that she was viewed by the great aunt and by Florence herself as a little lower in status that Florence should associate with. They would talk over the garden wall as they grew up, but only occasionally went into society together, and almost always at Caroline's instigation.

Their houses were mirror images of each other, but in some ways, Caroline noted, Florence's was plainer, less richly furnished. Their maid did not live in as Annie did; she worked every weekday and walked from St James every morning, worked for two hours until eight, then returned at four and worked until nine. Caroline and Florence sat in the parlour, which was chilly despite a small fire glowing in the grate.

"So you see," Caroline continued, "the show is for the department store, but the photographs could be seen across the country. London even."

"And we might be able to keep some of the clothes?"

"That's what my friend says. I'd like to let her know today, and I will definitely be taking part."

"Then I shall too. It will be amusing. How shall we get to Gloucester?"

"By train I presume, unless you know anyone with a motor car?"

"I do. Josiah will drive us."

"Mr Curzon? Does he have a motor car? I thought he only had a lorry for his business."

"He bought one only last week. It is so inconvenient to rely on the railway."

"Florence, is that a new ring?" Caroline could not help but notice the diamond on Florence's left hand, as Florence had been fiddling with it the whole time they had been talking.

"This? Why yes. It was a present."

"Should you be wearing it on that finger?"

Florence lifted her head and looked directly at Caroline, "I believe so. Josiah has been a complete gentleman. Once the sale of the land is complete, we shall be married."

"What sale? What land? You mean his glasshouses? His business?"

"Yes. Josiah is selling the portion of his land on the other side of Queens Road to a business associate. I believe they will be building some houses there."

Caroline was shocked. The glasshouses were a landmark in the town, and without them surely some of the men who worked at the nursery would also lose their jobs. Would that include Jim Cox? Then she registered the other piece of information that Florence had given.

"Did you say married?"

Florence giggled, "Yes! Isn't it just too amusing? Mother and Father are pleased, but Aunt Isobel was beside herself over it all! She refers to Josiah as 'the tradesman', but now that Josiah is selling the land she is warming to the idea."

Caroline shook her head. She could see clearly the attraction on both sides. Unlike Helen and Tommy's unconventional marriage, Caroline could not see this as being a happy one once the initial flush of good will had subsided. She made her excuses, wished Florence well, and returned home.

In her room, she emptied her carpet bag of the clutter she had accumulated over the weekend. Annie had taken care of the clothes in the case, but these were Caroline's more personal items. She took the keepsake box from underneath her bed and opened the lid. It was slowly filling, but mostly with half-tickets from cinema trips. Caroline added the raffia cross and trimmed the wire stem of the paper flower from the Pierrot clown so that it would also fit diagonally into the box. She smiled as she remembered the clown patting his chest to signify his beating heart. A pretend love, but one that felt good regardless.

When she met her father that afternoon, Caroline had had time to digest Florence's news and had discussed it all with Elsa. The evening was dry, so father and daughter walked the short distance from the Building Society office through Sandford Park to the hospital. George was interested in the proposed land sale, particularly as it would lead to more houses being built near to their own. He was not altogether convinced that in the current climate that would be a good thing; there were already too many vacant properties in the town although they were mostly the large Georgian homes around Suffolk Square and Montpelier, and on the road to Charlton Kings.

"And you say Florence and Mr Curzon are to be married after the transaction has been completed? Well I never. Your mother's ambitions have succeeded, although in somewhat the wrong direction!"

"I would never have married Mr Curzon, father. He is much older than I am, though that doesn't seem to have put Florence off the idea."

"He is a good man, honest, industrious. I have no wish to blacken Florence's character, but it would seem that it is not necessarily Josiah Curzon himself that she finds attractive."

"I am learning that people marry for many different reasons. You and mother married for love though, didn't you?"

"We grew to love, to understand and to live together. Our families brought us together and all agreed that it would be a suitable match. Things were a little different then. Had our parents not contrived the arrangement, I may never have married at all. There are very few women in my field of employment as you know. I'm sure your mother would have found a match, but for myself a life of bachelorhood would have been most likely."

"Would you be terribly upset if I never married?"

"My dear, I would be terribly upset if you married because you felt you should. If you are to spend the rest of your life with someone, please make sure you at the very least enjoy their company!"

Elizabeth lay in the white metal bed beneath the white starched sheets with her eyes closed as Caroline and George approached. Matron had informed them that Elizabeth had been vomiting earlier that day from the treatment but that they could see her for a few minutes. Caroline hesitated as she recognised her mother; she looked so small, frail and paper thin. Almost transparent against the white surroundings. Elizabeth's hair, normally rolled and pinned in the Edwardian style was now draped in a single plait over her shoulder. There was far more white hair in it than Caroline remembered.

The noise of the chairs being placed by her bed stirred Elizabeth and she smiled at her family as they sat down. George took her hand, feeling it to be cold and as light as a feather in his own.

"Any better my dear?" he asked. What else could one say, he thought. Obviously, she was not better, the treatment was as Doctor Riley had warned making her worse, and they must trust that eventually she would turn the corner and regain her vigour.

"A little. I have slept and had some broth. Food makes me cough so," Elizabeth's voice seemed childlike and far away.

Caroline talked of the seaside and her ride in the big wheel. She carefully left out details of the wedding, of James, and also of Elsa's modelling opportunity. Neither she nor George mentioned Florence's engagement to Josiah Curzon. After ten minutes had passed the Matron came over and said she thought Elizabeth needed more rest. They said their goodbyes, and Caroline waited outside the hospital entrance while George had a few words with Doctor Riley. When he re-joined Caroline at the bottom of the steps, he looked ten years older.

"What did Doctor Riley say?"

"He wants to keep your mother in the hospital for another week to see how she progresses with the treatment. Her vomiting is a concern to him as she is taking so little nutrition. We must trust him Caroline and pray."

They walked home in silence, each with their own thoughts sent skywards.

Caroline decided to return to the engineering works the following morning, in the hope it might place her in good favour with the managers. Mrs Chandler was pleased in her understated and business-like way to have Caroline back again, and Lottie was desperate for news of her trip but had to wait until lunchtime for it. The girl from the dope room who had been standing in for Caroline was sent back again, and Caroline was paired as usual with Gwen. Mrs Chandler astutely guessed that Caroline would work most efficiently that day if she was not asked a thousand questions at the same time as trying to knot the rough thread through the canvas.

Their half hour lunch was insufficient for Lottie to glean every detail, and Caroline suggested Lottie might like to have dinner with her that evening to continue their conversation. Lottie was reluctant, suddenly ashamed of her work outfit, but Caroline explained that her father would be visiting her mother and it would just be the two girls. As they walked over the bridge that spanned the railway lines, Caroline pointed out the glasshouses that were to be sold.

"And your neighbour is to marry him?" Lottie shook her head in disbelief, "I know Mr Curzon, father knows him. But he's old Caroline, as old as father at any rate. I wouldn't marry a man that old. Would you?"

"No. Mother had ideas we might make a match, but I would never have agreed, and I don't think my father would have approved if it had come to a proposal. But you see Florence's parents are teachers and she wants more from life I suppose. They might be gloriously happy together and have fifteen children!"

"I'd only marry a man I loved," declared Lottie, "he'd have to have a job, and be taller than me, and have a good manner. I want him to make me laugh and take me dancing on a Saturday."

"Lottie that sounds suspiciously like Eric."

Lottie blushed, "Who would you marry then?"

James flashed into Caroline's mind. For goodness' sake she said to herself, how many times must he tell you he would not make a good husband? Better not say Bob though, or anyone remotely like Bob.

"Someone like my father," she replied.

Florence was standing at her gate as the girls arrived at number 20. Caroline introduced Lottie, and Florence announced she was waiting for Josiah to collect her in his motor car as they were having dinner with friends of his in Prestbury. Lottie complemented Florence on her hat, which was tied in place with a scarf knotted under Florence's chin. Florence smiled graciously, and the two girls went indoors.

"She thinks she's the Queen of Sheeba!" exclaimed Lottie when the front door was firmly closed.

Josiah's car adequately accommodated Florence, Caroline, Elsa and her photography equipment as they set out for Gloucester. They had agreed to leave Elsa's shop at five thirty so as to allow time for the girls to try on the clothes to be modelled and decide who looked best in which outfits. Elsa was dressed as usual in a man's suit, her hair freshly trimmed. She had had several conversations on the telephone with Oscar Gerrard to ensure the arrangements were satisfactory and had struck a hard deal over the rights to the photographs. He had wanted to retain the rights over everything Elsa developed from the show, but she had insisted that he could have two pictures of every outfit modelled and she would keep the rest.

Caroline and Florence were excited to be wearing the range of day and evening wear that would be all the rage in the Cotswolds the following spring. They were met by a rather stern, small woman with spectacles on her nose and a tape measure around her neck. She introduced herself as Mrs Gordon, head seamstress, and gave the girls a quick lesson in moving on the catwalk. Josiah mumbled that he would go and have a pint in the George Hotel bar opposite the department store and would see them later on.

Elsa set up two cameras; one at the end of the catwalk which had been constructed on the first floor of the store in what was usually the furniture department, and the other to one side behind the rows of chairs. She had arranged for Peter to catch the train and join them at six thirty so that he could operate the camera at the side, and she could concentrate on full-front shots. Elsa had a feeling that this could be a lucrative departure from her usual portraiture business, and despite his nerves, Peter was a fast learner and keen.

All of the one hundred tickets had been sold for the fashion show. It was a novelty in Cotswold society, and to benefit a cause such as the Royal British Legion with Remembrance Day still fresh in people's minds was a winning combination. The eight models each had four outfits to display. Changes between outfits were frantic, with zips getting caught and buttons needing to be resewn. Mrs Gordon hovered nervously, safety pin in hand and pin cushion around her wrist on a length of elastic, as she watched her creations float out on to the catwalk and then be hurriedly discarded in turn for the next.

Florence was in her element. It could be said that she was not exactly modelling the outfits but parading herself to the adulation of the crowd, but in that moment it didn't matter. She had the ability to pose, pause and turn with grace. She looked directly at the cameras despite being asked not to, forcing Elsa to take pictures she did not expect to use. Caroline enjoyed herself but knew she was not cut out to be a model. The flashes from the cameras made her blink with temporary blindness and she almost stumbled as she caught one flash full in the face. She also felt she didn't have the graceful flowing movement that Florence seemed to find so easy.

At the end of the show and the final parade of all eight models, the audience was ushered down to the women's wear department on the ground floor so that they could browse the garments and make purchases. Elsa left Peter to dismantle the equipment and found Caroline pulling on her sweater in a corner of the storeroom they were using as 'backstage'.

Florence had quickly gone down to the ground floor to mingle and continue her show as she had come to think of it.

"You were wonderful!" Elsa grinned over Caroline's shoulder into the mirror.

"I'm exhausted! And hungry. Those shoes didn't fit properly, I wish I could have simply worn my own," she turned to Elsa, "but it was fun. Did you get any good shots?"

"I won't know until I develop them, but I think so. Florence was certainly enjoying herself."

"She was made for this kind of thing. Pass me my bag would you."

Elsa handed over the handbag and Caroline dropped a brass safety pin in before pulling out a small brown paper bag which contained a cheese sandwich. Annie's emergency rations again. Elsa refused the bite Caroline offered and went to supervise Peter. She felt a flush of emotion as she had every time she had seen Caroline since she had first walked into the shop. She did not want to make a fool of herself, or to make Caroline feel awkward.

Florence would not leave until the last of the audience had gone and the doors had been firmly closed. It was almost ten o'clock and Josiah had been waiting patiently since half past nine when he and Elsa had finished loading his car with her equipment. Peter had gone to catch his train, and Caroline was trying to stay awake as she sat in her coat and hat on a chair by the door. The safety pin would be her addition to the keepsake box from the evening, as none of the clothes would fit inside. She had chosen a two-piece outfit in brown with geometric patterned borders and a matching jacket, and Florence had managed to acquire two outfits and a coat. Oscar Gerrard was entranced by Florence and was talking to her about a permanent engagement to be the Face of Gerrard's for 1926. Finally, Josiah took control and announced in his most official voice that it was time for him to take the ladies home.

14

LUKE

It was agreed that Elizabeth would return home for Christmas. George insisted that Caroline keep her engagement to visit Midge, and Caroline agreed but decided she would return on the Monday rather than the Wednesday as she had originally planned. Mrs Chandler had agreed to Caroline taking the Monday off; there was only one order on the books at that time and there was a general nervousness across the engineering works about the prospects for 1926. They would all have Christmas Eve, Christmas Day and Boxing Day as unpaid holiday, and there was no Christmas bonus to be had that year.

As she had managed to keep her job and not spend very much besides her train ticket home from Blackpool, Caroline's finances were in good order. She was confident she could remain in the black and still make some small purchases for Christmas presents while she was in Berkshire. There was a train she could catch at six-twenty on the Friday after work which with one change at Oxford would get her to Pangbourne at just after nine that evening. Midge would meet her at the little station, and it meant they could spend all of Saturday in Reading. That year's Christmas bazar had taken place the weekend before and there would be little else to entertain Caroline, Midge had said.

A few flakes of snow fell and mingled with the soot and steam from the train as Caroline stepped onto the platform at Pangbourne station again. A year had passed since she had been there before. She had learned a lot and felt that she was catching up fast with her peers at last. Midge called out to her from the platform entrance and Caroline picked up her case and went to meet her.

The tractor had been replaced with a small black car. Caroline expected to see at least one of Midge's brothers, but Midge herself climbed into the driver's seat and started the engine.

"When did you learn to drive?" Asked Caroline as the slowly made their way the short distance to the Vicarage.

"At college. One of the other girls has a car, and we've all been practicing in it. It's a little bigger than this one, and this old brute needs more brake, but it's more or less the same idea. Do tell me if I get too close to the hedge though, won't you?"

Midge parked the car in the road outside the Vicarage. As they entered the kitchen, Caroline was enveloped in Midge's mother's arms and welcomed heartily back to her home. Questions fell like raindrops; was she hungry, had she had a good journey, was the train crowded, was she tired, which room would she prefer (she had the choice of two this time)? Caroline answered in good spirits that she was thirsty but not hungry as she had eaten on the train, which had not been crowded until Oxford, and she would be happy in whichever room the Framptons could offer her. Midge put a kettle on the stove for tea and her mother disappeared to make sure Luke's old room was ready to receive her guest.

In the quiet of the kitchen, Caroline felt at home. She loved this rambling house and family the most out of all the places and people she had known over the past year. The way they took her in and made her one of their own immediately, and there were no airs or graces. Instead, there was lots of genuine laughter and a sense of support and closeness that would get them through the worst of times.

She was very tired though, and Midge was perceptive enough to insist that they take their tea up to the bedrooms and drink it with their shoes off and their feet up on the beds in her room. Caroline didn't protest as she might have done a year ago, though having food or drink in a bedroom when one wasn't ill at home would be unthinkable. Midge chattered on about the girls on her teaching course while Caroline sipped her tea. When they had finished, they went into Luke's old bedroom and Caroline apologised for being ready to fall asleep.

"That's alright," said Midge, "we have all weekend for you to tell me your news."

Caroline woke with a start the following morning, Saturday 19 December 1925. For a moment she thought she was back at Knapp House and was disappointed to realise that there would be no swimming in the pool or gazing out to sea in Pangbourne. She could smell bacon and dressed quickly. In the kitchen she found Midge, Reverend and Mrs Frampton, Mark and John around the big table. They made space for her between Midge and John, and a plate of bacon and eggs, fried bread and mushrooms was placed in front of her. The tea pot was refilled, and it became clear that she was the last to eat that morning. John excused himself shortly afterwards as he had to go to work. Mark left for his job at the garage half an hour later. The kitchen became quieter. Reverend Frampton would be visiting his parishioners in the hospital that morning and Mrs Frampton also had some calls to make.

"Matthew has his own home now?" asked Caroline as she finished the last morsel on her plate.

"Yes, he has one of the estate cottages. It's tiny but he says he'll add an extra bit on the side in the spring for a new sitting room and a second bedroom upstairs. Kate is looking forward to moving out of her lodgings too."

"They are to be married in February?"

"Valentine's day. A bit soppy, but they both wanted that date."

"I must tell you, Helen got married while we were in Blackpool."

"What! Helen? Who on earth to?"

Caroline retold the event of the Blackpool trip, this time not leaving out any mention of James. Midge was well aware of Helen's sexual preferences and was in agreement with Caroline that marriage to Tommy could be a success.

"As long as they stick to the rules they have set for themselves. I have never met Tommy, but he sounds like a jolly fellow. But tell me more about this James."

Caroline continued with her fragmented year, this time describing James' brief visit to Cheltenham and then moving backwards to her month in Dorset which she had already written to Midge about though not in much detail. Midge was enthralled. She was about to ask another question when she suddenly realised the time.

"Golly, shake a leg or we'll miss the train! Luke said he would meet us."

Caroline was expecting Reading to be somewhat similar to Oxford or Blackpool. While it was comparable in size, its architecture was very different. Almost every building was constructed of red bricks, with some patterning of white and grey bricks to show off the builders' skills. Much of the centre of the town had been built during the latter half of Queen Victoria's reign when the town underwent largescale expansion. Acres of workers homes, built in terraces radiating out from the commercial centre housed the railwaymen, brewers, biscuit and tin makers that flocked to the town from the surrounding agricultural villages across the county.

Unusually, Reading's great and good came from a Quaker background. The large Huntley and Palmer's factory employed several thousand townspeople, and its sister factory Huntley, Boorne and Stevens which made the biscuit tins and other metalware was the main alternative employment in the town. A third option was H & G Simonds, a brewery just out of the centre of the town. Famous for its red hop leaf motif, it owned over a hundred pubs around the town. Reading was famous for other things; the prison had housed Oscar Wilde, and King Henry VIII had plundered the town Abbey leaving the ruins to one side of the prison for the later generations to investigate and incorporate into the adjacent Forbury Gardens.

The town felt vibrant to Caroline. The shops were busy and there were several theatres and cinemas to entertain the populace. Caroline was amazed to see so many public houses; it seemed as if every other building was serving alcohol to the workmen of the town. She picked up the scent of beer on the breeze just a few moments after they left the railway station, and it mingled with fresh meat, fish and poultry smells that leeched from Union Street, an alley which ran between the main thoroughfares of Friar Street and Broad Street.

The girls skipped between the numerous trams and made their way over Bridge Street and up towards the Royal Berkshire Hospital. They agreed to return the same way and call into Jackson's department store which occupied a whole corner, later on. As they approached the hospital the crowds of people fell away, and the buildings changed from red brick to a style more familiar to Caroline; Georgian terraces and squares with gardens in the centre and substantial individual houses that she learned were mostly owned by the University College. They were heading to Luke's digs. He lived in a shared house a little way from his old halls of residence Wantage Hall.

Luke was closest to Midge in age, but the least similar of the five siblings to their parents. He was tall and blonde where the others were dark and of average height and Midge was the smallest of them all. There had been some comments around Pangbourne as one would expect, but he bore the same facial features of the rest of the family, and no one paid much attention to the gossips. All of the Gospels were good with their hands, but Luke's skill was with delicate surgery. He had been fascinated by the wounded soldiers who were sent to recuperate at Basildon House and had become determined to train as a doctor and specialise in surgery. Having achieved that earlier in the year, he had secured a position as a junior houseman at the hospital and worked extraordinarily long hours necessitating his lodging as close to the hospital as possible.

He met them in the street outside Wantage Hall.

"Dash it, I knew I was late. I'm so sorry, I truly meant to be at the station, but I had such a late night. How are you both?"

Midge gave her brother a hug, "I knew the way you'd walk so we thought we'd head you off at the pass. Caroline has had a guided tour of the town at any rate."

"What do you think of it?" Luke had turned back towards his home and the girls walked with him.

"It's rather crowded. But it has a nice feel to it. And the smells! I don't think I have been anywhere that has so many different scents on the wind as here."

"Do you know, I rarely notice them now, but when I first came to study here, I agree it utterly reeked of biscuits and barley. You will have come over the river, that smells rather rank in the summer. Oh and of course there are the horse sales that add to the mix, though I've managed to avoid the Allisons and their businesses so far."

He opened a wooden gate and ushered the girls up a brick garden path to a white rendered house with a dark green door. They went inside and through to the kitchen at the rear of the house. There was a walled brick courtyard outside the kitchen door with a privy on one side and a table with six chairs around it. Inside the kitchen the detritus of communal male habitation littered the surfaces. Luke looked around for some clean cups, failed to find any and suggested they walk down to a café on the London Road which he knew well.

When they were settled in the café at a table by the window, Caroline asked Luke what he had meant by 'the Allisons'.

"They are a big family here. Not entirely on the right side of the law the whole time, but respected – or perhaps feared – enough for it to not make much difference. They practically run the west of the town. They have a fish business, a horse business and various other irons in the fire."

"I suppose every town has its families like the Allisons. In Southampton there are the Fortunes. They are in the fish business too," Midge poured out the tea as she spoke.

Caroline tried to think of a similar family in Cheltenham, but she could not. There might be one, but her upbringing had shielded her from them.

"I can't imagine coming from such a large family," she said.

"I can't imagine not having my brothers around when I'm at home. It will be very strange when Mark goes away. It's been strange enough with you gone Luke, and you come home every couple of weeks."

"Do you have any brothers or sisters Caroline?"

Midge trod on her brother's foot under the table. "I'm sorry Caroline, my brother has a brain like a sieve. I did mention Freddie to him at least ten times."

"It's quite alright. My older brother Freddie was killed at the end of the war. It seems a lifetime ago now, but also as if it was just yesterday when we got the news."

"I'm so sorry. Midge is right, my brain doesn't hold everything that it should. What are you girls going to do for amusement today?"

"Shopping!" they both said at once.

The three of them walked back into town after Luke paid their bill. He also needed to visit Jackson's to pay his account. Caroline spent some time making her Christmas purchases, small items such as gloves and handkerchiefs, and an ink pen for Midge which she managed to hide in her bag after paying for it without the other girl seeing. She bought her father a navy-blue tie. She could not see anything that she thought her mother would like until the assistant who was attending to her mentioned some new jigsaw puzzles that had recently arrived. Caroline chose one with a bowl of roses.

When they had finished their shopping and had arranged to collect their purchases that afternoon, Luke suggested a trip to the museum. Midge yawned dramatically, but Caroline said she would like to go. As with their trip to Silchester, Luke's love of history meant he was able to give them an insightful commentary of the objects on display and Caroline was impressed at his knowledge. He was able to answer almost all of her questions, and the ones he couldn't he was not too proud to ask one of the room guides for more information. Invariably they knew less than he did. Eventually Midge found a chair to sit on and waited patiently for Caroline and Luke to emerge from viewing a collection of Elizabethan clay pipes. She wasn't entirely happy to play the gooseberry, but at the same time she found it intriguing how Luke was clearly enamoured by Caroline and she in turn was practically oblivious of it all.

Coming to the end of a long glass cabinet, Luke turned to Caroline, "Have you ever been to the Ashmolean Museum in Oxford? Or the Pitt Rivers?"

"No, never."

"Perhaps, in the new year, you would like to visit with me? I never tire of seeing their objects."

"What do they have?"

"Everything! The Ashmolean is much larger than this. They have many items of antiquity from all around the world. And the Pitt Rivers is, well, imagine an attic in a very old house stuffed with treasures and curios. I really couldn't do it justice by trying to describe it, you really have to see it for yourself."

"It sounds fascinating! I would love to Luke."

"Excellent! Do you have a telephone at home? My shifts at work are only agreed a week in advance and often change so I will need to let you know which day."

"No, I'm afraid we don't have a telephone. Any Saturday would be preferable though, I really shouldn't take any more time off work."

"Can we agree on the first Saturday in January, and then I shall send Midge to meet you if anything happens at this end. She knows Oxford as well as I do," he looked at his watch, "I really need to get to the hospital now. I hope you've enjoyed your visit here; I know I have."

They walked out of the gallery to find Midge.

"You are so very well informed, Luke, I very much enjoy talking to you and learning so much."

Midge got to her feet as they approached.

"At last!" she smiled.

"I need to get back to work, Midge. It's been lovely to see you girls today. If you are hungry, I recommend Benton's café in Harris Arcade. They serve an excellent Welsh rarebit."

He hugged his sister and hesitated, unsure how to bid farewell to Caroline. She smiled and offered her hand.

"Write and let me know when you are sure about visiting the Ashmolean museum," he said, then turned and loped off up the road towards the hospital.

That evening after dinner, the Framptons and Caroline settled in the library to listen to the news broadcast on their radio. Caroline was excited. Radio broadcasts were still a novelty to her, though she had listened to records on phonographs several times. The Marconi Company had begun to broadcast music, news and plays relatively quickly after their initial test messages, to encourage enthusiasts to try and pick up the signals on crystal sets further and further away from their base in Chelmsford. The newsreader spoke of the new Prime Minister in Portugal, of the filing for divorce in a Paris court of Natacha Rambova, wife of the screen star Rudolph Valentino, and a report from Italy on the banning of Christmas trees. The broadcast lasted for five minutes, and Caroline was spellbound the whole time.

When the radio was switched off, the family discussed what they had just heard. The fire burned brightly in the grate, the beer was comforting, and the atmosphere was calm and relaxed. Meg the black Labrador wandered in while they were talking and flopped down at the side of Caroline's chair, resting her head on Caroline's knee. The girl scratched the dog's head, which elicited a thump of Meg's tail on the wooden floor.

"She remembers you," said John with approval.

"I should like a dog one day. Though I think they would tie one to home rather," Midge said.

"Dogs are good company for children," Mrs Frampton said sleepily. "We have been fortunate to share Meg with the village. What are your plans for tomorrow, girls?"

"I thought we might go to church in the morning and then after lunch walk up to see Matty. If that's alright with you Caroline?"

"Of course. Oh, could I borrow some wellingtons?"

When Caroline woke on Sunday morning, the light had changed. The room felt very cold; she could see her breath as she sat up in bed. She got up and crossed to the small window to draw back the thin curtains. It had snowed in the night. The Vicarage garden was blanketed in at least three inches of snow. Caroline noticed there was no birdsong, just silence. She got back in to bed, pulling her clothes with her so that she could warm up again and then dress under the covers.

The walk to the church was picturesque. The snow that covered everything sparkled in the low sunlight and brought a rosy glow to everyone's cheeks. John remarked that it wouldn't take long before the snow turned to muddy slush, and they should make the most of the beauty of it all. Inside the church everyone kept their coats and scarves firmly on. Reverend Frampton, sensitive to the needs of his parishioners, instructed his organist to play with as much enthusiasm and tempo as possible and the congregation romped through the hymns with gusto. As John had predicted, the roads were already streaked with brown from car and cartwheels by the time they emerged again from St James the Less and headed back to the Vicarage for lunch.

The roast beef, roast potatoes and vegetables, smothered in rich brown gravy, was possibly the best meal Caroline had eaten that entire year. On her previous visit she had wondered how the Framptons appeared to have an endless supply of food. This time she understood that the villagers often grew or produced more than they could eat themselves and distributing the food around the village was the usual way of eliminating waste. This, coupled with the grateful donations of the Reverend's parishioners for his faithful service to their spiritual needs, meant the family's larder was always well stocked. On this occasion, the beef was from the estate farm, the vegetables from the root cellars of three homes, and the summer pudding was made from bottled red berries from the Frampton's own garden.

Caroline felt she would like a nap after the meal but knew that would be frowned on. She had brought the socks with her that Midge had given her before, and also the trousers that used to belong to Freddie. She changed into them after sitting for a few minutes on the bed with her feet up and then went to find Midge and the wellingtons. The girls set off through the melting snow, conscious that the sun would only light their way for a couple more hours. Midge took a wind-up torch along for the return trip though Caroline had half expected there to be quaint torches on poles.

The girls talked as they walked through the woods. It seemed they only had conversations with any depth when they were by themselves. Midge wanted to know more about James, and Caroline wanted to hear about the teacher training course and about Southampton. She mentally added it to her list of places to visit.

"How is your mother?"

"Not well I'm afraid. She will be coming home from the hospital for Christmas so perhaps that is a good sign. Doctor Riley is trying some radiation therapy on her, but it seems to be making her even more ill. I don't know Midge, I'm worried that it's more serious that anyone is saying."

"At least you'll be together for Christmas. Kate is going home to her parents, so we'll have Matty with us again this year. But next year they will be in their own home. It will be strange to not have him with us."

"Perhaps they will both want to spend Christmas with you at the Vicarage? Or at least come for Christmas luncheon. I would want to be at home for Christmas."

"Even when you have your own home? Wouldn't you want to spend Christmas there?"

Caroline considered the idea, "I think I might want to invite my family to spend the day with me. Or perhaps alternate each year. Goodness, how complicated things become when families start to spread out. I hadn't considered it before."

"I wonder what Christmas in Africa would be like," Midge climbed over a style and waited for Caroline to follow, "I wonder what food there will be."

"You will write won't you, and tell me absolutely everything you see and do there?"

"Of course. I just have to pass my final examination and then Mark is sure the community will offer me a position to teach in the school. And then there will only be John at home. I hope Mother will be alright."

They came to the crest of a small hill and turned left. Caroline could see a small cottage set back a little way from the track. Smoke curled from the chimney and the sound of a dull repetitive thump came to them across the hillside. When they reached to the cottage, they walked through the open garden gate and around to the rear of the cottage to where the noise came from. Matthew was in a small stone shed stacking a pile of wood that he had been splitting into logs for the fire. He had dragged the felled limbs from the woods the day before and explained to Caroline that they would need to sit in the shed and season until the following winter.

"These are not to use now?" She asked.

"No, this winter's fuel is in the store on the other side of the cottage. I brought that down on the cart in the summer. At least I don't have to buy much coal, the price is going up by the day I hear."

"Do put the kettle on Matty, we're freezing!" Midge stamped her feet and hugged herself to illustrate how cold she felt.

They did not stay long at Matthew's cottage. It was sparsely furnished; Matthew brought a chair through from the sitting room to the kitchen so that the girls could sit while he leaned against the chimney breast with a mug of tea in his hands. Caroline noted that his weaker arm did not appear to cause him too much inconvenience. He described the alterations that he had planned for the cottage, and how he wanted to build a chicken coop in the garden in the spring. He said Kate would be bringing linens back from her parents' house after Christmas, and they were saving for a large rug to cover the stone sitting room floor. They were hoping for a few small items for the cottage as wedding presents to help them settle in.

Caroline absorbed the information. Of course, she understood that new homes needed to be furnished, but she had only
thought about it on a superficial level. She was beginning to
understand that homes evolved over years rather than days or
weeks. Even Vic's apartment in London had furniture that must
have been in other homes before hers. She thought back to the
new house in Tavistock that Helen's father had bought; the rooms
there were much less cluttered than her own home because
the pieces of furniture and decorations had been placed there
deliberately and not accumulated over the years in that space. A
new home could be furnished how the owner wished and did
not necessarily have to accommodate too many of anything.

On their way back to the Vicarage, Caroline asked Midge
if she thought they would be making the same journey that
time next year.

"I hope so. It's becoming a tradition, and a long overdue one
if I might say so. I do wish you'd agreed to come and stay years
ago Caroline, it's so nice to have you here. I love my brothers,
but I have different conversations with you."

"Then let's agree now, if it's alright with your parents, that
I will stay again on the weekend before Christmas next year.
It will be something for us both to look forward to no matter
what happens or where we end up next year."

They linked arms as they walked the last stretch of road
towards the Vicarage.

Elizabeth was brought home two days before Christmas.
They used one of the doctors' cars and she sat in the back
seat with George at her side, her hand in his and a rug across
their knees. It was the first time she had been in a motor car,
as her trip to the hospital had been in an ambulance. Elizabeth
declined the offers to carry her indoors, or up the stairs. She
would not agree to be a spectacle again for the neighbours to
gossip about. Instead, she got slowly out of the car and walked

as upright as she could, clinging to George's arm until they were safely indoors. There she asked to sit again for a moment before tackling the stairs. Annie brought a chair from the dining room into the hall.

Eventually Elizabeth was returned to her bedroom. The fire burned in the grate, the curtains were drawn, and lamps were lit. It was almost three o'clock in the afternoon, but already growing dark. George stayed with her, sitting in the upholstered chair by her bed until Annie knocked quietly on the door and asked if they would like some tea. Elizabeth was asleep and George left the room and went downstairs.

George was in his office when Caroline arrived home that evening. She had been to visit Mary, Philip and Angelica as usual after work and had proudly finished the matinee jacket she had been knitting for the baby just in time for Christmas. Not wanting to linger, she had declined the offer of dinner and had left soon after sewing on the last button. Caroline went straight through to the kitchen to ask Annie to warm some soup up for her, and then went to find her father.

"Is mother home?"

"Yes, she is sleeping. Doctor Riley says she will sleep a lot and we are not to try and keep her awake. He believes sleep to be a good medicine."

"Does that mean there is no other medicine?"

"There will be no more radiation therapy, no. I'm afraid my dear that your mother may not recover from this," he could not meet Caroline's concerned grey eyes.

"I can sit with mother tomorrow if you are going into the office. I'm not due back at work until Monday." They both thought, like old times, but neither spoke of them.

"Thank you but I too am not needed until Monday. And I thought I might allow Annie to finish at lunchtime tomorrow if she can prepare us some meals that we can see to ourselves."

"I don't think I am in the mood for a large Christmas luncheon this year. If Annie can tell me what to do before she goes, I am sure I can cook for us and not burn the house down."

George smiled at his daughter. She had grown so much over the past year, in outlook and practicalities. He would not take that away from her now; he would engage a nurse if Elizabeth required one and not retract the freedom that Caroline had worked for. He knew she was in credit on their agreement, and he intended to honour his side of it and let her keep the fifty pounds.

Christmas Eve was cold with a heavy bone-seeking mist that lay across the town and muffled every noise. Caroline had given Lottie a hair comb with inlaid mother of pearl as a Christmas present, and also a small package which she asked Lottie to give to Bob. Inside was a woollen scarf of bright red, the same colour that Cheltenham Town footballers wore.

Before Annie left, Caroline gave her a small packet containing a pair of black woollen stockings. They had spent most of the morning together in the kitchen with Annie taking Caroline through the required cooking methods and times of the dishes she had prepared. Caroline made notes, as Annie was not a confident writer, and felt reasonably prepared given the tips she had also picked up from Mary.

"There was no need, really," Annie said, without opening the gift. "Your Father has been generous enough giving me the extra time off."

"You've been such a help to me this year, I wanted to get you something."

"I shall be back Sunday after church. You'll be going to Christ Church this weekend?"

"If Father wants to go, yes. I suppose we must see how Mother is feeling before we decide. I have felt no guilt this year when I haven't attended a service on a Sunday, and I doubt I shall if we decide not to this weekend either. Annie, I really think God finds us wherever we are."

Annie did not reply; she wasn't sure she understood what Caroline meant. Caroline went to the front door with her and as Annie waved from the garden gate, Bob appeared through the mist. Annie called out to stop Caroline closing the door and hurried past Bob to her family.

"Hello! This is a nice surprise, how are you? Do come in, it's so cold with this fog!"

Caroline stepped back into the hallway and Bob entered the house. He felt self-conscious in his work clothes as he had come straight from the early end to his shift. He had chosen not to take the extra pay and work on, so as to allow one of his workmates to reap the benefits this year. He would be back at the gas works early Saturday morning instead.

Bob tried not to stare at anything in particular, while taking in the Victorian style of the entrance hall with its polished wood and dark wallpaper. The mirror above the side table reflected his awkwardness and Caroline moved to stand in front of it.

"I've brought you a gift. For Christmas. Don't open it to-day, will you," Bob brought a very small packet out from his pocket, smoothed the brown paper with his fingers and then handed it to Caroline.

"Thank you! Did Lottie give you yours?"

"Yes, thank you. There was no need."

Why do people say that, thought Caroline. The need is Christmas, surely. To give and be happy in giving rather than receiving. Perhaps that was it, perhaps we should only give to people we know won't give us anything in return. She realised the silence was hanging between them.

"Would you like some tea? I know how to make that, and Annie has left us some scones. And we have jam," she smiled warmly hoping to ease Bob's obvious discomfort.

"Just a cup of tea would be nice, thank you."

George came down the stairs at that moment, "I heard voices." he said.

"Father this is Bob. Robert. Lottie's brother."

The two men shook hands.

"I am pleased to meet you, Bob. I hear you are a football devotee?"

"Would you like some tea Father?"

"Indeed I would. Let's go through to the parlour Bob while Caroline plays hostess."

Bob swallowed hard. This was not what he had expected at all, but he went with George into the parlour and took the seat offered to him. Caroline could not hear their conversation from the kitchen, but she was relieved to return with the tray of tea things to find them both laughing at something.

"Bob was just telling me how at last Saturday's match Cheltenham's goalkeeper kicked the ball all the way into the opposition's goal while all of the players simply stood open mouthed and watched! That must have been something to see."

George was skilled in talking to put others at their ease. He listened, asked open questions, and allowed the other person to feel that he was genuinely interested in what they had to say. Most of the time George really was interested, and he was especially interested in Bob. Any young man who had the courage to come to the house and see Caroline should be taken notice of, he felt.

Caroline was pleased to see her father and Bob getting along. Possibly Bob would require a mortgage to help purchase his little house in Prestbury one day, and it would do him no harm to have the sympathetic ear of the Building Society manager. For his part, Bob was pleasantly surprised that George would speak to him as if they had known each other socially before. He didn't want to outstay his welcome, so after finishing his cup of tea he handed Caroline the cup and saucer carefully and stood up to leave. George stood and shook Bob's hand again, and let Caroline see the young man to the door.

"It's been lovely to see you, Bob. Thank you again for my present."

"I wanted to ask, there is a New Year's dance at the Town Hall next weekend, would you care to come with me if I can get us tickets?"

"I should like that very much. Thank you for the invitation."

"Good. Well, I will let Lottie know to tell you next week. I'm sorry to hear about your mother, I hope she is feeling better soon."

"Thank you. I'm glad she is home at least. I think it would be horrid to spend Christmas in hospital."

"Yes. Well, goodbye then Caroline." He paused, gathered his courage, and kissed her cheek quickly, "have a happy Christmas."

Caroline closed the door as Bob reached the gate. She turned to find George standing in the parlour doorway smiling at her.

"A nice young man," he said, "hard-working, responsible position, serious."

"A little too serious sometimes. More tea?"

Elizabeth managed a slice of bread and butter and some beef broth that evening. George and Caroline dined on cold roast chicken, boiled potatoes and sprouts that were still rather crisp but were eaten without comment. They had discussed where they might put their presents for each other given that they had not had the foresight to obtain a Christmas tree or decorations that year. Annie had arranged some holly with red berries in a vase for the dining room table, muttering to herself that there should be some festive spirit in the house. They agreed to take their gifts into Elizabeth's room after breakfast and open them all together there.

In the absence of Annie to clear the table, father and daughter found a novel enjoyment in working together to take the crockery through to the kitchen and washing and drying it all. George mused that perhaps Annie would no longer be needed, which caused Caroline to explain in worried tones that Annie had hoped to stay in their employment at least until she and Jacob were married.

George placed his hand on her arm to calm her, "I have no desire to dismiss Annie just yet."

As they went back through to the parlour, there was a knock at the door.

"It's very late for callers. Carol singers perhaps?" George pulled back the bolt and opened the door letting the freezing air inside, "Ahh, it's you. Come in Miss House."

"I won't stay, and I'm sorry for calling so late but I had some prints to deliver this evening."

"Elsa, what a lovely surprise! Are you sure you won't stay?"

Elsa and George exchanged glances.

"No, I really just came to give you this and wish you a very merry Christmas." She handed Caroline an envelope, "It's payment for the fashion modelling. A cheque for you and one for Florence if you wouldn't mind passing it on to her?"

Caroline opened the envelope and pulled out the two cheques, both made out for seven pounds and ten shillings. She handed hers to George who took it into his study for safe keeping. The two women stood facing each other in the hallway. Caroline took a step towards Elsa because the gap between them seemed too great a distance.

"Thank you so much Elsa. I hate how difficult this is for us all. Will you be with family for Christmas?"

"Not tomorrow, but I am going up to London next week for a few days. Staying with an aunt and her three pug dogs. I've arranged to see a magazine editor while I'm there about the fashion photographs, he is very interested in moving away from the usual sketches so we might be in for a few more of those cheques by the end of it."

"You know I would invite you to have Christmas luncheon with us, but…"

"But it would be too difficult for us all, yes, I do know that Caroline. As you said before, one day when we are older no one will care, and we can stroll arm in arm wherever we choose. Just not now." She smiled a sad smile.

Caroline opened her arms and the women embraced. Elsa was the first to move away. She put her bowler hat back on her head and opened the door out onto the chill damp night.

"Happy Christmas, Caroline. Let's hope for good fortune next year, eh?" she closed the door behind her.

Caroline went into her father's study. He was sitting behind his desk with a large black ledger open in front of him. He looked up as she entered.

"You have done much better financially this year than I anticipated my dear."

"I know I am in the black as you say."

"Indeed. And with this contribution and your wages next week, you should end the year with around sixty-three pounds. Well done. Do you have any plans for the new year?"

"Bob asked me earlier if I would go to the dance at the Town Hall next week. And I am going to Oxford to meet Midge's brother Luke, he wants to show me around the museums there, though that very much depends on his shifts. He is a doctor you see."

"And what of this James fellow?"

Caroline found herself blushing, "He is very busy. He has talked of going to Europe or America, so I might not hear from him for a while."

George closed the ledger and sat back in his chair. "I am sorry that I did not encourage you sooner to go out and see a bit of the world. But as things are, if you work hard, you may be able to travel further next year. I have thought several times over the years that I might travel to France, to see where Freddie…

a pilgrimage of sorts. Your mother of course would not hear of it, but if you would like to perhaps that is something you and I could do together one day?"

Caroline had never given the prospect any thought. She enjoyed her father's company and decided it would be an interesting trip if somewhat emotional and lacking in excitement.

"Yes, I should like to do that one day."

In her room before she got into bed that evening, Caroline took out her keepsake box. She removed the lid and took out each item, laying it carefully on her bedspread. Each item triggered a memory, a smell, a taste. There was plenty of room still in the box and she knew she would continue to collect these worthless, priceless objects wherever she went in the future. They made a collage of an interesting year, and she thought that it would be a nice thing to paint, a keepsake of keepsakes. She would have some time before returning to work, it would give her something to do as the year came to a close.

The End.